Bella Books, Inc.
P.O. Box 10543
Tallahassee, FL 32302

Printed in the United States of America on acid-free paper
First published 2012

Editor: Katherine V. Forrest
Cover Designer: Sandy Knowles

ISBN 13: 978-1-59493-287-8

PUBLISHER'S NOTE

Other Bella Books by Ann Roberts

Paid in Full
Brilliant
Beach Town
White Offerings
Root of Passion
Beacon of Love
Deadly Intersections
Petra's Canvas

Other Spinsters Ink Books by Ann Roberts

Furthest from the Gate
Keeping Up Appearances

Author's Notes

Inspiration comes in many ways and the idea for this story stemmed from my father's memories of Phoenix during the forties and fifties. While I've taken huge liberties with city history, the enclave really exists, surrounded by a wonderful post-WWII neighborhood that I call home.

I'm grateful for my neighbors, who plan impromptu happy hours, or let me borrow a pound of pasta when dinner is twenty minutes from completion, and I finally realize what I forgot at the store. And none of them have a problem requesting the "lesbian babysitters" when they want a night out.

One such neighbor is my friend Alexis, another writer who'll get back to writing when her amazing little daughter doesn't need all of her attention. She read the manuscript and provided great moral support as well. It's wonderful to know such a person is just across the alley.

My partner Amy is my biggest fan and my most important critic. She always makes the story better, telling me which scenes don't work, when she's lost, or why a character's name needs to change.

Finally, I'm always honored when Katherine V. Forrest edits my book. I learn so much from her. And, of course, I'm thrilled to work with Bella Books, who support my passion and love of storytelling.

For Morgen
Cousin by blood, friend by choice

Definitely Friends First! – 27 (Central Phoenix)

Date: 2010-06-05, 11:18PM MST
Reply To This Post

GF, 27, ready to try again. I am a professional career woman who recently moved to Phoenix from Indiana. I love art, politics, hiking and a good debate. Looking for friends first and then maybe more. I'm gay, not bi, and I'm not into men or threesomes. No games, drama, drugs or addictions. Who are you? Carpe Diem!

Reply

CHAPTER ONE

October, 1953

"Vivian Lucille Battle, you are a complete moron! You could've been killed! No one with a brain would do something as ridiculous as jump off the roof, but apparently God handed your brain to the next child in line. Whoever *that* boy is, he'll probably grow up to be president seeing as he has *two* brains!"

I gazed up at Mama, a screaming silhouette against the blinding sun. A familiar pain chewed through my left arm, and I was pretty sure I'd broken it, just like I'd broken my right one two summers before. I held it against my stomach, praying that it didn't split in two. Douggie Kerns had told me he'd seen a guy whose broken hand fell into a well and he never got it back. I needed mine for drawing.

Mama yelled some more, and I hoped she'd finish soon because I knew she wouldn't take me to the doctor until she'd said her piece, and her pieces tended to run at least as long as a radio commercial when it came to scolding me.

She yanked me off the ground in one motion and my left arm swung free.

"Don't you expect any tea and sympathy from me, young lady," she said as she shoved me into the front seat of the Cadillac. "This is your own doing. If they have to cut off your arm, then so be it. Can't believe a twelve-year-old is so thoughtless."

She slammed the door shut and went to the other side. Her lips kept moving, but I couldn't hear most of the words. Those Caddies were well-made cars.

"This is just like what happened to Mopey," she added as she turned onto Missouri Avenue.

It wasn't anything like what I'd done to our dog Mopey a few years back, but I knew better than to argue. My brother Will had dared me to shake a leftover bottle of champagne, and poor Mopey was walking through the kitchen when the cork flew off. Blinded him in one eye, and for the rest of his days whenever he'd bang against a doorjamb or knock something over because his side vision was gone, Mama shook her finger and said, "There's a dog with more sense than my daughter, the moron!"

When we turned left I knew we weren't going to the emergency room. "Why aren't we going to St. Joseph's?" I asked, remembering the last time. I thought broken bones automatically meant the emergency room.

Her breath seemed to catch. "Can't," she said simply.

When we stopped at an intersection a young guy in a Ford called, "Hey, beautiful! You babysitting?"

Her face slid into a grin. "Hey, yourself. You plannin' on stayin' here all day?"

"If it means talkin' to you," he said coolly.

She laughed. This happened all the time, especially when she was forced to go out in her house clothes. She always wore her blonde hair in a ponytail and people thought she was seventeen, not thirty-seven. I'd noticed two tiny crow's feet near her eyes, but I didn't dare mention it. She prided herself on her appearance even when she was wearing pedal pushers and a simple cotton blouse, like she was now.

"Well, I need to get going," she said. "My *daughter* needs to go to the doctor."

I waved and his face fell. He tore away and she just kept laughing.

We drove to Dr. Steele's office. He'd been our family doctor for as long as we'd lived in Phoenix, and I'd been a regular visitor since I seemed to need stitches, splints and medications more than most kids. He enjoyed my *exploits*, as he called them. His most favorite story was how I busted my lip when I flew over my bike handlebars after Will convinced me that blind people could ride bicycles and I could close my eyes as I flew down the hill. Dr. Steele had laughed so hard he'd caught the hiccups. That visit had actually worked out okay because he didn't charge Mama since he was so amused.

I followed her inside and my eyes watered from the strong smell of rubbing alcohol. I went to my usual chair while she talked to the nurse. Soon they were both staring at me and frowning. My arm was killing me, but I didn't make a peep. That would make Mama yell more. Will had told me that she yelled to keep from crying because I scared her most of the time. I tried to stay out of trouble, but I'd get these pictures in my head and I wanted to see if I could make them come true. He said I needed to get out my sketchpad when those moments happened and *draw* them instead of *do* them. Sometimes that worked, but it didn't help that he dared me to do some of the stuff.

Even though there were other people ahead of us, the nurse took us right back like she always did. We never waited long, and I wasn't sure if it was because she worried I'd set the whole place on fire before I saw Dr. Steele or if he just wanted to spend more time with Mama. Men loved spending time with her—the plumber, the milkman and even the grocery delivery boy.

I hopped on the table while she checked her face in the mirror. She reapplied her lipstick and pulled the rubber band out of her hair. She shook and fluffed a bit and undid the second button of her shirt. When she turned around she looked different, not so much like a mother and more like a model in a magazine. By the time he walked in she'd lit a cigarette and was leaning against his instrument counter with one hand on her hip.

He ignored me and went right to her. "Lois, it's always good to see you."

"Hi, Hank," she replied with a broad smile. "We're back."

I guessed he was somewhat older than her since he had a lot of gray hair and a potbelly. He wasn't very tall, and he always looked tired with big bags under his eyes. But when he looked at her he found a bunch of energy. And for some reason when she talked to *Hank*, whatever I'd done was funny or amusing because she never sounded angry.

"What happened this time?"

She sighed and played with her hair. "Fell and broke her *other* arm, I think."

He chuckled and gave me a sideways glance before stepping closer to her. It was their little ritual. She sniffled, and then he'd put a friendly arm around her, assuring her that she was a great mother and my stupidity wasn't her fault.

By the time they got to this part, my arm felt like someone was pounding it with a hammer, but it was like I wasn't there. I opened my mouth to say something but they were giggling and whispering so I kept my mouth closed.

"Um, Hank, there is one thing," she said. "Chet can't make another shipment until Friday."

He nodded thoughtfully, and her face tensed while she watched him think. His arm was still around her but he wasn't stroking her shoulder anymore.

"Hmm. I seem to remember this happening last time, Lois. Everything okay in the orange growing business?"

I could tell he was making fun of Pops by the way he asked the question. It made me mad because I loved those trees even if Pops didn't make a lot of money.

"We're fine, Hank, but money's tight."

"Isn't it always?"

I didn't recognize the soft voice that answered. "Uh, well, I was also hoping you could check a mole for me. It's on my chest. It looks funny."

He licked his lips. "Let's take a look."

He led her into the next room, and I held my broken arm for

another five minutes. I thought about putting my ear against the door, but I was pretty sure that Mama would break my other arm again if she caught me.

I saw my reflection in the mirror above his sink. From a distance I guessed I looked like her, although I had Pops' dark hair, which I'd recently cut with her sewing shears one day. She'd been so mad that she had me wear a big hat with a sunflower on it when we went to church. She said that it looked like I'd stuck my head in a threshing machine and I deserved what I got. I said I'd rather wear Pops' fedora and she'd scowled.

The calendar on the wall caught my eye. Somebody had forgotten to flip the months and it was still on January and February. The picture was friendly. A boy sat in an attic room, showing a clock to his grandma, who sat on a bed. A cat curled up at the foot of the bed, right above the name of the painter—Norman Rockwell. I decided I liked Mr. Rockwell's pictures very much and would ask my art teacher, Mrs. Curry, if she knew who he was.

The door flew open and Mama went straight to the window. She lit a cigarette and stared into the sunlight. Her eyes were red and I looked over at Dr. Steele, who was writing on my chart. When he finally stepped to the table and took my arm in his hands, he shook his head.

"Vivi, Vivi, what are we going to do with you?"

*****

On the way home Mama said nothing. She kept her eyes on the road. I waited for the lecture that usually followed our return from the doctor or the hospital, but she only drove, which was a bad sign. I much preferred her yelling since I'd learned to block it out after the millionth time. Will had told me it was her way of showing she cared, and there was always plenty to yell about. My grades were too low, I continually did stupid things, and I just wasn't as good as him, a conclusion she'd made the last time she'd retrieved me from the principal's office.

She often said, "I'm almost positive, Vivian Battle, that

you were switched at birth. How your father and I wound up with such different children could only be explained by such a thing."

I didn't think it would be wise to mention that *Will* could have been the switched one.

I glanced down at the cast on my arm. It itched, and Dr. Steele said I'd need to wear it for at least six weeks before he could cut it off. He'd offered to sign it, but Mama had hurried me out of the office before he could.

"I'm sorry," I offered.

She puffed her cigarette. "Sorry is a word, Vivian. Don't be sorry."

"But I *am* sorry. I know it costs money to go to the doctor," I said, hoping I could show her I was mature. I knew Pops was struggling with the orchard, or as she called it, his harebrained idea to get rich.

At the mention of money, she shot me a cold look. "Yes, Vivian, that's right. Everything has a price, a *cost*. You should learn that."

Her eyes returned to the road and I stared out the window, ashamed that I'd caused so much trouble. I vowed to do better and thought about saying so, but I remembered what she'd said about words. I'd need to prove it to her.

I could tell she wasn't just mad at me. I guessed she was mad at Dr. Steele for some reason, but I knew she was mad at Pops, too. She was always mad at him.

We'd moved from Iowa to Phoenix in forty-seven when I was six. Pops had said Phoenix was "money land" because they were building so many houses. He'd heard stories of rich men pulling up in fancy cars carrying wads of cash that they showered on the folks fortunate enough to own the property.

So when he inherited the family farm, he sold it, moved us to Phoenix, and took every penny he had and bought thirty acres of orange orchards and a farmhouse that reminded him of home. Mama hadn't wanted to leave her family but after the first mild winter, she'd fallen in love with the dry climate.

But no one wanted to buy the land, and he wasn't very good at running the orchard. When they'd fight over money, she would point at the trees and scream, "There's the gas bill, Chet, and the kids' school clothes and the gasoline!"

He'd shrug and say, "If I'd wanted to be a damn farmer, I'd have stayed in Iowa. This is our way out."

We pulled into the long driveway, and I automatically smiled at the sight of the orchard in the distance and our beautiful farmhouse. On its walls built entirely of red brick, the white wooden windows looked like enormous eyes, and the long brick path that extended from the road to the large oak front door seemed to go on forever. We had a fancy dining room with a chandelier and something called a sun porch with glass walls. It got hotter than the oven during the summer, but Pops said it was a great place to sleep in the winter after he and Mama fought.

There were four bedrooms so Will and I didn't have to share anymore, but the best part was the backyard—rows and rows of orange trees. I'd tried to count them once and got lost after forty-eight. Right now the blossoms were just beginning to turn and by February there would be millions of oranges dangling from the limbs.

"Go upstairs and do your homework," she said wearily. "Tell Will he needs to do his chores."

I ran up to his room, glancing at Mama's amazing sweet potato pie as I passed through the kitchen. I found him hunched over his desk, his pen moving effortlessly across a paper. It was always easy for him. Once I'd asked him to explain my homework since he was two grades ahead of me, and he'd tried but it was like he wasn't saying the words in the right order. I knew he'd been speaking English, at least part of the time, but it was too confusing. I'd just nodded and never asked him again.

"Mama says you need to do your chores."

He turned and grinned when he saw my arm. "Was it broken?"

"Just my wrist."

He looked half like Mama and half like Pops. He had a friendly smile that Mama said would charm the ladies and Pops' thick hair and spindly build. And I loved looking into his pretty blue eyes. They always reassured me that everything would be all right no matter what happened.

"How'd Mama pay Dr. Steele?" he asked suspiciously.

"He was really nice. He said she could pay him on Friday."

He frowned and turned back to his book. "I'll be down in a minute. Go do your homework."

Instead of reaching for my schoolbooks I went to the window seat and gazed out at the orchard and the mountain. The acreage Pops bought was near the base of Squaw Peak and seemed close enough to touch. I'd wake up in the morning and stare over the treetops to the rugged switchbacks that crossed the face. Once in a while Will and I would ride our bikes to the trailhead and climb to the top. We'd look at Phoenix and he'd say something about how different it was from Iowa—so flat, no rolling hills or blue rivers. I knew he missed home a lot. He'd been eight when we moved so he remembered Cedar Rapids but Phoenix was all I'd ever known.

If we turned the other way we saw the tall buildings of the downtown and all the fancy stores. Central Avenue sliced the city in half and houses chewed up the sorghum fields. But nobody seemed to want our orchard. Mama had said once that Pops' price was too high.

He'd just laughed and said, "It'll happen. Just wait."

The day turned dark and he still wasn't home. He worked long hours and sometimes we ate without him. My stomach rumbled and I stole down the stairs to see what she was doing. I'd given up on my homework after only completing a few problems. Hopefully I could copy off someone when I got to school.

I sat at the base of the stairs in the shadows of the dark living room and faced the kitchen. Dinner was on the table but Mama sat alone, smoking a cigarette and drinking her water, which was what she called vodka. She didn't know I'd read the bottle one time before she put it away. She stared at nothing in particular, and the smoke twisted around her as if she were surrounded by a dream.

I wondered what she thought about. Did she think about us? Him? Was she worried he wouldn't like his dinner? Whatever it was I knew it didn't make her happy. She never looked happy.

I went back upstairs guessing that if he didn't show up in a little while we'd eat the dinner cold as usual. I'd learned not to say anything about the condition of the food, then, which tasted as if it had been sitting out all afternoon at a picnic.

I stared at my unfinished math homework, meaning to finish, but soon I was doodling and copying the picture I'd seen in Dr. Steele's office. I closed my eyes trying to remember the exact details, the light and dark as Mrs. Curry would say. With only a lead pencil it was impossible to re-create Norman Rockwell's colorful painting but I did my best.

"Get down here, Vivian!" my father's voice boomed.

I dropped the pencil and hustled down the stairs. He stood in the living room, his arms crossed. He was lanky and tall, with wavy hair that rarely looked as if it needed to be combed. It just sort of sat on his head naturally. He was tanned from living outdoors every day, and I thought he looked like a movie star, although Will always said Mama was the good-looking one. But whenever we tagged along on one of his errands to the store, he'd smile and laugh with the pretty cashiers, more so than he ever did with us or Mama.

He stood over me, his angry face a million miles away. He reached for my arm and studied my cast.

"Bend over," he commanded.

At least he hadn't brought out the paddle he kept on the bathroom doorknob, but the three swats still hurt and it was hard to sit down at the table. Will grinned, and I stuck out my tongue when Mama and Pops weren't looking.

"Meat's dry," he said, scowling at his pork chop.

Dinnertime was the main event, and Mama's cooking was usually the topic that started a fight. Even though we'd moved out of the Midwest, she still cooked as if she were there. I can't imagine why he would've thought that could change. She cooked what she knew and that meant meat at one o'clock on the plate, potatoes at six and vegetable at ten. There wasn't a lot of love in the meals but she tried.

The only thing he never complained about was her sweet potato pie. She made the *best* I'd ever tasted, and we always fought over the last piece but that fight was good-natured. The rest of the arguments weren't. He wanted to be proud of her for certain things—the ones he chose.

"Perhaps if we could afford something more substantial it would taste better," she remarked as she went to the cabinet for the vodka.

Ever since we'd moved to Phoenix, I noticed she'd taken to drinking at the table, which by our midwestern standards was bad manners, but he didn't seem to care.

"You need to keep your comments to yourself, Lois," he said sharply. "And I don't appreciate your fancy words. *Substantial.* What the hell kind of word is that? Maybe if you'd keep our children in line, we'd have some more money for food," he said, throwing a glare in my direction.

I hung my head.

"So how much did that little trip to Dr. Steele's office set us back?" he asked.

"Fifteen," she said quietly.

He harrumphed but never asked where she got the money. That's how it always was. Conversation between my parents was like Will and me playing catch. He'd throw the ball and I'd always miss it, since I wasn't very coordinated. Them talking was just like that—a lot of dropped balls.

"Well it won't be long until we can pay for everything up front. We're having a visitor tonight," he said, "a man named Rubenstein." He looked up and offered a little smile. "I think he wants to buy our land."

Will and I glanced at each other. Maybe if Pops sold the land they'd be fine.

"Now, when he gets here, I don't want any fightin' between the two of you, ya' hear?" He was holding out his fork like a weapon and we nodded. "You say your hellos and then you get upstairs."

We nodded again for salvation's sake. While we were scared of Mama, we were terrified of him, not just because he swung the paddle, but because we didn't know him. He was always in the orchard or at the bar with his friends. Once in a while he'd take Mama out for special occasions, but when he was home, he ignored us mostly.

"How did you meet Mr. Rubenstein?" she asked.

"He bought the grove next door. Came by the other day and said he wanted to talk."

I glanced at Mama, who opened her mouth to say something but decided to swirl her drink instead. He was the only one who could keep her quiet. When she was angry with me, her mouth was like a motorboat on a full tank of gas. She only stopped when she ran out.

He hated talking to her about anything that he thought was *his* business, like finances or major decisions. He thought she ran the kitchen and the kids but nothing else. She didn't think so. Their fights were so loud that Will and I heard everything.

We ate in silence until she excused herself and began the cleanup that Will and I would finish. In my entire life I'd never seen Pops pick up a single dish or cup to help. He entered the kitchen to eat and left when he was done.

Uncomfortable sitting at the table with him alone, Will and I gobbled the rest of our dinner, and I took over the washing from Mama while Will dried. She disappeared upstairs to change and fix her hair before Mr. Rubenstein arrived.

"Do you think he'll buy it?" I asked quietly, unsure if Pops was listening in the front room where he read the paper.

He shrugged. "I dunno. He already owns the land next to ours. It could be economically advantageous," he said. He liked using big words and sounding smart like Mama. I knew he wanted me to ask him what it meant, but I just kept washing since I was pretty sure I understood.

"Where will we go?"

He stopped drying the skillet and stared at me like he hadn't thought about that part. We'd waited so long for anyone to take an interest in the land that we'd forgotten what it might mean to our family.

The doorbell rang, and we finished just as Mr. Rubenstein shook Mama's hand. She looked like Rita Hayworth at a movie premiere. She'd put her hair up in a style called a chignon and reapplied her makeup. And like every other man who met her, he was laughing and patting her hand as if they'd known each other for years.

She waved at us and we were immediately at her side, wearing our own smiles of hope.

"These are our children, Will and Vivian." She'd said our names like she was proud of us.

He bent down and offered a firm handshake. I was surprised because his fingers were soft and his palm was warm, nothing like Pops' hands, which were like tree bark. He had a long face and his nose was like a beak. I tried not to stare, but it was hard because it took up a lot of his face. Pops said all Jews had a big nose—even the women—and that's how you could tell you were in the presence of one. His hair was slicked back, and he wore a dark blue suit with a red tie. He smelled like spice, and I resisted the urge to hug him just to be closer to his smell.

"Get on up to your homework," Pops said firmly, and we quickly charged up the stairs, only to tiptoe back down to the landing where we could watch and listen.

Pops led him to the dining room table while Mama went to the kitchen and retrieved some refreshments. They made small talk as Mr. Rubenstein opened his briefcase and looked around the dining room. He asked several questions like how many rooms our house had and what was the square footage, and I realized if he bought our land he'd probably live here.

When Mama returned with a tray of coffee and three slices of sweet potato pie, Pops scowled at her. I knew he wanted her to drop the refreshments and go away, but she planted herself across from the two of them, not really in the conversation but not gone.

Mr. Rubenstein complimented her on the pie and told them he loved the area and the orange groves. But like adults usually do, he rambled into a bunch of boring things I didn't understand, using words like fair market value, equity and water rights. I plunked my head against the wall feeling like I was stuck at school. I woke up when Will poked me in the ribs.

"They're talking about whether we get to stay," he whispered.

I'd been asleep for a while because the pie was gone, there were papers scattered over the table and Mama was sitting next to Mr. Rubenstein. Pops was studying something while she laughed at one of Mr. Rubenstein's stories. She touched his arm and played with her hair just like she'd done in Dr. Steele's office.

When she stopped laughing, she said, "You know, Jacob, I love this house. I'd really like to keep it. Would you ever consider purchasing the groves but not the house?"

She still held his arm, a look of pleading on her face.

"I don't know, Lois. This farmhouse is one of the reasons I considered buying the property."

"But to a woman a house is really a home. I'm sure your wife has explained that to you."

He coughed and said, "Um, I'm not married, Lois. Haven't met the right woman."

She gasped. "I'm shocked. A handsome man like you with your strong business sense?" She patted his arm again. "It will happen, and then you'll understand why a woman loves her home so much—"

Pops set down the papers and picked up a pen. "Don't listen to her jibber-jabber, Mr. Rubenstein. We'll be just fine in another place. Where do I sign?"

"Chet, now hold on a minute. You hate the idea of living in a ranch-style house." She quickly turned her gaze to Mr. Rubenstein. "No offense to you, Jacob. I'm sure the houses you'll build will be grand, but we loved this place the moment we saw it."

"No offense taken," he said.

I knew she'd hate leaving this place, especially the formal dining room where they were sitting. It would kill her to give up the chandelier and the white crown molding that bordered the ceiling. It was fancy, and there wasn't much in her life that fit that description.

"This is our home," she continued. "If we—"

"Lois, shut up," Pops said gruffly. "This decision doesn't concern you."

She turned red and started to rise, but Mr. Rubenstein shot him a hard glare and caught her arm. He whispered to her and she nodded. When they both looked at Pops, I knew it was two against one.

"Mr. Battle, I'm no longer interested in purchasing this house as part of the agreement."

He smacked the table and stabbed a finger at one of the

papers. "This is what you're costing us, Lois. This is what we're losing by keeping this place."

"Actually, Mr. Battle," he interrupted, "your wife's charming personality has *saved* you money." He turned to her and added, "I'll be happy to buy the groves, but you'll retain the house and two acres beyond, so the children have a yard. Initially, though, I'll need to borrow that property for some temporary worker housing, but I'll be happy to pay rent to you for its usage."

He looked like he was holding her hand, almost like he was her husband. I suddenly wondered if Jews were any different than us.

"Will that be acceptable, Mrs. Battle?" he asked, totally ignoring Pops.

She sighed and touched her chest. "That would be perfect."

PhoenixConnect.Com (Women Seeking Women)
Re: Definitely Friends First! – 27 (Central Phoenix)
Date: 2010-06-06, 1:07AM MST

I just read your post. U can see from the time that I'm a night howl(er), if you get my meaning. I also don't like games except the ones we play together. I'm a fantasy kind of girl and I'd love to be your friend—your bestest friend. When I'm done with you, you won't want any other friends. Give me a try.

Posted by: Nighthowler
Reply

Re: Definitely Friends First! – 27 (Central Phoenix)
Date: 2010-06-06 8:16 AM MST

DFF, I loved your post! I think we could make a real connection. I'm also a professional woman who relishes a good debate, a good bottle of wine and fine art. Why don't we meet? But I do have one question: are you totally inflexible about the threesome? My husband loved your post too!

Posted by: LesBIan291
Reply

Re: Definitely Friends First! – 27 (Central Phoenix)
Date: 2010-06-06, 2:13 PM MST

Hi DFF! I just read yur pst. U sound just like the gal I want to meet. I'm the girl u want to meet! I got rid of my issus long ago thanks to my incarceration. How do you feel about long distance relatunshps?

Posted by: 15GoesFast
Reply

CHAPTER TWO

June 10, 2010

Ding!

CC's gaze flicked from the red traffic light to her Droid screen. She had *another* reply to her personal ad. She dismissed the alert and punched in the rest of her text to her paralegal just as the light changed. She knew it was illegal to text and drive in Arizona, but as a new junior associate every minute of the day was a chance to impress her boss, even if it meant breaking a few minor laws in the process.

The computer reminded her to take SR-51, but a red Miata refused to let her merge.

"Son of a bitch," she cursed as the exit flew by.

She pulled into a gas station and immediately cranked the window down to counter the stifling heat. It was only the tenth of June and already the temperature had hit one hundred and five. She couldn't imagine how she'd survive August without air conditioning. The ancient Honda's compressor had died somewhere near Albuquerque during the move.

Curiosity demanded she check the latest reply to her ad, which she'd decided was a mistake. She calculated that of the nearly one hundred responses she'd received, half were bizarre or scary, and another twenty-five percent were from men. A fourth seemed to be authored by sane and competent women, but she couldn't bring herself to take the next step—actually setting up a meeting. She'd said she wanted friends and she did. So why was responding so hard?

She quickly deleted the reply, which listed twelve ways she could be "disciplined" for her own enjoyment, and reentered her route on the Droid's Navigator. As she was about to leave, an alert popped up. Alicia had sent a message.

I need my Melissa Ferrick CD back.

She gritted her teeth. It wasn't Alicia's, although she remembered when she'd shown it to her, the first night they slept together, and Alicia had coveted it since. They'd made a joke of it during their two-year relationship, Alicia always claiming it belonged to her.

"But it doesn't," she said out loud.

This was the third time since their breakup six weeks ago that she'd called demanding something back or asking how an electronic worked. Each conversation was like sunburn, and CC didn't feel the pain until hours later when she was sitting alone in the apartment and suddenly burst into tears.

Determined to win at least one argument, she called her while her hackles were still raised. Surprisingly, Alicia answered, and she felt herself sink in her bucket seat. She'd been praying for voice mail.

"Did you find my CD?" she asked evenly.

CC could hear the noise of the law office where she worked. "It isn't yours, Lish. It never was."

She laughed into the phone. "Of course it is. You gave it to me as a present for our anniversary."

"What?"

"Yeah, we'd just come home from that great dinner at Anthony's, remember? We were both a little drunk, and you wanted to give me something special. You knew how much I wanted it."

She shook her head. Most likely she was making up this story, probably as the words fell out of her mouth. She had learned from experience how well Alicia created instant fiction. Still, she did remember the night at Anthony's but she just didn't think...

"Look, if you didn't give it to me for our anniversary, what did you give me? I gave you the locket, remember?"

She fingered the tiny heart around her neck. She couldn't bring herself to take it off, and she didn't want to fight over a CD.

"Maybe I did give it to you. I don't think so," she quickly added, "but I really don't remember."

She chuckled. "You weren't one for details, but I'm sure that'll change with your new job." She paused and changed subjects. "So I guess congratulations are in order. Pretty big deal landing a junior associate position at Hartford and Burns."

"Yeah," she agreed, glancing at the new briefcase on her passenger seat.

"I saw that posting online and thought about going for it myself."

She narrowed her eyes. "You already have a job."

"But it's not like the big leagues. I'll never get anywhere if I stay here."

She glanced at her watch. "I need to go, Lish. Do you want me to mail it to Nadia's apartment?"

"No, um, what time do you get off work?" she asked.

"I don't know. I should stay at least until seven thirty to make a good impression."

"Well, if you still have it in your car because you play it *all the time*, then why don't we meet at Kinkaid's around eight?"

Yes, automatically jumped from her throat but she caught it, and Alicia only received a garbled sound of indecision.

"Was that a yes?" she asked confidently.

"I don't know, Lish." Her heart was still in pieces, and she'd only begun to move on, beginning with her month-old job at

Hartford and Burns.

"Just one drink," she coaxed. "I'm dying to see you."

She seemed so sincere. CC had loved her most when she was earnest. "Um, okay," she said hesitantly before she hung up.

She threw the car into drive when the robotic voice coaxed her onto SR-51. She hesitated, remembering that she'd seen construction on the other side of the freeway yesterday, but she decided to listen to the computer over her common sense.

She sighed. She'd made a mistake. She should've insisted on mailing the CD. No, in fact, she should've insisted it didn't belong to Alicia. Yet she gave in, just as she had throughout their relationship.

Sure enough as she approached the exit, she saw the cones and signage.

"Unbelievable," she muttered, smacking her palm against the steering wheel. She couldn't drive five miles anywhere in the valley without hitting construction. The Droid announced it would recalculate her route again, and she stuck out her tongue.

Her phone rang and she welcomed the distraction. "CC Carlson."

"Are you there yet?"

She instantly sat up straighter when she heard Blanca's voice. She was a senior associate and her boss.

"No, I'm stuck in traffic. I missed the on-ramp and I'm paying for it."

After a long pause she said, "I understand. You're still learning your way around the valley, and this is the first time we've sent you out in the field. Would you like me to Google the best route?"

"No, I've got it now. I'll be there in another five minutes."

"Good. Make sure you obtain a clearly legible handwriting sample, one that is written in cursive. Despite her advanced age, Ms. Battle is quite savvy, and she may offer up something inadequate, thus prolonging this case."

She couldn't decide what she hated more—her condescending tone or being treated like a five-year-old.

"Don't worry. I have it under control."

"Good. Seth Rubenstein is one of our most important clients. And don't forget you have the Morgans and the mediator at three o'clock."

Blanca hung up, and she felt sick to her stomach. The mediator was known around law circles as the Sweatinator because every time he lifted his arms to make a point, the attorneys got a great view of his sweaty pits.

Ding! Another reply to the personal. She'd have to check it later.

She changed lanes and watched for the exit. This wasn't what she'd expected when she'd earned her law degree, and she'd never planned on moving to Phoenix. *What we do for love.*

"Some Enchanted Evening" burst from the phone. "Hi, Mom."

"Hello sweetheart, I'm so sorry to bother you, but I just had to call. I'm sure you're in the middle of something terribly important."

"Not really. I'm just driving. What's up?"

There was a pause and then, "Honey, you're driving *and* talking on your cell phone? Is that okay?"

"Yes, Mom."

"Well, your father is set on you coming home for Thanksgiving, and he's found some flights that are quite reasonable. Do you think you could get a week off?"

She took a deep breath. Her mother would never understand the life of a junior attorney. "Probably only a couple days. I'm working eighty hours a week right now."

"Well, he'll be disappointed but he'll understand. It's just part of paying your dues."

"Yup," she said. She didn't have time for one of her mother's lectures about how hard she'd worked to become a certified C.P.A. thirty-two years ago when few places hired women.

"So the week is out, huh?" she asked again, but more matter-of-factly, as if she was coming to terms with her announcement.

"Can't pay my dues if I'm not here, Mom."

She regretted saying it the minute it came out of her mouth. She shouldn't have conversations with her mother while she was driving. It was dangerous to her health and their relationship. Her mother said nothing, and she knew she'd hurt her feelings.

"I'm sorry, Mom. I'd love to come home, but I can't."

"I know, sweetie. I know you work hard. I just wish you were doing it here in Bloomington, especially now that Alicia's out of your life—"

"I know."

They had circled back to the same issue as always—CC moving with Alicia to a foreign place that was fifteen hundred miles away from her family and friends.

"Is there anything else, Mom? I'm on my way to see a client."

"Just know how much we love you and how proud we are of our daughter, *the attorney*."

"I know, Mom. I appreciate everything you did to put me through law school. I'll talk to you this weekend, okay?"

"All right, honey. You're okay, though, aren't you? I mean you're enjoying your life?"

She phrased it as a question, but CC knew it was a statement, one that she had to agree with or her mother would worry and call her every day. It was one of the consequences of being an only child.

"Of course, Mom," she lied. "I'll talk to you soon."

She clicked off and sighed. It was a lie. She wasn't happy at all. After she and Alicia had moved to Phoenix, it had taken five months for her to find a job, and, apparently, Alicia had found another girlfriend in the meantime. New city equaled new opportunities, at least for her. So Alicia had moved out of their ridiculously priced apartment to live with Nadia the bartender, and CC was left with no social life and a job in probate litigation, which the seasoned junior associates ironically referred to as the *deadly* assignment. And after just one month she understood why.

There was nothing pleasant about estate planning. No one wanted to think about the inevitable death of a loved one, and CC's clients usually emptied an entire box of tissue each week as they sobbed over a recent death or planned for someone's eventual departure.

And doling out the assets was always a nightmare. She'd become quite cynical as people often disappointed her with their fake sympathy or greed that seemed to squat toad-like in her office. The minute a beneficiary realized he'd received less than expected, he turned into a victim demanding more and questioning the validity of the will. She'd called for security more than once when fists started flying during a meeting of beneficiaries.

The Droid sent her north on Seventh Street, where she stopped at practically every light. She glanced at the buildings around her, unimpressed by the stucco strip malls, disturbed by the amount of shuttered businesses and saddened by the lack of trees. It was as desolate as the landscape of her life. She'd found it was difficult to cultivate friendships. Everyone was so cliquish. She missed her Bloomie friends terribly, and every Sunday when she spoke with them they all begged her to come home. But she knew if she quit now it would be difficult to get work anywhere. She needed to stay for a reasonable amount of time to make a good impression—at least a year.

She made several turns until the street dead-ended, and she sat in front of a large retaining wall. *This must be the backside of the freeway.* She punched a button and the Droid indicated it was rerouting her again.

"Continue east on Colter Drive," the voice said. She looked around. She was on Colter Drive, and it was impossible to head east. "Continue east on Colter Drive," it repeated.

"I can't!" she yelled. "There's a damn wall right in front of me!"

She threw the phone on the passenger seat and decided to travel the old-fashioned way—with her common sense. She found a bridge that crossed the freeway and entered a quaint subdivision of post-World War II ranch houses with enormous eucalyptus and pine trees lining the streets and providing ample shade.

She pulled in front of a row of orange trees that formed a lovely natural fence. Two brick columns stood side by side, each supporting one-half of a black wrought-iron gate. A long brick walkway led to a unique two-story colonial that looked nothing like the rest of the neighborhood tract housing.

She pulled her briefcase onto her lap and coated her dry throat with a swig from her water bottle. This was her first meeting with an adversary—alone. She hated confrontation, and she'd called Blanca into three difficult meetings to help smooth the waters when she felt she was drowning. Even at twenty-seven, she still felt like a child playing dress-up. Her law degree had done little for her confidence.

She reapplied her lipstick and ran a brush through her auburn hair. At least she looked the part. She checked her briefcase and headed through the gate. It squeaked horribly, and she wondered if it had been opened in the last decade. An orange cat darted in front of her and she jumped off the path, her Kenneth Cole pumps landing in the soft grass.

"Shit," she said, noticing the heels of both shoes caked in mud.

She took a deep breath and circled around a plastic birdbath, wrinkled and parched from lack of use. A stone wraparound porch shaded the expansive windows that stared toward the street, and a white chimney peeked over the back of the house. An old swing rested in the far corner of the porch, and a claw-foot bathtub served as a flower planter next to the front door, absorbing as much sunlight as possible.

She pressed the bell several times, but no one answered.

Not surprising. This is why you're here. Because no one will return your calls.

She rang once more and decided to follow a fork in the path to the south. It arced away from the house, and she found herself sandwiched between colorful foliage and a row of orange trees that ended at an expansive patio and inviting crystal blue swimming pool. The backside of the house boasted twice as many windows, suggesting at least three or four bedrooms on the second floor that sat above a sun porch that provided a lovely view of the pool.

She knocked on the back door but still received no welcome. To return to the office without the required handwriting sample would be a career defeat, one that would count against her. Formulating a new game plan, she tapped her foot nervously.

The plush green yard extended past the pool. There was no fence, only trees, bushes and tall hedges that split at a southern point, providing a clear entry and exit into the backyard. She slipped through the opening and found herself standing in a large expanse of grass facing four cottages that curved around the border. She realized that the cottages and the large brick house formed a circle.

At the center were two palm trees, their trunks angled outward in a V-shape, a hammock secured between them. Redwood deck chairs, a chaise lounge and a free-standing swing surrounded a long concrete prism, the sides covered in bright mosaic tiles that formed hearts, suns, dog faces, flowers and words. *I choose* was spelled out in royal blue, red, green and yellow in several places. She assumed it was an art piece, until she stood close enough to see the granite slab top with an embedded backgammon board.

She turned a full three-hundred and sixty degrees, realizing that the hedges were so tall, the trees so mature and the foliage so dense that she couldn't see any of the nearby ranch houses that comprised the neighborhood. The four cottages and the brick house were completely closed off from the rest of the world except for the driveway that cut between two of the cottages and disappeared. She followed the blacktop back to the street and a set of locked mailboxes. A sign clearly stated that No Solicitors were allowed. Twelve foot oleanders hid the buildings from the front, and she'd unwittingly driven past the entry. She smiled at the thought of living in an area where access was limited. In the midst of a major metropolis these five homeowners had created their own little community.

She returned to the interior and noticed a long carport to the side. Only two vehicles were parked underneath the metal awning, a sleek BMW convertible and an ancient pea-green Chevy Nova in mint condition.

There was no one around. She headed toward the first cottage. A yellow placard with the silhouette of a dog breed she didn't recognize sat in the corner of the window, and the doormat read *A Devoted Dog Lover Lives Here*. She rang the bell. Suddenly giant paws crashed through the vertical blinds with a deep bark to match. She sprang back and gasped. He was big and brown with shiny teeth, nothing like the silhouette.

When no one came to the door she headed to the next cottage, which was an exact replica of the first. Underneath the house numbers was a square limestone sign, the words *Harpist Rest* chiseled in rich script. She rang the bell and a lilting harp played. *Of course.* She pressed the bell again just for fun when clearly no one was home. She assumed that at least two people were in residence somewhere, since two vehicles were in the carport and few people used public transportation in Phoenix.

The front blinds of the third cottage were open. When no one answered the bell, she peered through the window, curious about the layout. A stylish arch separated a small living room from a tiny kitchen, and a doorway led to at least one bedroom. She thought it was adorable, but judging from the stacks of moving boxes and takeout containers that surrounded the few pieces of living room furniture, someone had just moved in.

As she approached the final cottage she heard laughter and engines revving.

She rang the bell and a voice yelled, "Whatever you're sellin,' we don't want any! Read the sign at the end of the driveway!"

She rolled her eyes and pressed the button again.

"I'm serious! Go away! I'm not joining a religion, subscribing to a magazine or helping you finance your trip to Disneyland. And it's too late in the year for Girl Scout cookies."

Very amusing. She checked her watch. She only had an hour and a half before her next meeting. This time she knocked insistently until the door flew open and she faced the words *Life Is Too Short to Smoke Cheap Pot.* Her gaze flew up from the black T-shirt to the wearer's face, a handsome woman with very short curly brown hair. CC imagined her round face was cherubic when she smiled, but she wasn't smiling now.

"Hi, I'm sorry to bother you, but I'm looking for Vivian Battle?" She pointed at the brick house and added, "The lady who lives over there?"

"I know who she is. Who are you?"

"I'm CC Carlson, an attorney."

She pulled one of her cards from the side pocket of her

briefcase and handed it to her.

"Uh-huh. So what does CC stand for?"

She blanched at the question. "Uh, well, that's not really your business," she said tersely.

She chuckled. "That bad, huh?"

"No," she said automatically. "Look, I just need to reach Ms. Battle. Do you know where she is?"

She started to answer until a raspy voice called from inside, "Hey, Penn! Get over here. It's your turn!"

Penn turned away and shouted, "Just a sec!" She leaned against the doorway and eyed her shrewdly. "Attorney, huh? So what do you want to talk to Viv about?"

"That's also not your business." She pointed inside and played a hunch. "May I speak with her, please?"

"That's not Viv. That's my grandma. She's visiting from Palm Beach. Viv's out of town."

She stared into her cobalt blue eyes. She had a strong jaw and CC had already seen a hint of dimples. But now she was lying—and enjoying it.

"Where did she go?"

"To visit her sister, I think," Penn said with a straight face.

Ding!

She ignored the Droid's alert. "She's an only child," CC countered, her gaze focused on the center of Penn's amazing eyes, which seemed to darken the longer she spoke with CC.

Penn gasped dramatically. "That's right. How could I forget that?" She cleared her throat and leaned toward CC with a serious expression. "Actually, she's visiting her very hot, very wealthy and much younger lesbian lover in Mexico. I don't have any idea when and if she'll return."

"Really," CC said flatly.

Ding!

Penn looked at her purse. "You're a very popular person."

CC fumbled for the Droid and silenced it. "My apologies."

"Not necessary. Now, do you have a problem with lesbians or the idea that Ms. Battle might be one?"

CC sighed and checked her watch. "Not particularly."

"So you're okay with women being with other women?"

The look on her face made CC uncomfortable. She looked *intrigued*, and no one had looked at her that way in a long time. She was warm, and she couldn't tell if it was the Phoenix heat or her rediscovered libido. When Penn glanced at her shoes, she realized she'd been tapping her foot incessantly.

"Penn! C'mon, I'm going to take your turn if you don't get your fanny back here," the raspy voice yelled.

She flipped her hair off her shoulder and smiled pleasantly. Two could play this game. "According to my last lover I rocked her world." Penn's jaw dropped. CC donned her sexiest smile. "What? You can dish it out but you can't take it?"

Penn laughed suddenly, revealing two perfect dimples. Then she closed the door.

CC pounded and said, "I know she's around! She's probably inside with you. Who else but an old lady would drive a seventy-two Nova?"

Penn opened the door and stepped into the portico. "How did you know that's a seventy-two, and it's mine, by the way."

"That's *your* car? I would've thought the Beemer would be yours."

"Really? Despite how I'm dressed you really thought I owned a Beemer." She motioned to her T-shirt and ratty cutoffs. CC sensed her nearness—and her difference. If she were asked to make a list of appealing qualities Penn would score two points for her dimples and eyes. Nothing else. She was uncouth, unrefined and poorly dressed.

"Few women can identify a Nova and certainly not the year. So, how does a well-dressed and refined attorney identify a seventy-two Nova?"

She shrugged dismissively. "I grew up on NASCAR. I like cars, and you seem like the kind of woman who'd be into them."

"Because I'm a butch lesbian."

"Well, no," she sputtered. "I had no idea." Few people flustered her quickly, and yet Penn had managed to rattle her in less than three minutes. *Thank God I haven't had to go in front of a jury yet. I'd die.*

"Then why," she pressed.

When she thought she wouldn't scream into Penn's cute and amused face she said, "I'm leaving now. Please make sure Ms. Battle gets my card and calls me as soon as possible. And you can tell *whoever* owns the Beemer that I think it's a great car."

She turned to go as a new, raspy voice said, "Thanks, sweetie, I love my baby. I named her Bandit after that funny movie, *Smokey and the Bandit*."

The lady in the doorway grinned, but most of her face was hidden by a Diamondbacks baseball cap. Puffs of snow-white hair hung around her ears, and she wore a pair of jeans and a denim work shirt. She pointed a finger at Penn. "You took too long. I took your turn, and then I crashed again and lost. I gotta get home. I think I peed my pants when I got so excited."

She started down the path while CC and Penn followed.

"You're Vivian Battle?"

She glanced back and shuffled along. "I am."

"Don't say anything, Viv," Penn advised.

CC shot her a look. "I'm here on a legal matter."

Viv continued to power walk toward the break in the hedge, and CC was impressed by her quick stride. According to her records, Viv was sixty-nine.

"A legal matter?" she asked. "I don't know any reason a lawyer would need me. I'm not getting divorced, I'm not in a dispute with my neighbors and I'm not dead."

"No, ma'am, it's none of those issues. My name is CC Carlson. I'm with Hartford and Burns, and I do have an important matter to discuss with you. It's very urgent."

She glanced at her. "Honey, here's what I know. When you get to be my age, your body calls the shots and you answer. Right now there's nothing more important than the bathroom. Whatever you need to discuss will have to wait at least five minutes."

She charged up the back steps and through the door. Penn turned and prevented her from following Viv inside, crossing her arms like a sentry.

"Hartford and Burns?" she asked with disdain. "Otherwise known as Heartless and Burned?"

She ignored the nickname that went around the legal

community and asked, "Can we please be civil?"

"If this is so urgent and important then she needs to have her attorney present, especially if it involves Heartless and Burned."

She checked her watch again. "And who would that be? How long will it take for him to get here?"

Penn leaned forward and she took a step back. "*She's* already here. *I'm* Viv's attorney."

Her jaw dropped. "You're serious?"

"Cal Berkeley class of two thousand. You?"

"Indiana University."

"What year did you graduate?"

She hesitated and looked away. "Recently."

She chuckled. "I thought so. You're fresh blood. Right out of school and going to work for the big dogs. I hope you don't get eaten."

"Not likely," she said without much conviction. Determined to shift the conversation she asked pointedly, "So are you a *real* attorney or did you lose your license?"

Penn offered a crooked smile. CC realized it wouldn't be easy to rattle her. *Not like you. Your fuse is an inch long and you wear your emotions like a sandwich board around your neck.*

"So which is it?" She smiled and a flicker of heat registered in Penn's eyes.

"My license is current. How and when I choose to use it is my business."

"And what kind of name is Penn?"

"It's short for Pennington, my last name."

"And what's your first name?"

"Tell me what CC stands for and I'll tell you *my* first name."

She shook her head. "Not gonna happen."

They stared each other down until the door opened and Viv appeared. "Okay, c'mon in. The sun is shining, my fanny's dry and I've got some fresh iced tea and sweet potato pie for you girls."

As they entered the sun porch, CC stopped suddenly. Tacked on the walls were dozens of images she recognized from childhood, Chloe the Chameleon. Some were simple pencil drawings while most were brilliant watercolor illustrations that she remembered from the series of books she'd loved growing up.

Carts and racks filled with watercolors, pastels and pens covered most of the floor space as well as bookshelves crammed with papers and design books. A drafting table sat against the bank of windows, facing the pool, displaying five photos of antique stagecoaches and a sketch of Viv's own rendition of them.

She turned to her and exclaimed, "You draw Chloe! I love Chloe the Chameleon." She realized she sounded incredibly stupid and quickly added, "I mean, as a child I read all of the books."

She smiled graciously. "Which one was your favorite, dear?"

She shook her head. There had been so many and it had been so long ago. "I guess *Chloe Goes to School*. I remember my mother reading it to me the day before I went to first grade so I wouldn't be scared."

"And did it help?"

"It did." She glanced down at the drafting table. "I saw your name on the case file, but I didn't make the connection," she said absently. "Are you still writing Chloe books?"

"Of course!" she said, excitedly, her voice cracking from the effort. She picked up one of the stagecoach pictures. "Chloe's about to take a trip to the old west. This will be her thirty-third adventure. She should've been dead about six times over since chameleons have such a short life span, but only a few children have ever commented on that. She just keeps going. Like me."

"Wow."

She leaned over a worktable and studied several discarded sketches. A supply cart sat nearby, overflowing with markers and trays of watercolors. She was so tempted to scavenge through the contents of the drawers that she gripped her briefcase tighter to prevent herself.

"Do you work exclusively in watercolor?" she asked.

"For Chloe, yes. Her adventures have always been watercolor, but I dabble in other mediums. Are you an artist, dear?"

She shook her head. "No, not an artist. I've just always liked to draw. I did it in school." Completely lost in the moment, she added, "I invented my own character because I loved Chloe so much."

Viv touched her heart. "I'm flattered, my dear. You've paid me the ultimate compliment. If I die today, it will be with a smile on my face."

"Viv!" Penn groaned.

"Maybe you could show me your character sometime?"

She blinked, suddenly remembering why she was here. Her gaze fell on Penn, leaning against a filing cabinet, her chin resting in her palm.

Viv grabbed her by the arm. "How about some tea and pie?"

They followed her through a completely updated home. She expected a seventy-year-old woman to have dark oak furniture with doilies and knickknacks scattered about the tops of multiple hutches, buffets and tables, but there was none of that. The floors were bamboo, the walls adorned with contemporary art and the furniture minimal and functional. Viv's tastes mirrored her own, not her grandmother's. She thought of Grammy's Iowa townhouse, a mausoleum filled to the brim with family history. Viv was the exact opposite. Two framed black-and-white photographs sitting on a sideboard were the only traces of personal memories.

They sat down on a leather couch facing a sixty-inch flat screen TV, while Penn went and retrieved the tray of refreshments.

"That's for watching my Cardinals play," she said.

"Your house is beautiful. I love what you've done with it."

Viv leaned closer and whispered, "It wasn't always this way. It took me a while to realize what I wanted in life."

"I'm still figuring that out," she said.

She patted her arm again and offered a smile full of wisdom. "You're young, sweetie. It takes time."

She immediately decided she liked Viv very much. Her clear blue eyes were kind, and CC could still see her outward beauty between the age spots and wrinkles. It made it that much harder to do what she had come to do. Her gaze wandered to the far corner of the room. An oil painting of a young African-

American woman wearing a white dress was the only piece of art on the wall and a display light hung over it. Alone, it looked important.

"That's an exquisite painting," she said. "Did you do it?"

"Yes, it's the only oil I've ever finished."

"It's exceptional. No wonder you've displayed it so prominently."

"No dear, that's not the reason. I've displayed it as such because of *her*."

Penn reappeared with a tray while CC opened her briefcase and withdrew a file. "I'm here on behalf of the Rubenstein family. Do you know them?"

"Of course. Jacob Rubenstein was one of the most important people in my life. He bought my family's land, everything except the farmhouse and this piece of property, the enclave."

"The what?"

"That's what we call this area," Penn interjected. "An enclave is a piece of territory unique unto its own. That's us," she said proudly.

"Before we talk business, you eat your pie."

She quickly obliged as it postponed the reason for her visit that much longer. Sweet potato pie wasn't one of her favorites so she readied a lie—until she ate the first bite.

"This is fabulous," she said.

"Thank you, dear. It's my mother's recipe. In fact, Jacob Rubenstein liked it so much he served it at his restaurant. As far as I know, they *still* serve it."

"Well, it's the best dessert I've ever had," she said honestly. She devoured the rest in four bites and withdrew a map of the subdivision while Viv and Penn finished.

"Tea's too sweet," Viv scowled. "I put too much sugar in it."

"It's fine," Penn said flatly, and CC noticed the shift in her tone. Penn was watching her carefully, not with interest but with wariness—like a lawyer.

She took out a pen, hoping her hands weren't shaking. Penn's gaze felt like an arrow stuck in the side of her neck.

"Now, this is the original piece of property that Mr. Rubenstein purchased, correct?"

They all studied the square half-mile that now sat in prime Phoenix real estate and Viv nodded. "Yes," she said, pointing. "All of this used to be beautiful orange orchards when I was a girl."

CC took her pen and drew a circle around the farmhouse, the carport and the cottages. "And so this is the area you refer to as the enclave?"

"Uh-huh, that's us."

"And your family has retained the rights to this property, correct?"

She nodded assuredly. "Absolutely. That was the deal. He bought everything around it and we kept this."

"And as far as you know, that's never changed?"

"What's your point, Ms. Carlson?" Penn interrupted. "Apparently there's a dispute or you wouldn't be here."

She took a sip of the too-sweet tea. She felt like she was standing in a desert. There was nothing friendly about Penn's tone now. She reached into her file and withdrew a photocopy of a handwritten note dated August of nineteen fifty-five and watched as they read it together, while her foot clicked against the bamboo.

She knew what it said. She'd read it several times over the last few days after Blanca had dropped the file on her desk. She'd read it carelessly, while she was eating lunch or taking notes on the case, recognizing none of the ramifications. But as she sipped tea and watched Penn's face turn angry and Viv shake her head, she realized she'd missed a critical piece of processing the case.

She heard Blanca's monotone voice say, "We'll make it easy for your first time in the field."

"This is bullshit!" Penn exclaimed, jumping off the sofa. "Have you authenticated it?"

She couldn't look at them. She withdrew the next paper in the file, for she'd made sure she was highly prepared, and handed it to her.

She turned to Viv and said, "It's a request from the court, ordering you to produce correspondence from your father that can be examined by a handwriting expert."

"Why are we hearing about this now?" Penn asked acidly.

She avoided the question and looked at Viv. "We've attempted to make contact several times, but you've never returned our calls."

She shrugged. "Well, thanks to caller ID I don't answer the phone unless I know who it is. I'm too busy. I guess your number came up as unknown caller. I thought you were a salesman." She looked up at Penn. "What is she saying?"

Penn glared. "You tell her. I'm not doing your dirty work."

She swallowed hard. "If this is valid, it means that in nineteen fifty-five your father sold the enclave, and you've lived here illegally ever since."

CHAPTER THREE

February, 1954

By the time I'd climbed halfway up the orange tree, my legs and arms were covered in scratches. Thin and spindly, the tree was nothing like the solid oaks in Iowa and the limbs sagged under my weight.

I was a tree expert, having fallen out of practically every type that grew in the Midwest. After so many times Mama no longer ran outside with her hands covered in flour or furniture oil. Instead she'd just call from the back door, "Vivi, are you hurt or just being a moron?"

"Just a moron," I'd call back most times, but once in a while she'd have to haul me to the doctor. Yet my falls never stopped me from climbing up high.

I wasn't sure what she'd say when she saw me in the orange tree. She was at the store, and I was staging a protest against the destruction of the orchard now that I finally understood that to build all of his homes, Mr. Rubenstein would be *killing* my beautiful trees. I'd assumed men with big shovels would come and gently remove each one and plant it somewhere else, just like Pops did at his new job with Harper's Nursery. People came in and purchased huge trees that sat in enormous square boxes, and then he went out and planted them in their new yards. I'd imagined my beautiful orange trees waiting to be picked up by Pops' truck.

But instead I'd come home from school to find a bulldozer smashing against the frail trunks until the trees toppled against each other. Without thinking I'd climbed up the nearest one while a man maneuvered the huge steel bucket. When he saw me, he jumped down and stared up between the limbs.

"I haven't got all day, missy," he called. "I'm on a schedule."

He was a large black man wearing jeans, a work shirt and a green baseball cap that covered most of his face. I couldn't tell how angry he was, but his tone was much nicer than Mama's would be when she found me. I knew she'd yell and carry on, and I imagined I wouldn't be listening to the radio any time soon. But I didn't care. I loved the trees and it wasn't right to cut them down.

A breeze sifted the leaves and the heady smell of blossoms made me dizzy. I sulked, thinking about the oranges that would never grow again.

Our new black Cadillac, that was the first purchase with Mr. Rubenstein's money, growled up to the house and I prepared myself for Mama's wrath. The workman took off his cap and squished it in his powerful hands. I thought he might be just as nervous as me.

She wasted no time confronting him and pointing to the quiet bulldozer. "What's going on, Mac?"

"Well, ma'am, we have a situation." He pointed up and her gaze followed until she saw me.

"What in the world?" she asked. "Vivian Battle what are you doing? Get yourself down here right now!"

"No!"

She moved closer to the trunk and stared up at me, her gloved hands resting on her tiny hips. Although she wore a simple cotton dress, she'd put her flowing blonde hair in the chignon.

"Get down," she said slowly.

I shook my head. "I don't want them to take the trees."

She glanced at Mac, and I could tell she was trying to hold her temper in front of him. Normally she'd be shrieking at me after the first *no*, but it wouldn't be proper to call me an idiotic moron in front of a stranger.

"Vivi, this isn't ours anymore. We sold it, and you need to get down or you're going to get in real trouble."

I imagined I was sitting at the edge of a waterfall and was about to plunge into the rapids. "No!"

She threw up her hands and whispered to him. I was fascinated. I'd never seen either of my parents talk to a black person.

He cleared his throat. "Vivian, you need to come down now. You're upsetting your mother."

"No!"

Mama screamed, "Vivian!"

He held up a hand and she closed her mouth just like she did with my father. Maybe it was the universal way women responded to men, but I couldn't imagine ever silencing myself because a man wanted me to.

I'd barely blinked and he was in the tree. He moved like Spiderman, standing on a limb about four feet from the ground. He was probably a little older than Mama with soft brown eyes and a bald head. He had a square jaw and his shirt clung to the muscles in his arm. Everything about him looked strong, and I was a little scared until he smiled. His bright white teeth consumed his dark face and I felt the corners of my mouth turn up.

"You didn't think I'd come up here, did ya?"

I ignored him and gripped my limb tighter in case he wanted to grab me. Mama paced below smoking a cigarette. She always looked so glamorous when she smoked, just like those ladies in the magazines.

"How old are you, Miss Vivi?" he asked.

I blinked in surprise. Adults rarely asked me a question outside of school, and then it was usually in a tone that only half expected me to know the answer.

"I'm twelve."

"That's awfully old to be sittin' in trees, don't you think?"

"No."

To show my complete disinterest I pulled my Wonder Woman comic from my pocket and pretended to read *Earth's Last Hour.*

"Hm. She's one of my favorites," he said, trying to read over my shoulder.

I ignored him and the pointy limb poking my thigh through my dress. If I wiggled around too much I might tumble to the ground.

"How would you like to see the *first* Wonder Woman comic book?"

I couldn't stop myself from looking up. I loved comic books, and I loved to draw. His expression seemed sincere but I was doubtful. Adults lied.

"Now *that* got your attention," he said. "You get outta this tree and I'll show it to you sometime."

He *was* lying. Adults always said things like that when they wanted kids to do something right away. They'd make a promise for the future and then never keep it. Pops did it all the time. I'd lost count of all the ice creams he'd said he'd buy me, the movies we were supposed to see together or the pony ride that never happened.

"I think I'll stay here," I said, turning the page.

"Can't let you do that."

I was in his arms before I could protest, and in just two steps we were out of the tree, but not before I heard a loud rip behind me. He stepped away and Mama spun me around.

"Now look at this," she barked, grabbing the back of my dress and holding it up so I could see it. "This is what your shenanigans have caused, young lady. Now, you get upstairs and change. We'll see what your father says when he comes home."

She swatted my bottom as I raced past her. I didn't want to be near the bulldozer when the trees started shrieking again.

I ran to my room and peered through the window. She was still talking to Mac so I lifted it slowly to eavesdrop.

"I'm sorry you had to do that, Mac."

"Not a problem, Mrs. Battle. The girl loves her trees. I'm gonna call it a day. Sun's startin' to bend, and there's no point in upsettin' her more."

She laughed. "You're far too nice to her. What she needs is a good whupping."

"I'll leave that up to your husband, ma'am," he said, tipping his hat and heading to our neighbor's property where the workers lived.

We watched him go, walking away like an easy breeze.

****

Coming up the driveway the next day after school I was greeted by the same horrible growling and the pathetic high-pitched cry as a tree fought back in vain. I ran faster determined to stop Mac but I slipped on something and fell, landing on my side in a deep groove from the bulldozer's tire.

I was wet, covered in pulpy juice mixed with dirt and surrounded by thousands of crushed oranges. I sat up and assessed his progress. While I'd struggled with fractions during math and played dodgeball at recess, he'd destroyed a few hundred trees and piled them into a disgusting pyramid.

I started to cry. The perfectly straight rows had been reduced to thousands of twisted roots, broken trunks and tangled branches. The huge bucket clawed at the earth and the machine strained underneath a slim trunk until a popping sound overpowered the drone of the engine as the tree lost its fight to stay planted in the ground. But the claw eventually hefted it up and dropped it onto the pile of bodies.

I gazed at the thousands of smashed oranges strewn across what was left of our lawn, victims of the bulldozer's enormous treads. A few had managed to roll out of harm's way near the back stairs. I picked one up with a plan to enjoy the sweet, delicious fruit, but as the bulldozer backed up and turned sideways, I saw Mac position the claw against another innocent tree.

"No!"

I threw the orange with all my might and it hit him in the arm. He jumped and the claw dropped as he let go of the controls.

He looked surprised, and I wondered if he might scoop me up as punishment, but instead he leaned against the bulldozer's steering wheel and shook his head in disbelief.

That just made me angrier. I grabbed several oranges and tossed them in his direction. And when I couldn't find any more oranges I hurled pebbles and then dirt, my arms flailing like windmills. As I readied to pelt what felt like a good-sized rock, a force of pink flowers and lace knocked me to the ground.

"Don't you be hurtin' my daddy!" a high-pitched voice screamed. "I'll break you!"

"Kiah! Get off her," Mac ordered.

We rolled over a few more times until his strong arms demanded she release me. I stood up and faced a beautiful girl with eyes like his and smooth, milk-chocolate skin. He held her in a bear hug while she squirmed to free herself. She was tall and skinny and probably a little older than me. Her short, wiry black hair was smoothed away from her face and cut unevenly at her jawbone.

"Now, Kiah, you be a good girl."

She nodded and he stepped away. I saw my chance. I barreled toward her but he was quick. He grabbed me by the middle and held me like a football.

"Now, quit wiggling, Miss Vivi."

I paid him no mind and squirmed and kicked. When I heard him grunt, I knew I'd done damage.

"You stop it, you hear?" he said roughly. "Or I'll tell your mama to give you another whuppin'."

At the mention of a spanking my body went limp, still sore from the last night's paddling.

He set me down and I looked up. All I saw was kindness.

"Well, Miss Vivi, your mama's right. You are a holy terror."

"I am not!" When he laughed I asked, "How do you know Mama calls me that?"

He squatted down and faced me. "Honey, everybody knows it. And your mama told me."

I made some sort of disagreeable sound which only made him laugh harder. It was contagious and I cracked a smile.

"This here's my daughter, Kiah."

She stood by the bulldozer, her hands on her hips. Unlike me, she clearly followed her daddy's directions.

"Say hello, Kiah." When she shook her head, he added, "Young lady, please be courteous."

"Hello," she said in a very unfriendly tone.

"I think the two of you oughtta be friends seein' as you're both the only girls around here."

We exchanged glares and he shook his head. "I have to get back to work." He studied the remaining trees before meeting my gaze. "You love 'em, don't ya?"

"Yes."

He tipped his hat to me. "Then I'm sorry my work is painful to you."

No one had ever apologized to me. I nodded dumbly.

"Now, it's good to have more friends, Kiah," he said seriously.

They gazed at each other as if they were talking without speaking. I was surprised because I couldn't talk to Pops even when I used words. We'd certainly never be able to read minds like them. Eventually she grudgingly stepped toward me.

"I'm sorry for beating you up."

"You didn't beat me up," I argued. "I'd a had you if your daddy hadn't stepped in."

She gave a lopsided grin. "Maybe you would have."

Obviously he thought we weren't going to kill each other, so he climbed back into the bulldozer. Before he started the engine, he said, "We live across the way in the quarters. Kiah, why don't you offer Vivi some lemonade?" he said.

And then the horrible motor rumbled to life and he went about his business of ravaging the orange grove. I took a step forward, but she put a gentle hand on my shoulder. I looked into her eyes and saw Mac's kindness. She nodded and I knew there was nothing I could do. We watched for several minutes as he effortlessly lifted up the trees and added them to the pile. All the while she kept her hand on my shoulder.

She turned to me and asked, "How old are you?"

"Twelve. How old are you?"

"Fourteen. I'm going to high school already."

I knew that meant she went to Carver downtown, the only high school for black kids. She trudged through the smashed fruit and retrieved a stack of books sitting on the driveway. The back of her dress was covered in a huge dirt streak from her neckline to her hem, and I wondered what names *her* mother would call her.

I glanced at the huge brown smudge on the front of my shirt. It looked as if I'd been making mud pies. I groaned. Mama would certainly offer her standard comment when she saw me. "Vivi, I should just let you run around naked seeing how you treat your clothes. A bath don't hardly cost nothing and your skin comes mostly clean except for those awful knees of yours. I've seen potatoes come out of the patch cleaner than your knees."

But for now I was lucky. It was Tuesday and that meant she was at her sewing group with the ladies from our church.

"Are you comin'?" Kiah called.

I followed as she slid between the rows of trees to an irrigation ditch on the east end of the property. She leaped over it and disappeared into an adjoining grove.

"We live over here," she explained. "Mr. Rubenstein bought up all this land too."

"Does your daddy work for him?" I asked.

"Uh-huh, he's one of the head guys," she said with pride.

Then suddenly the trees were gone and we were standing in a flat field, the earth newly turned. In the distance huge yellow machines rumbled over the soft dirt where rows of little houses would sit. They would all look the same: red brick or painted masonry block with a pop-out front window and a single-car garage.

On our first trip through the city, as we had driven through west Phoenix, Mama had asked Pops what he thought of the tiny houses and he'd remarked, "Don't think much of 'em except the money we can make."

She led me past a row of cabins, and we went inside the one on the end. I could see the whole place from the living room since the bedroom and bathroom doors were open. Neither of the beds was made and I was jealous. Mama never tolerated an unmade bed or one full of wrinkles and poor corners.

Kiah threw her books on the small dining room table and went to the kitchen. I was surprised to see a sink, which meant they had running water. Dirty dishes were scattered on the counter and only two clean glasses remained on an empty shelf in the cupboard.

"Where's your mama?"

"She's dead," she said flatly. "It's just me and Daddy. She died when she was having me, but Daddy said it wasn't my fault. You want some lemonade?" she asked, removing a pitcher from the refrigerator.

"Sure."

She poured us each a glass and we sat down at the table. I didn't know what to say to this odd girl quietly sipping lemonade, who had thrown me to the ground just minutes before. I looked at her stack of schoolbooks, the one on top titled *Algebra I*. I'd been warned about algebra and told that I'd learn it next year as a freshman, if I got promoted. I wasn't a very good student, and sometimes I believed Mama when she called me a moron, especially after she got my report card or visited with my teachers.

"Vivi, a whole family of squirrels could take up residence in that empty area between your ears. Might as well seein' as you don't have any need for it. You better hope you're good at makin' babies."

I couldn't imagine what it would be like to squeeze a baby out of the tiny hole between my legs, and the thought made me study harder but nothing stuck. I'd be in the middle of writing an essay and suddenly I was doodling in the margins, drawing faces or scenery, the thought of the paragraph dropped like a used hankie. I knew it didn't matter anyway. I always got a D. Teachers gave me just enough to pass, but I thought it was because they liked my drawings.

"Why were you up in that tree?" she asked.

"I don't want your daddy to tear 'em down. They're *my* trees, at least they used to be."

She frowned but she didn't get mad. She just poured more lemonade in my glass.

"I think it's important to stand up for things you believe in," she said slowly. "I'm going to go to law school to fight for civil rights someday. You might find me sittin' in a tree somewhere, too," she added with a grin. If she was going to law school, I knew she was smart.

I pointed at her algebra book. "Do you like it?" I said. I figured I could at least be nice since she invited me into her house and served me some of the best lemonade I'd ever tasted.

Her whole face lit up in a way I didn't understand. Nothing about school excited me except art class. "I like math a lot."

"I don't," I snorted.

"Why not?"

"It's too hard. There's so many rules to remember, and if you miss one step, you get the whole thing wrong. I don't think that's right," I added, hoping she could appreciate the injustice of mathematics. "It oughtta be at least half right." She giggled into her glass and I sat up straight. "Hey, are you makin' fun of me?"

"No," she said, shaking her head. "I just never heard anybody explain it like that. But I guess that's true. You can't make a mistake or it's all wrong."

I hung my head thinking that she also thought I was a moron. My cheeks felt hot and I knew if I looked up she'd see my shame. "I need to be going." I went to the door, my eyes glued to the floor.

"Where you goin'?"

"I need to get home," I whispered. "Thanks for the lemonade."

When I heard the door shut behind me I broke into a run, heading into the orchard that we no longer owned. I was trespassing and I didn't care. I zigzagged haphazardly down the rows of trees that remained, changing direction in a split second and ultimately smashing my forehead into a low-hanging branch. I fell backward onto the ground and stared up at the offending tree. Instantly angry, I laughed, picturing the bulldozer clawing at the screaming branches as they ripped away from the trunk. My laughter died in the back of my throat and turned to sobs.

****

"How in the world did you manage to grow a goose egg on the front of your face?" Mama asked when I charged through the back door.

She was making supper and the sight of her daughter holding her throbbing head in filthy clothes did not deter her from stirring the gravy. When she saw that I was upright and mobile, she returned to her cooking, not particularly interested in my answer.

But she never was. She seemed to live with a perpetual scowl on her face, and I rarely saw her laugh except on her birthday or one of the few times Pops took her out. She was tiny and small-boned, and the stories she told suggested she'd been a spitfire, ready to take on the world. In the old pictures she'd looked happy. But Pops, Will and I had wiped the smile off her face for good. Her dislike of me probably should've made me mad but I felt sorry for her instead.

Today she wore a colorful blue apron with birds over her plaid pedal pushers and pink blouse. Even though she looked angry she was always a good dresser. She bent over the oven to check on the casserole, and I pictured Pops playfully swatting her bottom and making a raunchy comment to draw her wrath. She wasn't as slim as she was in the old pictures and he called her curvy, but he seemed to like it. And I knew that other men thought she was pretty because they always whistled when she walked by.

And she'd make a point of saying to me, "You see, Vivi, they'll be whistling at you someday if you ever decide to fix your hair, quit jumpin' off the roof and start behaving like a lady rather than a moron."

I shuffled across the linoleum, anxious to get upstairs and change my clothes before she put me to work peeling the potatoes. I slipped on some jeans and a T-shirt and started on my homework, but it didn't take long before the doodles and drawings covered my math paper, leaving little room for the fifty mixed fraction problems I was supposed to complete. I was only on number four and my pencil was already dull from shading the portrait of Kiah that I'd started. I was in awe of her beauty and her dark skin and straightened hair fascinated me.

I heard a tap on my window and jumped a foot in the air. She was outside waving.

"What are you doing?" I asked, opening the window.

"I was worried about you when you left. You looked like you were mad or sad."

I shook my head and lied. "No, I just needed to go."

She leaned closer. "What'd you do to your head?"

I automatically rubbed the goose egg and it started to hurt again. "I just ran into a tree branch."

"That looks bad. It's turning purple."

"It's okay."

I glanced at my door, knowing that Mama would appear soon and announce dinner. I couldn't imagine what she'd do to Kiah if she found her in my room. "You should probably go."

"I know. I just wanted to check on you."

"How did you get up here?"

She pointed to the trellis against the house. "It's easy. You just climb up and walk across the edge of the roof. Seein' as you're a holy terror, I'm surprised you've never tried it."

We laughed, and I thought of my math homework. "Could you show me how to do mixed fractions real quick?"

She held up the paper, and I remembered that I'd been drawing pictures of her. I tried to grab it but she turned away. I closed my eyes and prepared for a big sock in the jaw.

"Vivi, this is really good. I think it looks like me," she said with tears in her eyes.

I smiled sheepishly. Will was the only one who ever liked my drawings. "Thanks."

She grinned and we stood there staring at each other stupidly. Then she looked down and her brow furrowed as she studied the little bit of math I'd attempted. "I don't understand what you're doing. Let me see your book."

I showed her the original problems and she shook her head. "Vivi, you're not doing this right."

"I know," I said. "I don't get it."

"No, that's not it. Look, you're not copying them correctly.

You wrote down four problems and in three of them you mixed up the numbers. You're getting them backward. It's not supposed to be fifty-two and two-thirds; it's supposed to be *twenty-five* and two-thirds. That's why you're messing up."

I followed her finger as she showed me the difference. In three problems I'd written numbers backward. "I don't know why I'm doing that. That's really stupid," I muttered.

Mama was right. I was a moron. I was twelve years old and I certainly should know the difference between fifty-two and twenty-five. I crumpled up the paper.

"Don't!" she cried. She took it and smoothed it out. "I really like the drawing. Let me help you. I'll write the problems down and then you solve them."

She wrote out the first one and we worked it through.

"See, you know how to do the math, but you get stuff backward. Do you do that with your letters, too?"

I nodded. I never admitted it to anyone, but I remember Mama had yelled at me after the last conference. "If you wanted to take the time to spell the words correctly, Vivian, you could. You're just being lazy."

"Geez, no wonder you don't like school," she said.

Mama shouted up the stairs. Pops was finally home.

"I gotta go."

"Okay, I'll just stay up here for a few more minutes and write out the rest before I slip back down the trellis."

"I...I don't know—"

"Don't worry about it. It's cool."

I looked at her funny. "Cool? What's that?"

She laughed. "It's the new way of saying it's fine. Just go and make sure you take care of this bump."

She gently rubbed her thumb across my forehead and turned back to my desk. My body froze, and, fortunately, she didn't see my jaw drop before I ran out of the room to answer Mama's call.

For the first time in my life a black person had actually touched me.

Re: Definitely Friends First! - 27 (Central Phoenix)
Date: 2010-06-07, 10:19AM MST

Hi. You don't know me. Well, of course you don't know me—yet. But I think once we met you'd like me, maybe. Maybe a little. If you haven't guessed I'm new to this whole personal ad stuff and I've never answered one and I've always thought about it but I couldn't bring myself to reply but I'd right the reply and then I'd sit there with my finger over the reply button and I couldn't bring myself to actually hit it you know, and send it off into syeberspace because what if it's going to a raving loonatic or someone who'll turn out to be a stalker or worse one of those serial killers who prays on dates. But you sound ok. Reply back, pleeeeasse!

Posted by: Chattylady1
Reply

Re: Definitely Friends First! - 27 (Central Phoenix)
Date: 2010-06-07, 7:10PM MST

DFF—
I'm gonna be honest. I'm nothing like u. I didn't finesh high school cuz I couldn't stand the teachers. But I'm street smart and I been a bartender at the Incog for six years. had my share of women and relationships. You didn't say what kind of woman you liked and I'm cool with that. Sounds like u r open to different types. I've got tats, a nose ring and a nip piercing that drives my lovers wild. Down- I'm a big butch and I'd like to meet. What says u?

Posted by: Buck
Reply

Re: Definitely Friends First! - 27 (Central
Phoenix)
Date: 2010-06-08, 1:01AM MST

You sound hot. Fuck me.

Posted by: Ladyinblack
Reply

CHAPTER FOUR

June, 2010

"How can you do this?" Penn hissed. Viv had left the room in search of the requested handwriting sample. "You call yourself a *fan*?" Her voice was trembling above a whisper but the anger and disdain were evident.

"It's not me. It's the client," CC said through clenched teeth. "As an attorney I'd expect you to understand."

"I don't," she shot back. She dropped onto the couch and shook her head. "That note doesn't make any sense. I don't know that much about Viv's past, but I'm telling you there's either a really good explanation or it's a forgery. Jacob Rubenstein was a friend."

Viv returned with a birthday card that Chet Battle had given to her sixty years ago. "I save everything," she explained. She held up the card and the note and compared them. "Yep, it's his," she said glumly. "I just don't understand."

"Why are you helping her, Viv?" Penn pleaded.

"What can I do? It's the truth. Pops always had the oddest ways of making his e's. He did it backward and half the time they looked like o's with a tail." She showed them the card and pointed to some of the odd letter formations.

"So what? Make her figure it out herself. Don't help the enemy," Penn said sharply, glaring at CC, who quickly placed the note and the card into her briefcase.

Viv patted CC's knee and offered a little smile, which only made her feel worse. "Don't you listen to Penn. Anyone who loves Chloe is all right by me." She looked her in the eye and said, "Please call me Viv. All my friends do. And next time bring your sketchbook."

"Thank you," she stammered. "I'm very sorry about all of this."

Viv nodded but showed no other emotion, which surprised her, given Viv was faced with losing her home. CC had expected tears and perhaps screaming but she seemed calm, almost accepting. She had been surprised by the existence of the note, of this CC was certain, but as the conversation progressed, or rather, as their argument escalated, she noticed Viv had grown quiet, as if she'd reached into a bag of memories and pulled out a very unpleasant one that might explain the situation.

Penn followed CC out, carrying some books under her arm. "Yeah, you can bring by your sketchbook with the eviction notice," she said acidly.

Tears welled in her eyes. She noticed a banana yellow Smartcar had pulled up next to her Nova.

"You can't be serious about this case," she continued. "Are you really going to put a little old lady out of her house?"

She turned and faced her. "There's nothing I can do."

"Of course there is."

"I don't have a choice," she said, her heels clicking down the blacktop toward the street. She walked faster hoping Penn would turn back.

"Of course you have a choice. Just tell them no. Tell them you're unwilling to toss a national treasure out on her ear. You know I'll fight this," she said, leaning against the car. "The media will love this story. This won't happen."

Her stomach flipped at the idea of a media firestorm and her hand shook as she manually unlocked the door to her beat-up Honda.

Penn stared at the car. "I'm totally unimpressed."

She smirked. "This is what all the high-powered attorneys are driving right now, didn't you know that? This is why I can't say no to this client. I have a senior associate who is totally riding my ass in a job I need to pay off my unforgiveable student loans." She pointed at her chest. "I just started a month ago! No isn't in my vocabulary."

Penn grabbed her extended finger. "Lawyers rarely point, counselor. It's confrontational. You need to learn that." She let go and pointed at her heart. "I choose." Before she walked away, she thrust three Chloe books into her hands.

She leaned against the Honda, her foot madly tapping the curb. She'd never spoken to anyone with that much fervor. She should have felt victorious since her client was going to win, but instead she felt like a loser, a card-carrying member of Heartless and Burned.

****

When the elevator reached the eleventh floor, she stood taller and clenched her briefcase as she crossed the marble floor. Hartford and Burns was classy and no expense was spared. Finely coiffed receptionists greeted clients and motioned to the Italian leather sofas while they retrieved beverages served in crystal glasses. The dress code was incredibly strict. She'd heard an attorney had once been fired after he'd lost a cufflink and dared to attend a meeting without changing his shirt.

She settled into her small office and checked her calendar. She felt strong after her confrontation with Penn, and she picked up the phone to cancel her plans with Alicia. Then she heard Blanca's voice in the hallway. Like all of the attorneys she was dressed in a sharp power suit with a conservative blouse and business pumps. Her short black hair was pulled back in a clip revealing stern brown eyes and a long forehead that was constantly creased in displeasure. She didn't bother to come in as she was far too busy and important to cross the threshold of a junior associate's office.

"Everything went well, I hope," she said in her robotic voice.

"Yes, I've got the sample." She held it out in case she wanted to inspect it. "I just wish our client wasn't evicting an old lady."

"I understand," she said in a voice that implied she didn't care. "Emotionally this is more difficult, but our focus must be on Mr. Rubenstein. Correct?"

"Absolutely," she said assuredly. She tapped a stack of folders on the edge of her desk and set them in her outbox for show.

Blanca offered a single nod. "I'll see you in the conference room in ten. I expect you to take the lead."

She continued down the hallway and CC deflated in her chair. She swiveled toward the window and stared at the mountain range in the distance. It used to be called Squaw Peak but had been changed to something more politically correct. It jutted toward the sky, and she could see the gray trails carved into the side. It was relaxing to think about hiking up the switchbacks, which she'd done a few times with two of her co-workers. Of course, Alicia would never do something so dirty. She abhorred hiking or sweating.

Her phone buzzed and the receptionist announced the Morgans had arrived. She raced into the bathroom and locked herself in a stall. At least five times a day she hid for a few minutes, unable to sustain a self-assured expression on her face for more than two hours at a time. She didn't know how the other juniors did it. She heard confidence in their voices and saw the way they swaggered into meetings. Yet, she felt like an impostor and often resisted the urge to scream, "I have no idea what I'm doing!"

After three deep breaths she charged out of the bathroom and glided into the smallest conference room, the one reserved for the junior associates. She glanced across the table at opposing counsel and nearly toppled over—Alicia. She was scribbling notes on a legal pad and only offered a passing gaze as CC slid into a chair next to her client Hailey Morgan.

She hadn't seen Alicia in six weeks, but she looked as she always did—completely put together. Not a strand of her blonde hair had escaped the tight bun she wore and the Armani suit fit as if custom made. CC imagined her own locks wildly situated on her head after baking in her non-air conditioned car, and she knew her cotton dress shirt was horribly wrinkled.

And how Alicia found the precise choice of jewelry and shoes amazed her. She spent hours trolling the accessory department just to find a belt that had a speck of color that matched a chosen blouse while CC's focus on shopping only lasted long enough to buy a few outfits.

Alicia sat in the chair next to Dusty Morgan, Hailey's brother. He'd only surfaced after a public notice advertised the death of Carter Morgan, their father. She imagined he wouldn't have paid any attention to Carter's death if three million dollars hadn't been at stake. He leaned back with his hands across his chest as his sandy brown hair flopped in his face.

At the head of the table was Steven Kraft, the mediator who'd been assigned by Judge Fitch after their one court appearance ended with him breaking off the head of his gavel as he attempted to silence the shouting siblings. At the time Dusty had been represented by a different law firm, and she hadn't realized he'd changed representation. *Is it coincidental he picked my ex?*

Blanca sailed into the room and quickly introduced herself to Alicia and Dusty before taking the seat next to Hailey. She carried no files nor held a legal pad, indicating CC was on point.

Kraft glanced in her direction before his gaze shifted back to the papers in front of him. When the Sweatinator scratched his head, she caught a glimpse of the puddle underneath his arm.

"Let's begin," he said. "Our goal today is to find some common ground so we do not waste any of the court's valuable time. Ms. Carlson?"

She nodded and cleared her throat, thinking of the most persuasive and succinct way to present her argument. "Miss Morgan has always been in her father's life. She made sure he was placed in an excellent care facility—"

"Yeah, right," Dusty interrupted. "Put him away so she could spend his money."

"That's not true!" Hailey shouted. "I've always cared for Dad!"

"That's such B.S.!" he shouted back and they were off.

Two minutes later, after she and Alicia had practically crawled onto the conference table to separate them, both had returned to their respective chairs.

Kraft looked up, nonplussed. "If that happens again, I will leave and make a decision without input from either of you. Continue, Miss Carlson," he directed.

"Miss Morgan paid the bills," she said firmly, "and she visited regularly, which is documented in the visitors' logs, and yes, she used some of the funds to ease her suffering."

"Some of the funds?" Dusty exclaimed. "You call twenty thousand dollars on clothes, makeup and shoes *some* of the funds?"

She grabbed Hailey's arm before she could react and her client slumped back in the plush leather chair. She had said nearly the same thing to her when she'd reviewed her finances but that was her right as the attorney.

"Mr. Morgan has appeared at the eleventh hour to claim half of an estate that doesn't belong to him. We agree that as the son, he is entitled to an inheritance; however, it should only be a fourth, not half."

"So seven hundred fifty thousand instead of one and a half million," Kraft summarized, writing in his notes. "Okay, your turn Miss Dennis."

Alicia folded her hands on the table. "We believe he should have half. Yes, Mr. Morgan made some decisions he regrets regarding his relationship with his father, but..." She paused and stared sympathetically at Hailey. "So did Miss Morgan. She misused his money, which in our opinion, is just as neglectful as absence. Thus, both of them have committed transgressions that are unfortunate and irreversible, so let's stop fighting and call it even."

He scribbled in his notes and opened a file. She glanced at Alicia and her unreadable expression. She'd never watched her work and only knew she was regarded as a solid attorney. She'd stated her case plainly while CC didn't feel she'd argued the facts well. It was always hard to justify a split between siblings that wasn't equal unless one child truly deserved to be lionized and the other demonized.

Such was not the case with Hailey and Dusty Morgan. Both were spoiled children, but if she lost it was significant to H and B since they were guaranteed twenty percent of Hailey's cut.

"Is that all, Ms. Dennis?" he asked.

She frowned. "Actually, no. I believe there is one more matter that the court needs to consider." She pulled a file from her briefcase and three eight-by-ten photos dramatically spilled onto the conference table. "Oh, I'm sorry," she said. "How clumsy of me."

Hailey gasped and CC knew they were in trouble. Before Alicia could scoop up the photos, CC caught a glimpse of three shadowy figures standing outside a building with a lighted sign that read Popperz.

"We need to talk," Hailey whispered. "Now."

CC smiled at the Sweatinator. "Could we have a few minutes with our client before Ms. Dennis continues?"

Kraft looked at Alicia, as if gaining her approval. "By all means," she said confidently with a blithe smile.

CC knew that expression. She'd seen it every time Alicia proved her wrong during their relationship.

Blanca joined them in her office. "What's going on, Hailey?"

She looked troubled and her gaze couldn't find a focus. "I've struggled with a little drug problem. I've got it under control now, but I'm pretty sure those pictures show me making a deal."

"Shit," Blanca hissed. She turned to CC. "You didn't know about this?"

"No, I—"

"I'm taking over," Blanca said heading out the door.

They returned to their seats and Alicia still wore her pleasant smile.

The Sweatinator looked at her. "Continue."

She handed him the photos. "These photos show Hailey Morgan outside Popperz, a bar known by local PD as a drug haven. You can see Miss Morgan in the presence of two men who are known dealers. And this is the affidavit from Officer Laura Calhoun, the beat cop who patrols that area and has confirmed their identities." She paused long enough for him to study the evidence before she continued. "We contend that Miss Morgan has used much of the money to support her cocaine habit and her inheritance will most likely go to such endeavors in the future."

"Endeavors?" Blanca rolled her eyes. "May I interject?"

"By all means," Kraft said, leaning back in his chair.

"These pictures are inconsequential. My client is clean and who she chooses to converse with is her business." She turned to Alicia. "She's never been arrested for selling or possessing?"

"No."

"Never been picked up for DUI?"

"No," Alicia said slowly.

"In fact, she's never even been questioned as a witness. True?"

"Yes, but—"

"No buts. These photos prove nothing. I'd like to have my client drug-tested."

"That doesn't mean anything," Alicia said. "Just because she's clean now doesn't mean she was then. It doesn't mean she hasn't used her father's money to purchase drugs in the past."

Blanca waved a hand. "Wait a minute. You just said that we need to set aside the mistakes of the past."

CC resisted the urge to smile when Alicia started to squirm, remembering that it had been *her* job to put Alicia in this position, not Blanca's. While the firm might still prevail it would be Blanca's credit—not hers.

"We would stipulate future drug tests as a condition of the inheritance," Blanca added, looking at Hailey, who nodded.

Kraft wrote furiously on his pad and then set his pen down. He stared at the pictures for a long time before he let them fall to the table. "Frankly, I'm sorry your mother's not around to inherit this money. I find both of you equally distasteful. Therefore, you're splitting it fifty-fifty, and Miss Morgan will consent to monthly drug tests for a period of one year."

They shook hands and everyone filed out. Blanca and CC said goodbye to Hailey, but when the elevator door closed, Blanca glared at her. "What happened?"

"I don't know."

"You *should* have known. That hurt us."

She disappeared and CC wondered if she'd find one of Blanca's notorious pink slips sitting on her chair. According to firm legend Blanca kept a pack of them in her desk drawer.

When Alicia exited the restroom, she saw CC and followed her into her office.

"We need to talk," she said, closing the door while CC hunted for some antacid in her desk. "I'm sorry I didn't tell you I was the opposing attorney."

She glared at her. "Are you really? You didn't think you could bring it up this morning when you called about the CD? Do you even *want* the CD, or were you just feeling me out, seeing if I knew you'd be here."

Alicia looked hurt. "Of course I want the CD. You gave it to me." She threw a glance at the antacid bottle in her hand. "I didn't realize you were so nervous and uptight."

"I'm not." She threw the bottle—evidence of the truth—into the drawer and dropped into her chair. "I was just surprised to see you."

Alicia perched on the edge of her desk and adopted a concerned look. "Honey, I know you. Your foot was bouncing like a basketball, you were speaking in that little high-pitched voice you get when you're nervous and when Blanca took over you looked like a ghost. Was this your first time with a client?"

She couldn't contain her surprise. "No, I've handled several cases." Alicia raised her eyebrows and her insides churned. "Did I really seem that green?"

"A little," she admitted.

Her door flew open. "CC, you need to rewrite this pleading," Blanca said, looking up from the papers she held. Her gaze landed on Alicia. "Why is she still here?"

"I'm a friend," Alicia said.

"I wish you would have told me that you knew the opposing counsel to avoid conflict of interest. We might have come off better with Kraft."

"She didn't know I was on the other side," Alicia explained. "Dusty Morgan just changed firms." Blanca looked skeptical until she added, "You know I saw your closing argument in the Swanson case. It was amazing."

Her stony demeanor cracked. "You were there?"

She nodded. "I was waiting for a hearing to start and I slipped into the courtroom. You were just hitting your stride."

"That was my first closing. Thanks for noticing." She dropped the report on CC's desk. "Please rewrite this." Before she left she said to Alicia, "Good play with the photos today, especially dropping them on the table. Very smooth. Too bad we didn't know our client was a user."

After she left Alicia looked at CC the way she used to when they were having a serious conversation in bed. "You need to learn how to suck up, babe. Bitches like that."

"But I'm not good at it," she whined. "You were always the persuasive one."

"Yeah, remember the time I convinced the neighbor's cable guy to hook us up for free?" She went to the door. "I've got to get back. I really am sorry I didn't tell you. Kinkaid's at eight?"

She knew there was a fifty-fifty chance Alicia was lying and had deliberately surprised her to throw her off her already shaky game.

"Please?" she pleaded. "I've got a surprise for you."

"Sure."

****

Kinkaid's was a two-story office building in its previous life, but a young upstart chef had seen the potential to convert it into a pub and restaurant with a loft. The exposed red brick walls created an edgy feel and a large metal garage front door allowed for indoor and outdoor seating. Cars cruising down busy Camelback Road could see all the action inside. It was the premier Phoenix happy hour spot for the younger generation, and CC had been propositioned there more than once but had never said yes.

When she saw Alicia sitting at a pub table outside she felt unbalanced again. She disguised her sexiness in lawyer attire every day, but now her bun was gone and her hair flowed suggestively around her face. CC was sure she'd reapplied her makeup with much bolder colors and her suit jacket was nowhere in sight. She'd undone an extra two buttons of her purple silk blouse exposing deep cleavage and her breasts cradled a gold pendant.

Alicia glanced her way and when their eyes met, Alicia remained expressionless. She picked up her Cosmo and took a sip, her gaze still locked on CC, who didn't know if she should join her or run out of the restaurant. Then Alicia flashed a killer smile that nearly knocked her over. This wasn't the same woman who'd sat on her desk just a few hours ago.

"Hey," she said, and CC breathed in a lovely jasmine scent she'd never smelled on her before.

"Is that new? The perfume?"

"Yeah. Nadia picked it out. I already ordered you a martini," she said.

"Oh, thanks, but I've actually switched to vodka tonics."

"Really?" Alicia asked in a clearly disapproving tone. "Thanks for the FYI."

She slid the CD across the table. "Here you go. Listen to it in good health."

She held it up. "You know, I lied," she said, still not looking at her. "You didn't give this to me for our anniversary."

She was stunned, but she held her response until the busy waiter delivered her martini and left. "I didn't think I did. Why did you lie?"

Ding!

She checked her phone as another alert for her personal ad appeared.

Alicia leaned forward seductively. "Because I wanted to see you and I was testing you."

"What do you mean?"

"I miss you, babe. I don't know what I want to do about that yet, but I acknowledge that I miss you and I still have feelings for you. But you failed the test."

"Oh?"

"The test was to see if you'd give me the CD if I badgered you for it. And you did. You let me run over you just like I always did during our relationship. Just like I did this afternoon," she added.

CC picked up her purse. "Okay, I don't need this. And, for

your information, I've started dating again, or at least I'm trying to. I took out a personal ad and I've had numerous hits."

She stormed out.

"Honey, wait!" Alicia was behind her.

She knew that Alicia would catch up once she reached her car. Unlike Alicia's Mercedes, which had automatic door locks and didn't even need a key to start, the old Honda only opened after the lock was finessed just right. She turned around since a confrontation was inevitable.

Alicia sashayed across the blacktop, gaining the attention of several men on their way to dinner in the company of their wives and girlfriends. But she was immune to the looks and stares—except when she wanted to be noticed.

"I'm sorry I was a bitch," she said, pulling her into a tight embrace. "That isn't how I wanted this to go."

She'd forgotten that Alicia was a fabulous hugger. She held her close against her enormous chest and CC closed her eyes. She missed it.

"Okay, try again," CC said. "If we skip the badgering and testing part, we left off where you told me that you missed me, which I find hard to believe since Nadia was your soul mate. Those were your exact words the day you left."

Alicia swallowed hard. "I know, but I think I was wrong. I think it's over. She was using me, if you can believe it."

She stifled a laugh. "Oh?"

"Yeah. I think she just wants a roommate to split the rent. She fed me a whole bunch of lines and I bought it."

She knew that was a lie. No one read through bullshit like Alicia. If she'd been with Nadia it was because she wanted to be there.

Alicia reached out and squeezed her hand. "I miss you, babe. I want to show you something that will spice up our relationship."

"We have no relationship. You left me."

"I know," she admitted. "I won't deny that I walked out. But I'm beginning to think it doesn't have to be an ending. Are you serious with someone right now?"

"No, it's been completely casual," she lied.

"I want to give you a test you'll pass."

She shook her head. "I don't know."

Alicia held up a finger. "Give me one hour. And if I don't show you an amazing time, you can delete me from your e-mail, unfriend me on Facebook and remove me from your contacts. Go out and screw every woman who answers your ads. Just one hour."

She's always most persuasive when she's cute. The way that little nose turns up and her whole face sparkles.

"Fine," she agreed. "One hour."

She followed her to the valet, who retrieved her Mercedes, a gift from her parents for law school graduation. Unlike CC's family, hers was wealthy and regularly showered gifts on their little girl.

"Get in," she teased.

She cruised through Kinkaid's back lot, passing CC's old Honda, and heading through the neighboring residential area. As she turned onto Camelback Road, the soft glow of the old suburban porch lights was replaced by millions of high-watt bulbs that filled the stretch of auto showrooms all the way to Seventh Avenue. She could see Alicia's profile, which projected a calm that was foreign to her, and amid the din of the massive traffic, she heard her humming with a soft rock song on the radio.

"So where are we going?" she asked, hoping she wasn't slurring her words.

"You'll see."

She made a right into a four-story office complex at the corner of Central and Virginia. As the Mercedes flew into the underground parking garage, CC noticed a for rent banner hung from the building's long glass panes. She imagined much of the building was unoccupied since commercial real estate faced a huge slump with the hard economic times. And the empty garage confirmed her suspicions. Only a handful of cars and SUVs filled the spaces.

She pulled into a corner partially hidden by a concrete pillar and popped her seat belt in a second. CC followed her into the backseat, and she noticed the pillar obstructed their view of the rest of the garage.

"Here?" she asked slowly.

Alicia kissed her and unbuttoned her own blouse. "Exactly.

Nadia's taught me a new way to have fun, and I want to share it with you. One of the reasons I think I strayed was because I wanted more adventure."

She glanced at the stark cement walls. "Sex in a parking garage?"

Alicia slid out of her bra. "No, sex in a public place. There's a sense of danger and defiance that add to the experience. Let me show you." She gave her a luscious kiss and continued disrobing.

"Aren't you worried about cameras or security guards?"

"There are none. This is the first place Nadia took me so I knew it was perfect for us. It's about to go into foreclosure. Don't worry. Just relax."

She froze. "*Nadia* took you here?"

"So what?"

She pressed her down into the soft leather and hovered over her, unbuttoning her blouse and exposing her breasts to anyone who walked over and peered into a window.

"Don't worry," she said again, clearly reading her mind. "There's no one around." She pushed up her skirt and straddled her waist. All CC saw was her perfect lips. "I want you to touch me while I touch you."

She guided CC's hand to the warmth between her legs and words became impossible. She was focused on pleasing her and worrying about public indecency laws as they undressed. But the jasmine perfume and Alicia's expert touch buried her nervousness as she rocked her hips and pressed her stocking feet against the window behind her head for support.

Ding!

Alicia grabbed her phone and glanced at the display. CC knew she was reading whatever response had come up on the personal ads. She snorted. "This one sounds charming. She wants to cover you in egg batter and pretend you're a quiche. Shall I save it?"

She grabbed the phone and turned it off. "You need to be honest with me. Did you play me at the meeting today? Did you deliberately try to throw me off by surprising me?"

"No way," Alicia mumbled.

She let their passion unravel and said, "Honest?"

"Yes," Alicia replied before she buried her lips in CC's neck.

The answer was ambiguous, and if they weren't groaning and moaning closer to climax she would have grilled her like a cross-examination.

Then a car alarm chirped.

"What's that?" she asked, suddenly paralyzed.

Alicia kissed her and stroked her breasts, unwilling to lose the moment. "Somebody's going home, that's all. They're not coming over here. They'll get in their car and drive away. Stay with me," she commanded and thrust her tongue into CC's mouth.

It was easy to believe her given the heat between their bodies and their mutual wetness.

"Come with me, baby," she gasped.

Instead of a car ignition, CC heard the whoosh of the trunk closing and the audible baritone of the driver chatting on his cell phone. She couldn't make out the conversation, probably because Alicia was sighing heavily, sitting on the edge of climax.

"Now, baby, now," she cried, and CC had no choice. She was too talented not to obey.

Their orgasms were loud—too loud—and the click of heels approaching echoed in the empty garage.

Alicia flashed a wide grin. "Gotta go!"

She jumped from the back seat into the front and threw the car in reverse, the tires screeching in protest. CC hunkered down shielding herself with their discarded clothes, realizing Alicia wore only her stockings. As they passed the stunned middle-aged man, he dropped his cell phone when Alicia turned and flashed him.

They sailed out of the garage and down a dark side street. She stopped suddenly and faced CC, who was holding a pair of panties over her breasts. She laughed hysterically, and when CC imagined how it looked, she laughed too and it was another ten minutes before they could stop.

Once they'd dressed under the cover of moonlight, Alicia drove CC back to her car.

"Don't tell me that wasn't great," she said, stroking her hair over her ear.

"Yeah, that was memorable," she admitted. She took her hand. "Are you sure you don't want to come home tonight?"

"I have to go back to work, and I think it's still too soon. I'm not sure what to do about Nadia. But I loved being with you again," she whispered against her cheek.

Her voice was like a fabulous dessert and CC wanted more. She cupped her breast and Alicia chuckled.

"Oh, no. Not here. This is a bit *too* public, but I promise we'll do it again, okay?"

She nodded and watched her peel away. She climbed into the Honda, instantly disgusted by the torn upholstery and the funny little smell that lingered regardless of how many air fresheners she hung. Alicia had always insisted they take the Mercedes when they went out because the Honda was an embarrassment, and although she agreed, she wished Alicia were more sensitive. Not everyone came from a family with money.

She shifted in her seat. Her bra wasn't sitting right, her skirt was on crooked and she was rather certain her French bikini underwear was on backward. But she didn't care. Everything tingled and she had to resist the urge to shed her clothes and drive home naked. Instead, she sat in her car for fifteen minutes and grinned at her ability to toss aside her midwestern sensibilities. Her mother would *die* if she ever knew.

But I liked it. I have to admit it. I liked the risk and I liked having sex in an unusual location.

But she wasn't really thinking of the term "having sex." She was playing with a much dirtier word, one that she normally couldn't stand to hear people say but nothing else fit for the little rendezvous in the Mercedes.

It was after nine by the time she crossed the threshold of her small condo. It wasn't anything special, and she'd already decided to move once the lease was up. If Alicia came back, she'd have to convince her since Alicia was the one who'd picked the location, which was close to the Scottsdale nightclub action. And when she'd left with most of the belongings, CC hadn't bothered to purchase another TV or a proper bed, instead choosing to sleep on a futon mattress on the floor.

She showered and washed away the lovely jasmine scent and

threw on a tank top and yoga pants before plopping onto her futon with a Lean Cuisine and her briefcase. She grabbed the Chloe books Penn had given her and randomly flipped back and forth between pages, studying the structure as well as the artistic talent. Watercolor was difficult for her and she preferred the bolder effect achieved with pen and ink, but she couldn't imagine the Chloe series in any other medium. It was a perfect choice for the moments when Chloe changed colors to disguise herself.

Ding! That was ten responses to her personal ad today, but she ignored them for now, far more interested in Viv's artwork.

She appreciated her approach: illustrate the entire page from corner to corner and insert the dialogue at strategic places. For small children the words were secondary to the artwork and Viv's detailed animals were enthralling. As a child, she'd been mesmerized by Chloe's scaly skin and pointy tail.

Once she'd absorbed the artistry she decided to start at the beginning and reread each book. She grabbed *Chloe Goes to the Symphony* and saw it was written only two years ago and dedicated to someone named Siobhan. She looked up the pronunciation and said, "Chevonne," out loud, which she learned was Irish for Joan.

The story featured a harpist and the theme was to try new things like listening to classical music. She paused for a moment remembering the cottage and the harp music.

She picked up the other book, *Chloe Makes a Friend.* It was nearly forty years old and dedicated to someone named Kiah. Although she was rather certain she'd read this story as a child, she couldn't recall the plot which described Chloe's unlikely friendship with a hawk—a predator who was nothing like her. The ending was predictable to an adult: accepting friends who are different. *If life were only this easy.*

She'd had a strong interest in art when she was in school, but it was foolish to think she'd ever make a living at it. Although her art teacher had told her she was a natural, her parents had convinced her otherwise.

"Honey, if you're going to spend all that money on college, you need to make it back," they'd said repeatedly during her years in high school. "Find a career."

By the time she was a senior her fear of failure and her unwillingness to disappoint them had suffocated her passion. One afternoon she'd carried all of her art supplies to the basement and put them in a corner. Then she'd gone upstairs and cried for an hour. Whenever she thought of drawing, a pang of regret tapped her on the shoulder and the memory of the trek to the basement sent her into a funk.

Ding!

She finished her dinner and stood and stretched. She still tingled all the way to her core. Was it Alicia's superb skill, or was it the thrill of being in a public place and knowing they might get caught? She laughed out loud when she remembered holding the underwear up as a shield. Her cheeks were warm and she knew she was blushing, but she realized she didn't feel lonely. That hadn't happened in a while.

This time her phone rang but the number was unfamiliar. "Hello?"

"So have you thought about what I said today?" Penn asked.

She put her hand on a hip. "What happened to, 'Hi, how are you CC? This is Penn.' Didn't your mother teach you any manners?"

Penn gave a sigh of exasperation. "I'm sorry, but there's not a lot of time here. After you left I tried to get Viv to open up and talk about the past but she wouldn't even though she could lose her place. I wanted you to know that you may be her only hope. She'll hate me if I go public with this and I'm just being honest with you. Can't you do anything?"

She raked a hand through her hair. "I don't know what to do without jeopardizing my job. He's my client and I'm sworn—"

"You don't need to lecture me, CC. I passed ethics class."

She glowered. "Then why are you calling me?"

"Because I thought you cared."

She disconnected and CC stared at the phone.

Ding!

She rolled her eyes. She had no interest in reading the replies, but as she glanced around the bare walls of the empty apartment her finger automatically hit the view button and she scrolled through her latest round of prospects. Only two replies of the six were grammatically correct and free of craziness. She saved those into a folder and saw that she had seven actual prospects if she ever chose to respond.

It almost made the thought of facing her briefcase bearable. She unloaded her files onto the pub table and fired up her computer. She needed to complete the request for the handwriting analysis despite Viv's insistence that it was real, and Blanca would expect the rewritten report first thing in the morning. She groaned. She hated writing.

Then why did I become a lawyer?

Her mother's voice answered the question as it had a million times before. "Because you like money, dear. You like nice things and you don't want to risk your future."

She skimmed through the Rubenstein file for the fiftieth time wondering if there was some clue as to why Viv's father had signed away the land. And why had the Rubensteins held on to the note for so long?

She imagined Viv losing the house, the place where she created Chloe. Then she thought of Penn, so strong and definitely smart. And those dimples. She covered her face with her hands and willed away the tingling feeling shooting through her body.

Penn had said, "I choose."

How could she choose to help Viv without getting fired?

She reread Seth Rubenstein's bio. He and his brother were heirs to a chain of family-style restaurants called Della's, named after the Rubenstein matriarch, Jacob's wife. Seth had inherited the family business after Jacob passed the previous year. Despite the challenging economy Della's quarterly reports showed a steady profit margin for a company worth millions. Only after the family had perused Jacob's personal files did they come across the note from Chet Battle, Viv's father, to Jacob. Seth Rubenstein had put the pieces together and realized he was entitled to the enclave.

She tapped her pen on the table. Why? Why hadn't Jacob Rubenstein claimed the property back in the fifties? He could have forced Lois Battle and her children out of the farmhouse decades ago.

"Why, Jacob?" she asked out loud. "What were you hiding?"

CHAPTER FIVE

April, 1954

"Hey," a voice whispered.

I nearly fell off the window seat, too lost in my sketching to hear Kiah shimmying up the vines for her nightly visit. Mama never heard her when she was smoking out on the sun porch because Kiah was quite athletic and the trellis lined the backside of the house, away from the other bedrooms.

"Is that Mr. Rubenstein out there with her?" Kiah asked, crawling through the window. "He was just at our place."

"Uh-huh. He stopped by to see Mama after he visited with your daddy. Did the same thing last week, too."

Laughter floated up from the sun porch and Kiah said, "They sure sound like they're having a good time. I don't think I've ever heard your mama laugh."

It was true. Mama rarely laughed and it was usually at

something stupid I'd done that didn't cause danger, doctor bills or embarrassment to her. Just the week before I'd managed to get my head caught between the banister spindles and she'd left me there for an hour, laughing every time she passed by.

It was odd hearing her speak in an unfamiliar way. Her voice was usually hard and bitter like a cold wind, but with him she sounded like a song on the radio.

"What does your daddy think about Mr. Rubenstein sitting on the back porch with his wife?"

I could tell that she didn't think Pops would approve, but I didn't think he'd care. Lately he was gone in the evenings, spending time with people from the nursery after work. We ate dinner without him and then Mama sat outside for hours. I never knew when he came home but it was after I'd gone to bed.

"Why's he always late?" Will had complained one night at dinner. I knew he wasn't happy that Pops wasn't around much.

"He's working overtime," Mama said absently.

"But the nursery closes at five," he said. "And I thought we had a whole lot of money now."

She wouldn't look at him. "Young man, the family finances are not your business. And there's still much to do after a business closes. That's when the crew can get the real work done."

He hadn't bought it. "In the dark?"

She gripped her silverware so tightly her knuckles turned white before she threw them down onto her plate, causing a terrible clatter. She'd stormed out to the sun porch and we watched her pace. We didn't understand why she'd exploded, but we hadn't discussed it since.

"I've got a surprise for you," Kiah said.

She wrapped an arm around me and pointed to a row of three cabins that had been built after Mac killed the orange grove. They were identical to the one she lived in on the adjoining property, but I knew those were being torn down to build more houses for the subdivision.

"Do you see that one right over there?" she asked, pointing to the one that sat closest to our house. "Daddy says that Mr. Rubenstein is going to keep him on as the foreman. He's going to help build this subdivision so we don't have to move again."

My eyes widened. "You aren't leaving?"

"Nope," she giggled. "We're gonna live right there. I'm going to be next door. You can come over whenever you want and play Scrabble with me, and we'll keep eatin' your mama's sweet potato pie. Daddy says that was the best he'd ever tasted, by the way."

We hugged each other tightly and squealed with delight. I stared into her rich brown eyes, still amazed at how dark they were.

Ever since that awful afternoon when I'd attacked Mac we'd been best friends. After school I'd run to the bus stop and wait for her. She was always one of the last off, letting the white kids go first and hoping to avoid Billy Smith, a teenage boy who routinely picked on her.

We'd walk home together, and she'd help me with my math while we drank lemonade. She was whip-smart and finished her homework long before I did. She often complained the work wasn't hard enough.

"Why would you ever want harder work?" I'd asked.

"Because I like school and learning. That's why I'm going to Tuskegee."

She constantly talked about going to a university that was all the way across the country in a city called Birmingham, where the rest of her people were.

I hugged her again, happy that we were still together at least for now. While I had a few other friends none of them was like Kiah. They were all stupid in some way, either very immature or prejudiced. I'd discovered recently that I couldn't stand listening to them say awful things about black people. Kiah said they were ignorant, but I had a different word for it—one that wasn't so nice.

"I like holding you," she said quietly and I knew what she meant.

"Me, too."

Everything felt better when we were together. I felt stronger. I wondered if this was what it was like to have an older sister, but we didn't feel like sisters. Maybe it was because she was black, but that didn't make sense either.

I squeezed her tighter and she cried, "Ow."

I backed away. "Did I hurt you?"

She rubbed her shoulder and shook her head. "No, it's nothing."

I pulled up the sleeve of her dress and stared at a huge welt on the side of her arm. "What happened?"

"I just got in the way of Billy Smith's fist," she joked.

He was a dropout and a greaser. I'd heard from Will he'd been kicked out of high school for beating up a freshman, and now he worked downtown as a gas jockey at a service station. Unfortunately he left work at the same time Kiah got out of school and took the same bus back up town.

He didn't seem to bother her as much when I was around, so I made a point of meeting her bus whenever I could.

I may have been younger, but I had no problem whacking Billy Smith with Will's baseball bat and drawing blood. Most likely the root of my courage was Billy's fear of Will, who was an excellent fighter and had won all his fights. Not that he went looking for problems. Will was exactly the opposite. He only fought when challenged and Billy had taunted him the year before he got kicked out. Will had taken him down in two punches.

I gazed at the purple and black welt. It was harder to see against her dark skin, and I imagined how bad it would look on a white person.

"What happened?"

With her back to me she said, "I got off the bus and he asked me for money. When I said I didn't have any, he said I'd have to pay in another way."

"What was that?"

"He wanted to kiss me. He said he'd never kissed a nigger. I'd be his first. But I got scared and started running. When he caught me he punched me in the arm and walked away. There were a lot of people around so I knew he wouldn't do nothin' too serious, but it scared me."

Her voice choked and I held her gently. She pressed her cheek against mine like she was preparing to tell me a great secret, sharing her tears with me. But she said nothing, and I closed my eyes enjoying the softness of her warm cheek against my own.

"I need to go," she said sadly, drying her eyes. "Do you need me to show you how to do your math before I leave?"

"No, I still got it from yesterday."

"Good. You're so smart."

"Not me. You're a good teacher. That's what you ought to be when you go to Tuskegee. I don't know anyone who can explain things the way you can."

She kissed me on the cheek. "You're sweet. But I'm not going to be a teacher. I'm going to be a *lawyer* and fight for civil rights."

"What are civil rights?"

"They're the things black people don't have now. It's bein' able to sit on the bus wherever we want or eat at restaurants or go to any school we want. It's all of those things."

Her voice was angry and I was afraid she was mad at me. "I think you should have civil rights," I said quickly. "Can I help you get them?"

She shook her head. "No, Vivi, you can't, not really. You don't have any power."

That was true. I was just a kid. What could I do?

"But it's nice of you to want to help me, to help *us*."

"I want to help, Kiah, I really do."

She took my face between her palms. "I'm so lucky you're my friend."

"Me, too," I said back.

She kissed me on the lips and hurried out the window and down the trellis. I touched my lower lip as if I could press her kiss into my skin so I wouldn't forget it. I'd never kissed anyone so I didn't know how I was supposed to feel, but it felt nice, like the smell of freshly baked cookies or the sky filled with puffy clouds.

A car started and I realized Mr. Rubenstein was leaving. I peered through the window as Mama trudged up the back steps and returned to the divan on the sun porch. I imagined if she'd seen Kiah kiss me she wouldn't have approved. It wasn't right. Blacks and whites weren't supposed to kiss but maybe that was part of civil rights, too.

Staring down at Mama I felt incredibly sad for her. I had something she didn't, a best friend. She had those ladies in the sewing club that she talked with on Tuesdays, but none of them ever came over for a private visit. That wasn't like Kiah and me. I couldn't imagine a day passing without seeing her.

I grabbed my sketchpad and turned to a portrait of Mama that I'd drawn for a class assignment. I erased some of her features—the turned-down mouth and deep lines in her forehead. I imagined what she'd look like if I could sit right next to her while Mr. Rubenstein made her laugh. I drew a broad smile and bright eyes. When I finished it an hour later, she wasn't just happy, she was overjoyed. I held it up to the window hoping I could wish it true.

****

The next day I raced to the bus stop just as it rumbled to the curb. Billy was one of the first off, pushing aside a young girl and laughing about it. The other whites followed in his direction toward our neighborhood. Kiah was one of the last people off. She said goodbye to some of her friends who walked in the opposite direction toward the poorer neighborhoods, before she ran up to me.

"How was that math quiz?"

"I got a B," I said proudly.

She jumped up and down with joy, and I knew if we weren't in public she would've thrown her arms around me. "That's great, Vivi! Good job."

"It's all because of your help. I couldn't have done it without you."

She smiled and we rounded the corner and headed up a side street that bordered the property now owned by Mr. Rubenstein. Remnants of the destroyed trees rested in enormous piles until the refuse truck hauled them away.

Billy Smith sat against one of them smoking a cigarette. He seemed to be waiting for Kiah, but when he saw me his face twitched a little, and I could tell he was debating whether to change his plans.

He reminded me of a bulldog, with a square face and a lip that curled upward. He was plump in the middle and wore his dark brown hair in a typical ducktail, but he used too much goo and it always looked a little lopsided.

I stood in front of him, fearing nothing. "I got something to say to you, Billy Smith. You better leave my friend alone."

"That nigger's your friend?" he asked disgustedly.

Kiah took my arm. "Vivi, don't. Let's just keep walking."

But I wouldn't. "I'm telling you to stay away from her, you ignorant piece of shit."

I'd made the decision for him. There was no way he could back down now. He flicked his butt away and came toward me, his hands in the front pockets of his jeans.

"What are you gonna do about it? Fight me?" he added with a sneer.

"I might," I said. "If my brother can take ya, I think I can, too."

His face turned red and in a flash he shoved me to the ground. Kiah grabbed his arm but he threw her to the side and she landed on her knees, book and papers flying everywhere.

"Vivi!" she cried. "Run!"

I sat up, but everything was spinning. There wasn't any way I could run even if I wanted to.

"You got a big mouth and need to learn some manners." He stepped back and kicked me in the thigh like he was punting a football.

I fell on my side in agony. I forgot he wore steel-toed boots. He sauntered over to Kiah, who was sitting on the ground sobbing. He circled her, whistling, his arms behind his back. She hugged her knees and wouldn't look at him. I sat up again and felt a searing pain shoot through my leg that brought tears to my eyes.

He leaned over, whispering, and she stood up slowly— apparently too slowly—since he grabbed her and pulled her up the rest of the way. She was terrified, her face nearly unrecognizable. He pushed her against one of the tree piles and hugged her.

"C'mon, nigger, gimme a kiss."

She twisted from side to side, screaming, "No!" in a hoarse

voice, which only excited him more. If he'd really wanted to kiss her, he would've, but I knew he didn't. He'd *never* kiss a black person. It was all about torturing her.

I grabbed a tree branch and pulled myself up. Her screams turned to moans, and she was loud enough to be heard in the next county. I trudged toward them holding the branch over my head, the pain in my thigh nearly unbearable.

"You son of a bitch!"

As I brought the branch down in the general vicinity of his head, an arm sailed in front of my face and snatched it from my hand.

"Whoa, there, missy," Mac's voice said.

Billy whirled around and shuddered at the sight of what had almost happened.

Mac threw the branch away and stared at Billy, who still had his arms around Kiah. The look Mac gave him made me nervous. He didn't need a tree branch.

"Move away from my daughter."

Billy gazed at him with hatred, his fear tossed aside with the branch. He let go of her but not before he caressed her shoulders. "Not a problem, nigger," he said. "She's not my type, anyway."

Mac clenched his fist and took a step toward him.

"Mac!"

I turned and saw Mama hurrying up the road, still wearing her apron. She stepped between them and said sternly, "Go home, Billy."

She knew his mother since they were both part of the sewing circle. He wouldn't look at her and kept his eyes on Mac. She put a hand on his shoulder and said softly, "Please, Billy. Don't make this any worse."

He glanced at her long fingers resting on his shoulder. I guessed it was the first time she'd ever touched him, and he seemed amazed that she was so close. He gave a slight nod and walked away. She went to Kiah, who fell into her arms and cried. They whispered while Mac and I stood nearby in identical poses—our hands tucked in our jean pockets. Eventually she stopped crying, and I gathered her books. When I tried to hand them to her, she walked away.

I knew she was mad. It was my fault. If I'd kept my big mouth shut, Billy would've probably just teased us while we walked by, but I had to confront him and make a mess of things. If Mama ever heard the whole story, she'd call me a moron and have Pops paddle me.

Kiah walked ahead and I lingered back near Mama and Mac, who were walking slowly behind us.

"You didn't need to do that, Lois," I heard him say.

"You were ready to pummel that boy. I couldn't stand to see that happen."

"He was molesting my daughter," he said.

"I know. It was horrible, Mac. Kiah's a lovely girl who doesn't deserve anything like that."

When we reached the edge of the property Kiah turned and waited for me to catch up. She took her books and looked at me kindly.

"Thanks," she said. "Do you want to come over?"

I looked at her expectantly. "You're not mad at me?"

She sighed and shook her head. "Just a little. You well-meanin' white folks get us into a whole lotta trouble sometimes." She glanced back at Mama and Mac who'd stopped walking. They faced each other and he was pointing at himself while she nodded. "I think Daddy's tryin' to explain that same fact to your mama right now," she said.

It was odd. The way they looked at each other, nodded when the other one was talking. And eventually they both smiled. Mama and Pops never looked at each other that way.

I turned back to Kiah and said, "I didn't mean for any of that to happen, really I didn't. I'm so sorry. But I wish Mac had let me clobber Billy."

She put her hand on my shoulder. "No, Vivi, you don't get it. It doesn't help. It just makes it worse. If you'd hit him with that branch, then the next time I got off the bus, Billy and some of his friends would've done something worse to me. That's how it goes."

"But then how do you get civil rights if you never stand up for yourself?" I asked. "Isn't that what it's all about?"

She started to say something and stopped herself. "It's just different," she finally said. "My daddy says that there's a time and a place to make your stand and you've gotta pick carefully. A dead nigger ain't no good to anyone. There's strength in numbers and violence isn't the way."

I knew that was something else her daddy said. I'd heard him talk about race issues a lot in the last few months, and I knew how much she admired him. But this wasn't a race issue in my mind.

"I didn't hit Billy because he was picking on my *black* friend," I said. "I hit him because he was trying to kiss you and that made me angry."

A little smile tugged at the corners of her mouth. "You were jealous?"

I hadn't thought of it like that. "Yeah."

We reached her front door and she paused with her hand on the knob. "Here's what I think. I think that making Billy mad wasn't a good idea but not letting him kiss me was a great idea. And maybe I'll kiss you again sometime."

Sometime turned out to be right after we got inside and shut the door.

Re: Definitely Friends First! - 27 (Central Phoenix)
Date: 2010-06-09, 9:36PM MST

Greetings!
As you can see by the time stamp, I'm replying later in the evening, which is the only time I have to look at e-mail. If you know the meaning of carpe diem, I'm guessing you're a teacher like me or a lawyer, but maybe not. I really am looking to make friends—no games, no addictions and no promise of a gay wedding. I'd love to get together for coffee. And I promise I'm sane.

Posted by: AZNative1
Reply

Re: Definitely Friends First! - 27 (Central Phoenix)
Date: 2010-06-10, 6:11 AM MST

Well, shit, DFF, I'm just damn interested in you! I'm a little redneck in case you didn't guess but don't let that stop a potential love connection. It just means I'm honest and up front about my beliefs that include my recent membership in the Tea Party, my disbelief in global warming and my pride in my handgun collection. I'm guessing you're my opposite, except that we both like fish apparently (carpe). But don't opposites attract?

Posted by: BrooklynBornBaby
Reply

Re: Definitely Friends First! - 27 (Central Phoenix)
Date: 2010-06-10, 12:04 PM MST

Hello DFF,
As a way to distinguish myself from the other replies I will amaze you with my poetic talent.
There was a young woman from Texas,
Who drove to Phoenix in a Lexus.
She came here for work,
And socially met many jerks
But she's optimistic she'll make a nexus.

Posted by: JaneAustenRocks!
Reply

CHAPTER SIX

June, 2010

The crowd had peaked at Della's Restaurant when CC arrived. The hostess seated her in a booth and promised to watch for Mr. Rubenstein. This was the original Della's, which looked like most every other diner she'd ever visited—a row of booths against a bank of windows and a U-shaped counter with old-fashioned stools. It was quaint and charming with an aqua and tan color scheme. The wall behind her displayed a large chalkboard listing two dozen types of pies, and underneath it was a long old-fashioned sign that read *Farmhouse Pies*.

Her foot tapped the linoleum incessantly as she waited for Seth Rubenstein. In a moment of reckless boldness she'd phoned him at seven. He hadn't sounded thrilled about joining her for breakfast, but he seemed more amenable when she offered to meet at his restaurant. She knew Blanca wouldn't approve of her summoning a client to a meeting without her knowledge, but after spending most of the night doodling across the report she still hadn't rewritten, she'd made a decision to help Vivian Battle as much as she could. She'd figured that solving the mystery of the note was the key to Viv keeping the enclave.

She flipped open the file and read his bio again. His father Jacob had built houses in the late forties and early fifties, but after he married he changed careers and opened Della's. It grew into a chain of ten diners across the state. Seth became CEO of the Della Corporation when his father passed away a year before. His brother, Ira, was an architect and had no role in running the company but received a share of profits.

She wasn't sure what a restaurant CEO would look like, but it wasn't the short, plump, balding man, wearing a Hawaiian shirt and chinos, that appeared in the doorway. He scanned the restaurant, looking for his idea of an attorney, and when his gaze settled on her dark blue pantsuit, he pointed and joined her at the table.

"Seth Rubenstein," he said, and she held out her hand but he waved her off. "Sorry, I'm kinda OCD about the handshaking stuff. All the years of working in the food industry. Millions of germs passed along because we've insisted on greeting each other with our most bacteria-laden appendage. Just another reason why the Japanese are ahead of us. They never get sick. Between eating a ton of vegetables and all that bowing, they stay out of the doctor's office. Why can't we learn, you know?"

She nodded her head in agreement. "Absolutely—"

"But if you don't shake hands with new people they think you're a bastard or a clean freak, which I kinda am, but it just makes good sense, you know? Have you ordered yet? I strongly recommend the Denver omelet or the waffle combo with hash browns. They're both fabulous."

"Great," she interjected. "I love waffles."

"That's what me and my brother always order. We always seem to get the same things wherever we go. When we were growing up, I always thought he did it to copy me, you know? Like he just wanted to frustrate me because I was his big brother. But when we started hangin' out as adults and he still got what I got, I finally realized we just had similar tastes. Happens all the time when we're both in the mood for a Philly cheese steak."

He motioned to a waitress carrying a pot of coffee in their direction, and CC listened patiently as they exchanged pleasantries about the morning rush. Five seconds after she'd taken their order and disappeared he asked, "So how's my case?"

She smiled and launched into the script she'd written at four a.m. "Mr. Rubenstein, I appreciate you meeting me this morning. I know you're very busy and I won't take much of your time, but I had some questions about your father."

She quickly pulled out the file and a pad of paper while he peered at her over his coffee. She hated doing business over a meal since inevitably she wound up speaking with food in her mouth, but she'd learned that eating and litigation went hand in hand and it was best to get most of it done between ordering and serving.

"Why do you think he didn't put the farmhouse property in his will?"

He shrugged. "Not a clue. We had no idea the place belonged to us. Dad got out of the construction business by the end of fifty-six, or it might've been early fifty-seven. I'm not sure on that part. He didn't like it. Too much time outside, too many employees. He didn't mind working hard, but he wanted to enjoy what he was doing. It was right after Mom had me."

She calculated the timing. The subdivision had been completed by the summer of fifty-six so the timing suggested he'd sold the last house in the neighborhood and turned his attention to Della's. She sipped her coffee and calculated her approach. He was quick and bright, and she sensed a strong streak of family loyalty.

"Your father sounds like an extraordinary man with a lot of business savvy."

Rubenstein nodded. "He was. He and Mom took this little diner with ten menu items and two cooks and turned it into a business. They were totally devoted to each other and us kids. Brought us up right, not like so many of these absentee parents today who don't have a clue where their kids are or what they're doing. Me and my wife Belinda, we always knew where Seth Junior and Moira were when they were teens. It's important, you know?"

She shifted in her seat uncomfortably. "Here's what I don't understand. Your father was such a great businessman, there's no doubt about that, but if that note is real and Chet Battle gave him the property in fifty-five, why didn't he add it to the subdivision? It wasn't completed yet, and he could've built two or three more houses and sold the farmhouse as well. That would've been quite a profit."

"No doubt," he agreed. "It doesn't make any sense. There must've been a reason. Dad always had a reason for everything."

"Why do you think he might have left the place with Vivian Battle, despite the note?"

"Again. No clue."

"Do you think your mother knew about it?"

Their breakfast arrived and her question hung in the air for the time it took him to chat up the waitress, dress their waffles and dig in. She was about to repeat it when he said, "I imagine she knew because she was his partner in everything. They had an odd relationship for that time, not like the typical man and wife thing where the wife just cooks, cleans, sews and deals with the kids, you know? She'd been a teacher before he married her so he knew she was smart. She was his equal. I'd be surprised if he hadn't told her, but I suppose it's possible. Knowing her, she would've told him to add it to the subdivision and take the cash, so the fact that he held on to the note makes me wonder." He shook his head. "Weird. I never thought there were any secrets between them."

She said nothing and kept eating. Since entering probate law, she'd learned there were *always* secrets in families, like a trump card held in a bridge hand, just waiting to be played at the most advantageous moment.

"So when do we wrap this up?" he asked abruptly.

"Well, we're still verifying the handwriting, and Ms. Battle has lived in the farmhouse her entire life. Did you ever meet her?"

He shrugged. "Maybe. You know how it is with parents. They drag you everywhere when you're a kid."

"Did you ever read the Chloe books?"

He cracked a smile. "I've got 'em all. First editions, too."

She nearly sighed before she said, "You know Ms. Battle wrote them."

She hoped she'd jostled his compassion, but he merely speared another hunk of waffle and chewed on it. Once he finished he looked at her intently. "That's not our problem. This is business, Ms. Carlson. I'm sure she has plenty of money, and I'm more than happy to pay her for the upgrades she's made to the land. But it's prime real estate. Claiming it is good business. Now I know you're young, but Blanca says that you'll do what needs to be done to please your client. Is that a fair assessment of your abilities and character as a lawyer?"

She swallowed hard, pressing her breakfast back down her throat before she said, "Absolutely. But just so you're aware, Ms. Battle's attorney has mentioned taking her case to the media. I'm not sure that would be a good idea."

He nodded. "You're right. It wouldn't." Then he winked. "And your job is to make sure that doesn't happen." He leaned over his waffle and added, "It's no accident that I hired the most ruthless law firm in town. You have my permission to do whatever needs to be done to get that property."

"I understand," she mumbled.

He laughed a belly laugh and turned the conversation to mundane topics like the Phoenix Suns and the immigration problem and she feigned interest. He finished his meal quickly, gave a wave and reminded her not to bill him for the time since she'd called the meeting. After he stopped at several tables and introduced himself as the owner, he nodded to the manager, strolled out and got into his Lexus.

She needed the bathroom. She headed down a corridor filled with framed black-and-white photographs, a visual history of Jacob and Della Rubenstein's life. She slowed to look. Several of them showed the Rubensteins standing outside their newest diner on the day it opened. They were a handsome couple, and both wore beaming smiles in every picture. Some of the photos included a young Seth and Ira standing in front of their parents, looking appropriately obedient.

She spotted two photos of the *Farmhouse Pies* sign, which she guessed originally sat on the side of a dirt road. While one of the pictures was solely of the sign, another showed a man and a woman standing on opposite ends of it. She easily recognized Jacob Rubenstein on the left, but she had no idea who the stunning blonde was on the right.

She turned to study the other wall and stopped suddenly in front of Jacob and Della Rubenstein's formal wedding picture, which was taken on the front porch steps of Viv's farmhouse. Her gaze strayed to the pictures next to it. In one photo, the bride and groom were sandwiched between a handsome black man and the stunning blonde, and in another, two young girls— one black and one white—had joined the four adults. She leaned forward, staring at the little white girl—almost certain she was looking into the eyes of a young Vivian Battle.

The handwriting request remained on the edge of her desk for the entire morning. Periodically she'd drop a file or a stack of papers on top of it, rationalizing that if it kept disappearing she wouldn't remember it. She knew that after she tossed it into the mailbag, the ever-efficient business department would process it quickly.

The receptionist paged her. "There's a woman here to see you. Alicia Dennis? She says it's very personal."

She could hear the disdain in the receptionist's voice. Personal *anything* was frowned upon in the workplace. And she couldn't understand why Alicia would be here.

"Send her back, please."

Ding!

She adjusted her skirt, hoping she didn't have lipstick on her teeth. Alicia appeared wearing a deep emerald-green blouse and a gray A-line skirt that clung to her buttocks and thighs perfectly.

"Well, I'm glad you still check me out."

She knew her face was red as she motioned for her to sit. "What are you doing here?"

She shrugged. "I was in the neighborhood and I thought I'd drop by and see if you wanted to go to lunch."

"That's nice but I can't today. Too much work."

Blanca popped in the doorway. "Don't forget that we need to review the Holsten trust at four, and where are we with Rubenstein?"

"It's coming," she said.

Blanca nodded suspiciously at Alicia. "What are you doing here?"

She held up a hand. "Strictly personal. I was inviting CC to lunch, which she declined in favor of work."

Blanca glowered at CC. "Good because her rewritten report needs a third try."

Before she could apologize for her poor effort, Alicia interjected. "Writing was never her strength in law school but she was fabulous in oral argument."

Blanca missed the wink that punctuated her sentence and asked, "You went to law school together?"

"Uh-huh."

Her eyes never left CC. "And where do you work?"

"I work for Alma Santiago."

"And are *you* a good writer?"

She shifted in her seat. "I think so, I—"

"Are you happy there?"

"For the moment."

CC imagined a hedge—as tall as the one that bordered Viv's pool—surrounding her and separating her from the conversation. Blanca and Alicia openly sized each other up before Blanca offered a single nod and walked out.

"Thanks a lot," CC hissed.

Alicia shook her head. "For what? I was just answering her questions."

"No, she was offering you my job and you practically took it."

"Honey, you are so paranoid," she sighed. "She's just pissed at you because of the report. Big deal."

"It *is* a big deal. I'm only allowed so many mistakes. You know how it goes."

"Do you want me to help you? I could write it."

"No, you can't." She glanced at the report sitting on her desk, next to the handwriting request that she still hadn't filed and started to cry. "I'm sorry I got angry."

Alicia took her hand. "What's wrong?"

Ding!

She glanced at CC's phone and noticed the alert. "Phoenix-Connect? Not exactly the best service for meeting quality women." Then she teased, "Have you had any dates?"

CC grabbed the phone and shoved it in her desk. "That's none of your business." She picked up the handwriting analysis to change the subject. "I'm totally bummed about this case. Our client wants to take away this beautiful house where an old lady has lived for almost her entire life. Once this handwriting analysis comes back it's all over."

Alicia tapped her chin thoughtfully. She plucked the paper from her hand and pulled an interoffice envelope from the stack CC kept on her credenza. She placed it inside and dropped it into CC's outgoing mail tray.

"But you didn't write anything on it," she said.

Alicia frowned. "Oh, my, that's right. Silly me." She picked it up and grabbed a pen. "Now, where was this going again… tax department, right?" she scribbled before dropping it into the mail tray. "You junior attorneys are just so overworked. And if I remember correctly from my internship days, the tax department is the worst. They get so much mail that by the time they figure out who to send this back to, I expect a week will have passed."

CC stared in disbelief and nearly pulled it from the outbox until Alicia said, "Let it go, CC. Just say thank you."

CC looked into her beautiful eyes, remembering why she'd fallen in love. Sometimes she'd so appreciated her bent morality. "Thank you. I don't know if that'll change anything, but at least it buys me a little time to figure something out."

Alicia smiled. "I'm hoping it bought me a little time too."

****

In the spirit of quid pro quo, CC asked Alicia to attend

the Arizona Bar Foundation's annual charity ball with her that Saturday. She'd purchased her expensive tickets, which all junior associates were expected to buy regardless of its effect on their monthly budget, but she'd decided not to attend. When Alicia learned she had tickets, she prodded her to go.

"It'll be fun," she said.

She disagreed, desiring to spend her Saturday night at home with her new sketchbook. Meeting Viv had inspired her, and she wanted to reacquaint herself with her love of art, regardless of how untalented she was. So, after slaving away in the cavernous offices of Hartford and Burns with the other junior attorneys bent on making a good impression, she'd stopped at the art store and spent the afternoon at home dabbling—with abysmal results.

When she looked at the clock, she gasped. Alicia would arrive in ninety minutes and she hadn't thought about what she should wear. She rifled through her closet, realizing she didn't own anything that would work for a semiformal affair. She pictured Alicia in an expensive silk dress with three-inch pumps and knew she couldn't compare. Her clothes were for work or relaxation with only a few date outfits in between, and she didn't think any of them was stylish enough.

She flopped onto her futon and buried her head in her hands. She was a failure swimming in debt. The student loans from law school were killing her, and when she thought of the fifteen-year payment plan she'd agreed to, she felt like throwing up.

"Don't think of it that way, dear," her mother had advised. "It's an investment in your future."

She pulled herself up, determined to parse together an outfit from the clothes she owned. She found a pair of silk black harem pants from an old Halloween costume and a deep plum camisole that went great with her hair and eyes. In the back of the closet behind the coats, she came across a black velvet vest that Alicia had left behind, and although it was a size too large, it still looked acceptable. She threw on some pumps just as the doorbell rang. What she'd created struck her as slutty, but if Alicia didn't like it, then she could go alone.

Alicia was indeed dressed to kill in a washed-out black jersey dress with a very short skirt that seemed to wrap around her torso. The hem barely covered her thighs and CC knew every man in the place would stare at her long legs, imagining what lay an inch above the fabric. She herself certainly was.

"I like your outfit," Alicia said, waltzing into her tiny apartment. She caressed the vest and asked playfully, "Where have I seen this before?"

She wandered into the bedroom as if she still lived there. She dropped onto the futon, her arms stretched behind her seductively. "I do miss this room," she said.

"We could skip the ball," CC offered.

She laughed and patted the mattress. "Come here. I need to see how those pants work."

She reluctantly sat next to her, feeling like a mouse about to be eaten by a python. But Alicia remained in a supine position, staring at her. The jasmine perfume announced its presence and smothered her overpowering female scent that lingered underneath the dress.

"You keep staring at my legs," she observed. "Is my skirt too short or too *long*? I actually debated taking it up another half inch. What do you think?"

"Then it would be a belt."

Alicia sat up threw back her head, laughing, exposing her creamy neck and the silver chain that rested against her bronze skin. "God, I miss your wit."

It was too tempting. She pressed her lips into the gorgeous flesh and Alicia responded by undoing her pants.

"Let's stay here," CC whispered.

"We can't."

"We can," she insisted, placing Alicia's hand on her breast.

All she wanted was her. She'd forgive everything that happened if Alicia would succumb to her charms and let her win. They fondled and kissed for another minute, their passion a seemingly powerful persuader—until she tried to push Alicia down.

"No, no. We can't, babe," she protested. "Not right now. I have to make a bid at the auction. I really need to go."

CC sat up completely frustrated, doubting she would ever get her way, and Alicia immediately pulled her into her arms. "I promise I'll have you tonight."

****

The Phoenix Museum of History sat in Heritage Square, a specialty park juxtaposed with several historical houses that sat with the Arizona Science Center. Ironically, the museum was a modern concrete and glass building. It contained displays celebrating the role of Native Americans and Hispanics in the city's development as well as pictorials and books dating back to the eighteen hundreds.

They crossed the courtyard toward a huge banner announcing the Arizona Bar Association's Alzheimer's Charity Benefit. The crowds were thick at the entrance, and CC immediately sized up her wardrobe choice, which seemed to be on par with many of the guests except for the trophy wives who clearly lived to shop. They were adorned in dresses that she imagined were a month's pay for her, as well as matching shoes and fashionable bling.

They checked in and Alicia scanned the crowd. "Isn't that your boss?" she asked, pointing to Blanca, who was standing next to Stoddard Burns.

"Yes, and that's my boss's boss," she said already feeling a sense of inadequacy creep over her.

Alicia grabbed her hand. "C'mon, let's say hello."

"No." She refused to budge. "I've never even met Mr. Burns. He doesn't know who I am."

"He will now," she giggled and pulled her across the floor like a child being dragged through a grocery store.

When Blanca saw them approaching, CC sensed she was more pleased to see Alicia than her own employee.

"Good evening, CC, Alicia."

"Good to see you again," Alicia said, heaping on the sugar.

Stoddard Burns leered at both of them. His suit and expensive haircut screamed money and when he stuck out his hand, it was to greet Alicia. "I'm Stoddard Burns."

"Alicia Dennis," she said.

"And this is CC Carlson, sir," Blanca added. "She works for us."

Burns tore his gaze from Alicia to glance at her but he continued to grasp Alicia's hand.

"Alicia's on the Morgan case," Blanca said, the disappointment in her voice apparent. "She was the one who literally stole money out of our pocket this week."

"Really? Impressive." Burns' smirk was light-hearted and he didn't seem to mind that the firm had lost thousands of dollars— as long as it was at the hands of a beautiful woman.

"I just got lucky," Alicia purred.

"Would you ladies care to peruse the tables with us? Blanca is serving as my date tonight, but we have specific instructions from Mrs. Burns regarding a spa day she wants to win."

Alicia wagged a playful finger at him. "I'm going to have to fight you on that as well, Mr. Burns. My boss Alma Santiago wants that package."

He laughed. "You work for Alma? Really?" He leaned closer. "We had a thing back in the eighties. Shh. My wife doesn't know."

They all laughed and turned toward the tables. Except CC. "I need to use the restroom," she said, but no one seemed to hear her.

She strolled through the exhibit, immediately recognizing Squaw Peak, now called Piestewa Peak, the mountain she saw through her window at work. The picture was dated 1936, and thousands of orange trees surrounded its base. This was the land Jacob Rubenstein had purchased.

A sign indicated that the museum library was just down the hallway. Since there weren't any barricades or security guards to prevent her from snooping, she hurried into the library and came upon several glass cases with memorabilia from the early twentieth century, including photos of the downtown and the desert landscape. She quickly scanned them until she came to a post-World War Two era display.

After the war thousands of midwesterners had trekked out to Phoenix for the warm weather, creating a housing boom. They'd purchased thousands of the familiar ranch houses like the ones in Viv's neighborhood, the ones built by Jacob Rubenstein.

The headline of a newspaper article caught her attention: "Phoenix Named one of the Most Desirable Cities in America." The story detailed the mild weather and low prices and showed proof of happy families enjoying their new tract homes, all with smiles on their faces.

A separate sidebar contained a headshot of Jacob Rubenstein. She scanned the article about the man many proclaimed to be the creator of Central Phoenix, and his wise decision to turn ten thousand acres of orange groves into family housing. The article mentioned his recent marriage to Miss Della Noyce, a non-Jew, and some subsequent setbacks that included a vandalized job site and workers who'd walked off the job.

A non-Jew. She winced at the choice of words and realized it was typical of the anti-Semitic attitudes of the time. She could only imagine what kind of prejudice Rubenstein faced because of his marriage, and she suddenly questioned his motives for abandoning the building industry. At the bottom of the article was another picture of him surrounded by several members of his crew, including a large, handsome black man—the same man in the wedding photos she'd seen at Della's.

"I wondered where you went."

She nearly jumped out of her shoes. Alicia stood in the doorway grinning.

"Brushing up on your Phoenix history?"

She shrugged sheepishly. "I just like looking at old photos. This is a picture of my client's father."

Alicia studied the photo and scanned the sidebar. "It sounds like this family was pretty important."

"Yeah, that's what Blanca keeps telling everyone. I'm working with an important client. Like I'd ever forget."

She massaged her neck, feeling a knot of tension settle near her shoulders. Alicia moved behind her and took over.

"Let's take a walk," she said, nibbling on her ear.

"What happened to Blanca and Mr. Burns?"

"He already left, and she's power networking. But she invited me to lunch next week. Maybe she'll offer me a job."

She could hear the excitement in her voice and wasn't sure how she felt about the two of them working in the same place.

Alicia took her hand and they proceeded down a cross-corridor. Piano background music and the endless chatter of three hundred people seeped through the adjoining wall, and CC felt like a kid who was out of bounds.

"What will we say if someone asks us why we're back here? Aren't we supposed to be at the party?"

"You started it. You're the one who wandered off. Now I'm just capitalizing on your idea with one of my own." She squeezed her hand. "I made you a promise, and I'm determined to find a way to keep it."

She was immediately wary. Alicia had that seductive look in her eye. She started to protest, but she pulled her into another room, one dedicated to transportation. Pictures of early buses and the new light rail covered the walls. But the showcase piece was a vintage trolley car with two-tone burnt red sides and yellow windows. Alicia chuckled and pushed open the creaky wooden door. "C'mon."

"We need to go," she said but Alicia pulled her up the three steps.

The oak casement windows were well preserved, and the black leather seats had retained their luster. Small advertising signs perched above the windows—the Coffee Pot restaurant and the Central Avenue Dairy, as well as Tom Chauncey Jewelers. She was amused by the five digit phone numbers that began with a lettered prefix.

"This is really something," she marveled. "What a great old car."

She imagined it in its heyday, filled with men in suits on their way to work, reading the newspaper, their hats in their laps, while the women tugged at their white gloves and reprimanded the wiggly children next to them. She guessed Jacob Rubenstein once rode the trolleys as well as Viv.

"Let's take this thing for a spin," Alicia teased. Her right foot perched on the driver's seat and she gripped the metal pole for support. Her skirt was hiked up indecently and CC could see everything—most notably that she wasn't wearing any underwear.

"You're kidding."

"Get over here," she said, swaying back and forth on the pole. "I love the transportation industry."

Only a few work lights illuminated the room and the car, but one shone brightly through the front window, casting an antique film over Alicia. She swung into the conductor's chair and pulled CC onto her lap, unbuttoning her pants in one motion.

"You know, I looked up your personal ad," she whispered. "It was incredibly easy to find. I almost answered it."

CC was only half listening as Alicia removed her vest and explored her breasts. "How would you have replied?" she managed to ask.

Their hips found a rhythm that Alicia matched with the cadence of her voice. "Gay gal wants ex-lover back for nights of passion and maybe more. Smart, funny, likes long walks in the park, mornings in bed and film noir."

CC moaned. She was so close.

"But...most of all...she wants...a great orgasm."

It was so wonderful that she thought she heard applause when their bodies fell limp against the old wooden seat. Only then did she feel the chill on her nipples from the air conditioning and notice her camisole wrapped around her neck. And when had she splayed her legs so far apart? One foot pressed against the side window and the other rested on the conductor's door handle.

Alicia laughed. "I doubt this trolley ever saw this much action."

"Definitely not," she agreed. "People used to have decorum and followed rules of etiquette in public."

"Then I fail," she snorted. She pushed her up and kissed her neck. "Let's go before we both get disbarred."

They quickly dressed and stole back into the main room unnoticed. Her legs were wobbly, and the tingling sensation had returned. She normally had sex in a bed and enjoyed basking in the afterglow. Peeling out of parking garages and rubbing elbows with socialites weren't her usual post-coital activities.

Yet Alicia seemed invigorated and quickly downed a flute of champagne and reached for another from a passing waiter. She checked the silent auction bidding, rewriting her boss's name again after she'd been out-bidded. CC blinked when she saw the amount was a thousand dollars.

"Your boss must really like a good massage," she said.

"She does, but that's as high as she wants me to go."

"You'd better not be bidding on Mrs. Burns' spa day," Blanca said. "She'll do anything for Elizabeth Arden."

It was a joke, but her delivery varied only slightly from her usual robotic tone. Alicia laughed and carried the light-hearted conversation for both of them while CC excused herself to the bar, remembering how often she'd felt excluded whenever Alicia talked to someone else.

"Let me guess. You're a white wine kind of woman," a voice said over her shoulder.

She rolled her eyes at the pickup line before she turned around—Penn. She was momentarily speechless at the sight of the butch in a black suit and tailored striped shirt.

"Do I look that good?"

"What?" she gasped. "You're so full of yourself."

She whispered, "No, it's just you have a lot of tells. If you're ever gonna make it in a high-stakes poker game or a courtroom, you need to stop transmitting your feelings."

"I am not," she insisted, knowing how lame she sounded. "And I don't like white wine."

"Scotch?"

"Vodka tonic."

"Well, then allow me."

She signaled the bartender and ordered the vodka tonic and a scotch for herself.

"What are you doing here?" CC asked.

"What are *you* doing here?" Penn echoed. "I'd understand if I ran into old man Hartford, but you're a lowly junior associate."

She could feel the heat rising in her cheeks. She didn't want to explain who she was with or what she'd been doing since she got here.

"I'm representing my firm."

"Oh, then," she said, raising her drink, "I'll offer a toast to Heartless and Burned and their quest to destroy one of the sweetest people I've ever met."

Her shoulders sagged and she glared at Penn. "Thanks. I'll have you know that I took Seth Rubenstein to breakfast and tried to reason with him."

Her sarcasm evaporated. "And?"

"And nothing. He's an ass and he doesn't care."

She attempted a smile. "Thanks for trying." She held up her glass again. "To chance meetings."

They studied each other, and CC saw in Penn's eyes that Viv wasn't the only one with secrets. "You still haven't told me why you're here."

"I do a lot of legal work for the association. Family members don't know what to do when their spouses or partners start losing their memories. And if they have to put them in a facility, there's a ton of paperwork. It's such a rotten disease." Her voice cracked and she looked away.

"It's great that you help like that."

She looked up, obviously disarmed by the kindness of her tone. "It was Viv who got me involved. She's on the board of directors."

"Really? Is she here tonight?"

"Yeah, somewhere." She looked around and her eyes settled over her shoulder. "I think your *associate* needs you."

She turned as Alicia sidled up next to her, standing just close enough to seem possessive but not overtly demonstrative. She stuck out her hand. "Hello, I'm Alicia."

Penn assessed her shrewdly. "Hello, I'm Penn. Do you work with CC?" CC and Alicia glanced at each other, and Penn picked up on the awkwardness immediately. "I see. You're not *work* friends."

"Actually, we're exes," Alicia said. "At least for now."

Penn raised an eyebrow and CC looked away. "Well, I should go find Viv. It was good to see you, CC. Nice to meet you, Alicia."

"Who was that?" Alicia asked as she wandered away through the crowd.

"She's Vivian Battle's attorney. Apparently she and Viv are affiliated with the Alzheimer's Association."

"So that's the attorney you're against?"

She shrugged. "I suppose, but I'm hoping there's a way to fix this."

"Don't count on it," she said.

She realized Alicia was working the room. Her eyes landed on Blanca. "So what's it like to work for her. I mean, really? She comes across as a grade-A bitch, but she's so good in court."

"I guess she's okay," she said simply. "I'm—"

Alicia touched her arm. "Hey, I'm going to go mingle. Can we meet up in a little while?"

"Sure," she said.

She disappeared and CC felt completely discarded. She headed in the direction she'd seen Penn go. Perhaps she could locate Viv and tell her she'd started drawing again.

She'd nearly crossed the entire room when she spotted them chatting with an elderly Hispanic man. He barely filled out his suit jacket and was severely hunched over. She guessed he was over ninety.

She didn't want to intrude but perhaps if she caught Viv's eye, she'd invite her to join them. "Where's your ex?" Penn asked, making her jump.

"She's back there," she answered absently.

"So are you two getting back together?"

The warm connection she and Alicia had enjoyed for a few fleeting moments had disappeared.

"I have no idea."

"Do you *want* to get back together?"

"That's a tough one. I don't know."

She shoved her hands in her pockets and rocked on her heels. "Probably an important question if you're still having sex."

She blinked and nearly fell backward. "What are you talking about?"

Penn leaned very close and CC's arms immediately sprouted goose bumps. "Your vest is on inside out."

Her gaze shot to her top, and it was only when her fingers found the tag in the back did she realize she was right. "Oh, my God."

"It's okay," she assured her. "I'll stand here and block the view and you fix it."

"Please," she said.

She stepped in front of her and CC quickly slipped the vest off and back on.

"The tag's stuck out." Penn shoved it back inside, her cool fingers trailing across her neck. "So are you dating, getting back together or just hooking up?"

"We're not hooking up," she said acidly. "We were together for two years."

"Then you're dating again?"

"Well, maybe. I'm not sure. Stop asking me questions. This isn't court." She flared her nostrils. "I don't appreciate your judgmental tone."

"I wasn't being judgmental at all. You're as scrupulous with your personal life as you are professionally."

"There. Right there. That wasn't judgmental?"

"Yeah, I guess it was. I take it all back. I'm totally judging you."

CC turned on her heel, determined to storm away when she saw Viv motioning to her.

"CC, how wonderful to see you!"

At the most awkward moment possible, Viv had finally noticed her. She pulled her into a tight embrace like an old friend, and CC imagined *everyone* was her friend after the first meeting.

"Are you a supporter of the Alzheimer's cause?" she asked.

"My firm is. But I hear you're a member of the board of directors."

Tears filled her eyes. "It's the least I could do. A lot of people were there for me when my mother got sick in the seventies, long before they knew what to call it."

"I think it's wonderful that you give back."

She took her arm. "I've often thought that if my dear Chloe wasn't a two-dimensional character, she'd have been sent to a home for reptiles long ago. And don't forget that I want to see your sketchbook soon."

"I'd love that," she said sincerely.

Viv introduced her to Manuel Munoz. His handshake was frail but his gaze was alert and he greeted her with a bow.

"Manny worked on our land. When things started to fall apart he was the one who held it together."

"Stopped a few fights as I remember. Your little community," he said with a cough, "was the talk of the town. I was surprised they didn't run you and your mama out of there."

Viv snorted. "We weren't afraid of them. They were the cowards. And when it was over we were still standing thanks to you."

"Well, *you* were," he said softly. "Others weren't so lucky."

CHAPTER SEVEN

July, 1954

"The key to sweet potato pie is the mashing," Mama instructed.

Kiah and I nodded dutifully. I was sure she was committing everything Mama said to memory since she was determined to bake one for her father. Mama made Mac a sweet potato pie at least once a week, and I thought Kiah was a little jealous. Every time Mama would drop one off, he'd fuss over her as if she'd handed him a million dollars. I think Kiah wanted the same attention.

We followed her around as she stirred and measured. I was already bored. I hated baking, but I'd learned not to complain or I'd face a long lecture about my unfortunate future as an old-maid spinster-moron.

"How in the world, Vivian, will you ever land a husband if you won't learn to cook? It's a wifely duty."

"Then I won't get married," I'd said.

For some reason that always shut her up. She'd look at me with a raised eyebrow, but it was almost like she was agreeing with me.

I wiped the sweat from my forehead with the bandanna I kept in the back pocket of my cutoffs. The July heat was worse in the kitchen and our old swamp cooler didn't help at all. I went to the icebox and stuck my head inside.

"Vivian Battle, get out of there! You're letting all of the cold air out."

I slowly closed the door, imagining I was sitting on an ice block in Antarctica.

There was a knock and the three of us turned. Mac stood on the other side of the screen door with his toolbox in his hand.

"Hello, Lois. I've come to fix your faucet."

"Hi, Mac. Please come in," she said brightly. She glanced at the clock. "Isn't this your lunch hour?"

"Yeah, but I don't mind." He knelt down by the sink and prepared to work.

"Oh, no, this can wait. You need to eat."

She went to the icebox and grabbed the fixings for sandwiches, the sweet potato pie forgotten. I slid against the open door for a few more seconds to cool down before I let it close. God, it was hot.

Kiah handed Mac the tools he requested while Mama made ham sandwiches. I wondered what Pops would say if he knew a black man was eating at his table, but I knew he'd never find out. I'd heard Mama tell Mr. Rubenstein, "Chet's gone all night and then tells me a story," but I wasn't sure I understood what she meant.

Will was gone too. He and Mama had a huge fight after the school had phoned because he was ditching and failing his classes. He'd called Mama a name and she'd slapped his face. Then he rode away and didn't come back often. He spent most of his time on his bike, riding the trails around Squaw Peak with a bunch of dropouts. He hadn't offered to go riding with me in months, which was fine since I spent every minute I could with

Kiah. For some reason I tied his absence with Pops' and didn't think much of it.

It became routine to have Kiah and Mac at the house. It never happened on purpose with a formal invitation, but we'd be coming home from the grocery store and Mac would be on his porch smoking his pipe and he'd offer to help carry in the bags. Then they'd start talking and Mama would invite them for dinner. If they met up between mealtimes, he was always ready for some sweet potato pie to go along with his lemonade. He *did* make the best lemonade I'd ever tasted.

"Mrs. Battle's teachin' me how to make pie," Kiah announced proudly as we sat down for lunch.

"Well, it's about time," he said with a laugh. "We can't be bothering these fine folks every time I get a hankerin' for some sweet potato pie."

"Oh, it's not a bother at all," Mama disagreed. "I enjoy it."

I blinked but said nothing. It was the first time she'd ever admitted to liking any type of work in the kitchen. While I knew she enjoyed the compliments about her pie, there was ample swearing during each phase of its creation, and I'd always thought she'd gladly stop making them if Pops didn't like them so much.

Mama pulled a cigarette from her case. "Well, you're about to get one all for yourself made by your daughter with a tiny bit of help from my daughter, whose only talent seems to be opening the icebox."

She scowled at me playfully while he whipped out his Zippo. She cupped his hand to steady the flame and leaned closer until it looked as if they were whispering. It was an odd picture, but Kiah obviously didn't notice.

"Yoo-hoo, Lois, dear!"

At the first syllable Mama dropped his hand and he stood up, knocking over his chair in the process. Ila Partridge waltzed through the door, assuming her announcement was enough permission. She glanced at the overturned chair, Mac, Kiah and the four place settings and immediately frowned. Mama took her elbow, leading her into the living room, away from the evidence that we were eating with black people. I crept to the archway, dying to know why she would come by. She didn't visit unless it was Mama's week for sewing circle time.

"Ila, what a nice surprise. What are you doing here?" she asked in a sugary voice.

They sat down on the couch, and Ila removed her gloves. Her yellow dress and shoes looked expensive but she was so homely that there wasn't much to be done. Her horn-rimmed glasses could barely stay on her tiny, upturned nose, and her eyes were huge like a squirrel's. I hated her because after church one day, I'd overheard her tell two of the other sewing circle ladies that some women weren't deserving of the beauty God had given them. She'd been staring straight at Mama when she'd said it.

"I was on my way back from prayer group and wanted to drop off this porcelain thimble before sewing circle tomorrow."

She held out a white thimble with a gold band around the bottom edge and presented it to Mama like a treasure. "I remembered how you'd told the story of losing your grandmother's thimble when the tornado struck your childhood home."

I scrunched up my face, puzzled. She'd never been in a tornado, and she'd lost Grandma's thimble when she'd thrown it at my head after I painted all the checker pieces the same color. She'd thrown a fit and the thimble happened to be on her finger at the time. After it bounced off my skull, it flew through an open window. I spent an hour crawling around her rosebushes looking for it, but all I found was a lot of thorns.

"This is very kind of you, Ila, thank you."

"You're quite welcome. I saw it and I just knew you'd like it. I knew if you were standing next to me you'd gush over how beautiful it was." She paused as if she was waiting. Mama gazed at her until she added, "I'll need a dollar."

She looked stunned. "What?"

"That's what it cost. Certainly you don't expect me to pay for it after I went to all the trouble of finding it for you and bringing it over."

She rolled it in her hand. "Of course not."

She got up and I moved back to the kitchen table. Kiah was doing her summer school homework, and Mac was cleaning off his wrench, having finished the sink. Mama went to the tea canister she kept on the second shelf and slowly pulled out a single from our grocery money. I'm sure she was already figuring what we'd have to cut from our list this month. A dollar was a lot to her.

She replaced the can and went back into the living room. I plopped down next to Kiah and muttered, "What a bitch."

She offered an understanding smile. I guessed she and Mac had heard most everything. He dropped his wrench into his toolbox and went to the cabinet. When he removed the tea canister, he held a finger to his lips. We watched as he pulled a dollar from his pocket and wrapped it around the small wad of money Mama had stashed. He quickly stepped back to the sink as they returned from the living room.

Ila stared at the table again. "Well, I'm sorry to have interrupted your...*lunch*?" she said, but like a question.

"Oh, Mrs. Battle is just the kindest woman on earth, ma'am," Mac gushed, a huge smile plastered on his face. "She's so good to me and my daughter. Helping us out when times are tough. And that happens a lot."

I thought he might cry as he stood there and wrung his hat in his hands, letting his head fall in shame. Ila was so moved that she touched her heart with her hand and sighed.

Not willing to be outdone, Kiah added, "And Vivian tutors me every day, helping me not to be such an ignorant Negro and catch up on my schooling." She pointed at the book for effect, and I pretended to look smarter than her.

Ila shook her head, overwhelmed by the sentiments. When she could finally speak, she grabbed Mama's arm and cried, "Lois Battle, you are indeed a saintly woman. I'm so glad I stopped by today to witness this act of charity. I am indeed changed. I'll see you tomorrow. God bless you."

I wasn't sure what she thought made Mama more saintly—allowing her daughter to tutor a black girl or actually allowing them to eat at the table with our kind.

Mac stepped to the window with her and they watched Ila drive away. When they were sure she was gone, they burst out laughing and Kiah and I quickly joined them. And just when we'd all managed to pull ourselves together, Mama held up her new thimble, dropped it onto the linoleum and crushed it with her shoe.

The next day when the sewing circle arrived, Kiah and I were curious to learn what Mama would say if Ila noticed the thimble was gone.

"Maybe there'll be another tornado," I said.

"There aren't any tornados in Phoenix," Kiah replied.

We had spent the morning cleaning the silver, baking the refreshments and making the tea. Mama flew around the kitchen like a sick bee trying to get everything ready. I was so grateful Kiah was there because she wasn't yelling half as much as she usually did. Kiah always knew just what to say and what she needed. I think she was just as grateful for Kiah as I was.

An hour before the guests arrived, she went to get ready. The woman who came back down the stairs wasn't the same one who went up. She looked stunning in a simple skirt and blue silk blouse. I couldn't understand why ladies got all dressed up to sew, but I knew none of them would look like her, with a chignon and makeup.

She smiled at Kiah. "Your mouth is hanging open, dear. Haven't you ever seen a proper lady?"

Kiah swallowed hard. "Yes, ma'am, but you're beautiful."

"Thank you. Now, I've got some leftover cookies and I know chocolate chip is your father's favorite." She glanced at her watch. "Isn't it almost time for his break?"

She nodded. "Uh-huh. We could take him some."

Mama shook her head. "No. I was thinking… Well, why don't you go see if he's nearby?"

We headed down the makeshift dirt roads that had been built for all of the trucks and equipment. It was still hard for me to look at the remaining orange trees and not see the whole grove. Sometimes at night I'd come out and stand on one of the cement foundations and breathe deeply, almost certain I could still smell the blossoms.

We found him talking to a man holding some blueprints and Mr. Rubenstein. When he saw us, he smiled.

"Mama wanted to know if you wanted some cookies," I said.

Mac grinned. "You know I do. Where are they?"

"Mrs. Battle wanted you to come to the house to get them," Kiah said.

He looked a little puzzled and scratched his head. "Well, I suppose I could do that. Mr. Rubenstein, would you like to come over to the Battle's with me?"

"I'd love to," he said. "I haven't seen Lois in a week or so. It'll be nice to check in."

When Mama came down the back steps, it was a contest to see who looked more surprised. She gushed over Mr. Rubenstein and he kissed her cheek, but at the sight of her, all dressed up with her hair and makeup done, Mac nearly fell over. He stood there like a statue even as the rest of us went for the cookies. I didn't understand why he looked so funny. He'd seen her dressed up lots of times.

"You look lovely," Mr. Rubenstein said to her. "What's the occasion?"

"Oh, my sewing circle's coming over, but I thought I'd get the rest of these cookies out of the way. I can always count on Mac." She giggled and glanced at Mac, who remained at the foot of the stairs, his hat in his hand. The giggle died in her throat. "Is something wrong? Mac, don't you want some cookies?"

He looked up slowly and something passed between them, a look written in a special adult code that she understood—and maybe Mr. Rubenstein.

"No, thank you, ma'am," he said quietly.

She took a step but Mr. Rubenstein gripped her arm. She glanced at Kiah, still watching her father walk away.

"Why is Daddy mad?"

"He's not mad, Kiah," Mr. Rubenstein said. "He's just not hungry." And he muttered in a low voice that only Mama was supposed to hear, "At least for cookies."

The four other sewing circle members arrived just as Mr. Rubenstein was saying his goodbyes. Mama stiffened as they got out of their cars and greeted him. Only Agnes McNulty flinched when his hand grasped hers. The rest of them acted as if it wasn't a big deal to touch a Jew, and Clara Drew, the youngest member, actually smiled and asked a few questions about his business. Then Agnes insisted they were wasting precious circle time so he took his leave.

Mama directed Kiah and me to the kitchen while the ladies assembled in the dining room. We served the tea and set out the cookies, listening to the idle chatter of the four women who knew each others' private lives intimately. Kiah and I excused ourselves with a stupid curtsy that Mama had insisted upon, and we went outside to climb the trellis and tiptoe back to the landing to listen.

"So who are all these ladies other than Ila?" she whispered. "Who's the lady at the head of the table with the bad wig?"

I almost laughed and gave us away. Agnes McNulty's wig, a clump of wavy brown hair, looked like a little dog lived on top of her head. She was an incredibly large woman today wearing a flowered dress that was definitely a size too small. The roses on her dress disappeared into the folds of fat like they were being pressed.

"That's Agnes. She's the head of the circle. She's the top lady at the church and in charge of a bunch of committees. When we moved here Pops told Mama she had to get to know her. She was very important to our orange business."

"Why?"

I shrugged. "Don't know. The one across from Ila is Mary Rose. Don't get mad, but that's Billy Smith's mama."

She leaned forward and stared sharply at her. Mary Rose wore a skirt and a long-sleeved white blouse that looked too hot for summer. "I see the resemblance," she murmured.

"And that's Clara next to her. She's actually really nice. She always says hi to us at church. I think she's just trying to fit in."

She was younger than Mama but not as pretty. Her blonde hair was in a bun, and she wore a silk dress so I knew she had money. But she kept her head down, focused on her needlework.

"I know I've told you this before, Lois," Agnes announced loudly, "but I do believe this is one of the most beautiful dining rooms I've ever seen."

"I agree," Ila said. "I told Lois that very fact just yesterday when I brought her the loveliest thimble." She searched Mama's hand. "Where is it, Lois? Certainly another tornado didn't strike last night," she said and all the ladies laughed.

Mama gathered her thoughts. I remembered the toe of her shoe smashing the porcelain to dust and smiled. But what could she say to Ila?

"Ila, I meant to tell you before we sat down that I loaned it to that very nice black girl you saw yesterday. Do you remember her?"

"Oh, the one that Vivian is tutoring?"

Kiah snorted and I punched her in the arm.

"Yes. She's a dear girl. Lost her mother, and she does all the sewing for her father. She asked to borrow it for a project and I didn't feel right saying no."

"Of course not," Clara said. "How kind of you, Lois."

"Absolutely," Agnes agreed, but Ila still looked upset.

Mary Rose shook her head and said, "It was a Christian thing to do, Lois, but I doubt you'll ever see that thimble again. Negroes are just so careless. I loaned a book to my Mabel, after she got on her high horse about learning to read, and she didn't return it for nearly a month."

"Maybe she wasn't finished yet," Mama said.

"Perhaps," Mary Rose said. "But I didn't make that mistake again. A month to return a loaned item is incredibly rude. I figured even the Negroes knew that," she added acidly.

"Lois, dear, you could take a lesson from Mary Rose," Ila said. "I think your Christian charity is admirable but perhaps misplaced. I wasn't going to mention what I saw yesterday, but since Mary Rose has brought up the shortcomings of the Negroes, perhaps you should reflect on her wisdom."

She set down her sewing and faced her. "What do you mean?"

She didn't bother to look up as she explained. "Just that there are limits. There's a point where charity becomes foolishness."

"Absolutely," Mary Rose agreed. "Have you heard that the school down the street is talking about letting those little Mexican children go to classes with white children?"

Ila gasped. "You mean they'd let them out of the basement?"

She shook her head. "That's exactly what I'm talking about. Lois, you need to hear all of this. Having Vivi tutor that girl is one thing, but allowing a black man to eat at your table—"

"What?" Agnes recoiled, pulling her fabric into her lap. Mary Rose seemed equally mortified.

"It wasn't the table in this room," Ila clarified.

"I would certainly hope not," Mary Rose said.

Mama looked like she was facing a death squad. The pleasantness and charm she'd shown when they arrived was gone. "There is nothing wrong with being hospitable," she said quietly.

Agnes sighed. "We certainly agree, Lois, but Ila is right about limits. Besides, I think you have other matters that need your attention."

"And they are?"

The women glanced at each other before returning to their sewing. There was something they knew that Mama didn't, and because Agnes was the head gossip she got to dish the dirt.

"Perhaps you need to attend to your *own* menfolk."

"Why?"

"Clara, why don't you explain?" Agnes directed.

She shot a dagger at Agnes before she touched Mama's arm. "There are stories going around. Will and his friends got in a fight with some boys from the other high school."

She looked shocked. We'd not heard anything about this. We barely saw Will.

"When?"

"About a week ago. Marvin said Chet came and got him from the police station."

I knew Marvin was Clara's brother—a police officer—so the story had to be true.

"Marvin agreed to let Will go with a warning, and Chet promised him it would never happen again."

"Chet never mentioned it," she said. She gazed at the table, avoiding Clara's stare.

"When do you see Chet?" Mary Rose asked.

"Every evening at supper," she lied.

"I was just wondering," Mary Rose said calmly as she searched through her sewing kit. "Since I see the nursery truck over at Shirley West's place most nights."

The comment silenced them all and no one looked at Mama. Pops made deliveries all over Phoenix for Harper's Nursery, and everyone knew he was the one driving the truck.

"And some mornings," Mary Rose added, dropping the bombshell and a spool of blue thread at the same time.

"And she certainly is preening about in all of her new dresses," Ila said. "Talks about them constantly at the beauty shop."

"I didn't know she could afford visits to the parlor, seeing as she's only a cashier at the nursery," Mary Rose said.

"Agnes," Clara immediately interjected, "I have been meaning to tell you how much my little nephew Aaron enjoyed your Sunday school lesson last week. He's still talking about Jonah and the whale."

She chuckled proudly and launched into a long explanation of her captivating lesson. She'd been the Sunday school teacher for years and she was a good storyteller. She'd been my teacher a few years, before and we'd all sit on the edge of our seats while she recounted a story from the Bible. In the end she always reminded us that we were just inches from going to hell if we didn't do what God or Jesus wanted. I remembered her directing those comments in my direction a lot.

I stared at Mama, who'd thrown her sewing onto the table. It wasn't really anything special. She'd been working on a dress shirt for Will since last summer. Sewing circle was the only time she ever brought it out, and I guessed that by the time she finished it Will wouldn't be able to get his arms through the sleeves.

She'd pulled out a cigarette and turned away from the table, facing the kitchen doorway. She sat and smoked while the four of them chatted about church and gossiped about other people. Nobody else spoke to her, not even Clara, although she kept stealing glances at her, like she wanted to make sure she was okay. She looked as if she was sitting on the sun porch, and I wondered if that's where she imagined she was.

I turned to Kiah. Tears were streaming down her cheeks. "I thought white people were nasty to us, but y'all save the worst of it for each other."

Re: Definitely Friends First! – 27 (Central Phoenix)
Date: 2010-06-13, 5:39AM MST

DFF,
I like your tone, baby, but who are u kidding? You want action. I'm interested in an NSA (that's no string attached since u sound like u r new to the game.) I m here 4 a week at the Holiday Inn by the Airport. Im a fine looking woman with a bald kitty who likes to eat pussy. Be honest with urself and text me.

Posted by: WorldTraveler
Reply

Re: Definitely Friends First! – 27 (Central Phoenix)
Date: 2010-06-14, 4:22AM MST

You should meet me. I have a nice car. A REALLY nice car.

Posted by: MustangMama
Reply

Re: Definitely Friends First! – 27 (Central Phoenix)
Date: 2010-06-15, 7:03PM MST

DFF! This is the SECOND time I've replied to your posting. I'm starting to get pissed. I was nice and friendly in my first reply so you should've ansered back. It's the polite thing to do! Or are you to high and mighty for us non-college educated girls. If you were so with it you'd already have a girlfriend!!!!!!!!

Posted by: BrooklynBornBaby
Reply

CHAPTER EIGHT

June, 2010

When six thirty rolled around most of the office staff were headed home grateful that Monday was over.

Her cell phone vibrated—Alicia. She hesitated for a second before dismissing the call.

She'd never seen this side of her—the daring risk-taker who screwed in public places. They'd always been rather traditional, and she imagined this brazen and bold approach to sex was due to Nadia's influence. And while she'd never forget her ride on the ancient trolley car, she couldn't fathom ending the first day of the work week fornicating in a movie theater or a bar restroom. As a girl from the Midwest she had her limits.

She stared at the files on her desk. For several more hours she could easily plod through the trivial cases Blanca kept dropping in her lap, but the files would be there in the morning. Since the Morgan debacle Blanca had only assigned her to grunt work either as punishment or a sign of her complete lack of trust in CC's abilities.

Ding!

She sighed and checked the alert—another reply from BrooklynBornBaby, who was quickly moving to stalker status. *Reply or else!* Not exactly a specific threat but definitely annoying.

She'd debated whether to delete the ad but if she did, she'd never be able to respond to the handful of promising women whose responses she'd saved. She decided to go home and send at least two e-mails.

But when she got to her car and saw her old portfolio in the passenger's seat, guilt overtook her as she recounted yesterday morning's conversation she'd had with her mother.

"You'll never believe what happened! We were at bingo last night and someone broke into the house!"

CC had nearly dropped the phone. "You're kidding. Did they catch him?"

"No, Mrs. Cox saw a young man go through the basement window. He was only there a minute, and then he was gone carrying a book or something. She said it was the oddest thing. We called the police, but nothing was missing."

CC's heart pounded. "Wow, that is odd, Mom. Maybe he'd stashed something there and was getting it back. Did they ever catch him?"

"No, CC, I already said that."

Fortunately her mother had drifted into her usual litany of praise about CC's work as a lawyer and the basement theft was forgotten. And better still, the teenage neighbor CC had hired to steal her portfolio and ship it to Phoenix hadn't been identified by old Mrs. Cox, who spent her days sitting at her front window, despite her limited vision.

She'd stolen from her parents. She couldn't think about what it meant in the scope of her life. It was too depressing.

Her cell phone rang and she nearly dismissed it thinking it was Alicia, but Penn's name popped up. "Hello?"

"Well, hello. What are you doing right now?"

"I'm going home," she said warily.

"Come over. We're having a barbecue and you're invited."

"I can't," she said instantly. "I'm not allowed—"

"We won't talk about the case, at least not directly. You can bring your maybe or maybe not girlfriend if you want."

"She's not my girlfriend, really," she said with exasperation.

"Then don't bring her. But come. Please."

The please got her. "I'll be there in ten."

The Honda easily found the enclave again, and she realized she wanted to know more about Jacob Rubenstein. There had to be a reason he'd kept the note, and still another reason why he'd never asked Viv's family to leave. She wondered if he'd ever intended for anyone to know about it. And there was something very important that had happened at the enclave, of this she was sure.

She'd just turned off the motor when Penn popped the lock of the passenger door and joined her in the car, grabbing her portfolio as she sat down. CC immediately felt her nearness. She was a tall woman who didn't naturally fit into an economy car, and her knees practically touched her chin as she contorted herself into the small bucket seat. She still wore the same cargo shorts but today her powder blue T-shirt read *If You Choke a Smurf, What Color Does He Turn?*

She flipped through the pages and stopped at one of CC's early attempts at landscapes—a meadow not far from her Bloomington home. She studied several drawings until she landed on CC's own version of a children's book hero, Danny the Dachshund, who was looking out a window, waiting for his next adventure. She couldn't remember exactly, but she was rather certain she'd picked a dachshund because it was the one dog she could draw well in ninth grade.

She waited for a sarcastic comment, but Penn eyed her with that look of interest she'd seen the day before. Suddenly the Honda seemed to be the size of a shoebox.

"You surprise me, Miss Carlson."

"You can call me CC," she offered, wondering what it would take for her to drop her suspiciousness. "Why did you invite me here? Are you trying to get me disbarred?"

Penn grinned. "Why would I do that? They'd just turn the case over to someone with more experience."

CC's temper rose. "And what are you implying?"

Penn ignored the question and jumped out of the Honda still carrying the portfolio. CC jogged to catch up with her. When she reached for it, Penn pulled it away.

"No, no. I think we need to show this to Viv."

"That's not your decision," she insisted, stepping in front of her. "Give me that back."

She clutched it to her chest. "I'll give it back, *and* I won't say anything to Viv if you answer three questions."

She thrust out her hand. "This isn't a negotiation."

Penn looked entirely unfazed, and CC made a mental note to practice the same expression in the mirror.

"Three questions."

She heard laughter in the common area behind them. She imagined if the other tenants learned who she was, they'd want to barbecue *her*.

She glanced over her shoulder. "Okay," she said. "What do you want to know?"

"First, what does CC stand for?"

She sighed, exasperated. "I'm not telling you that."

Penn grinned and held up the portfolio while CC glowered.

"Cleopatra Cinquain."

Penn's jaw dropped. "What?"

"I'm not repeating it!" she spat.

Penn bit her lip to stifle a laugh. "How did your parents ever come up with that?"

"My father was a huge fan of Egyptian history, and my mother is a poet of sorts." She reached for the portfolio, but Penn pulled it away.

"Not yet. Second question. Why did you quit drawing?"

She sputtered an incomprehensible response. She'd wondered the same thing many times, but no one else had ever asked since she left for college.

"Never mind," Penn said. "I get it."

The noise from the common area increased and she suddenly

realized she'd made a mistake in coming here. She just wanted to leave. "What's your third question?"

Penn glided past her, still holding the portfolio tightly under her arm. "I haven't decided. I'll let you know."

"What?" she cried.

She hurried to catch up before she rounded the corner and faced the other residents, but her Bandolino pumps and Penn's long stride made it impossible. Suddenly her right heel caught in a pothole and her ankle twisted as she dropped to the ground.

"Shit!"

Penn rushed to her side, and she yanked at her skirt which had ridden up her thighs. She caught Penn glancing at her legs, but when their eyes met she only saw concern. Penn helped her sit up and took off her shoe to examine her ankle. When she rotated it to the left, CC moaned.

"Yeah, I think you've sprained it, but I'll defer to the expert," she said, hopping up and jogging to the edge of the driveway. "Hey!" she called, waving her hand.

Viv and two other women joined them on the blacktop, along with seven of the homeliest mutts she'd ever seen.

"My Lord," Viv proclaimed. "What happened, child?"

"She tripped in that damn pothole I haven't fixed yet," Penn said.

A light-skinned African-American woman knelt beside her and manipulated her ankle until she winced.

"It's a semiserious sprain. I imagine with some ice and maybe a painkiller or two you'll be fine."

"I can help with those," Viv said brightly and headed for her house.

"This is Maya," Penn explained. "She's an ER nurse."

"Help her get up," Maya commanded. "I need to see if she can put any weight on it."

Penn and the other woman each took a side and lifted her, but the minute she tried to stand on her right foot, it buckled.

Maya sighed. "Okay, that's not going to work. Lynette, go get an ice pack from my freezer."

Lynette jumped to attention and saluted. She looked as if she'd stepped out of a secondhand store. She was chic in a long peasant skirt, lime-green blouse cinched by a fashionable black belt and a red bowler that sat on her head over very curly brown locks. It was a bold fashion statement, and CC thought it worked.

"Hi, I'm Lynette. I'm not sure if this is an appropriate time to be introduced but since I'm tending to your injury—"

"Lynette, go," Penn said.

"I'm CC," she said, returning the smile before Lynette ran off.

"Let's get her to a chair. We need to get this ankle up."

Followed by the pack of dogs, they set her in one of the chaise lounges. Bowls and platters of food covered the long concrete table with the mosaic sides, indicating their meal was about to begin.

"I'm sorry to be so much trouble," she said automatically.

"It's all right," Penn said. "It's my fault for not fixing that pothole."

When Lynette returned, Maya packed her ankle and she groaned. The pain and the cold made it ache.

"You'll definitely need some drugs," Maya said. "It'll get worse before it gets better."

She went back to her dinner responsibility of organizing the side dishes while Penn crouched beside her and held up the portfolio. She tried to grab it but Penn was quick.

"You still haven't told me why you invited me here."

Before she could answer, Viv appeared shaking a small pill bottle. "Now you just take two of these and a glass of wine and you'll feel a lot better."

"I have to cook," Penn said, handing her the portfolio and again ignoring the question.

"Oh, good, you remembered it," Viv said excitedly.

Penn offered a lazy smile, and CC handed Viv her life's work. "It's just some drawings I did during high school. I was a kid. It's not like I had any talent."

Viv's gaze shifted from her immersion in Danny the Dachshund to her. "And what idiot told you that?"

"I just…"

"These are excellent. You have a real knack for texture. Did you ever go to art school?"

"No, I went to college."

Her sympathetic smile told CC she understood. Perhaps Viv had chosen between stability and her passion decades ago—only she'd chosen differently.

Lynette handed each of them a glass of sauvignon blanc. "Viv's right," she said, raising her own glass in salute. "Wine helps."

She washed the pill down and chatted with Viv about art and drawing while the others finished the meal preparations. She felt light-headed and knew she'd soon be swimming in a pleasant stupor.

"I wanted to ask you about Jacob Rubenstein."

At the mention of his name, Viv smiled slightly. "A lovely man."

"So what happened with that note? Why do you think your father gave up your home, and why did Mr. Rubenstein leave it out of his will? Better yet, if he owned the property for forty years, why didn't he claim it?"

"Whoa, honey, you need to slow down. You asked a ton of questions, and I can't even remember the first one. Besides, we don't know each other well enough to discuss such matters."

She nodded at the kind rebuff and decided to let the subject drop. She was enjoying herself, and she realized it was the first time in a long time she'd been around a group of women. She missed their voices, their laughter and the camaraderie.

"Can I ask you about your art, about how you came to be an illustrator?"

She laughed. "Of course. What do you want to know?"

"Did you go to art school?"

"No, there wasn't enough money. And school was never my thing. I was dyslexic but nobody ever figured that out. I learned it from *60 Minutes.* My parents split up when I was in high school, and my mother had to support me. I went to work in a dime store as a cashier. I painted on the side."

"How did the Chloe series happen?"

"I'd taken an art class at the YMCA just for fun. The teacher was a student at the university. He saw my watercolors and invited me to meet one of the professors who knew a publisher." She smiled and added, "It's all about who you know."

"Well, as one of your biggest fans, I'm glad you knew someone who knew someone."

She was certain she wore a goofy look of sheer admiration, but she couldn't help it. Chloe was a true friend, and CC was completely inebriated. She had no idea how she'd get home, and she didn't care. One of Lynette's dogs, a huge pit bull mix with a terrible underbite, sat down next to her as if he was standing guard.

She patted his head and said, "Nice doggie."

Penn hovered over her wearing a frown. "Maybe you shouldn't be drinking."

She pinched her thumb and forefinger together. "Just a little. It's helping with the pain."

"I'll bet. Don't let Maya find out. She'll really give you a lecture, and you, too," she added, shaking a finger at Viv.

"I'm just being hospitable," she protested. "The woman's over twenty-one, so I'm assuming she knows her limits." She shot a glance at CC. "You do know your limits, don't you?"

"Yeah, and I'm not there," she said, holding her glass out when Lynette passed by.

"How will you drive home?" Penn asked, leaning over her like a possessive lover entitled to such close contact. She was rugged and independent and completely appetizing. She was outdoors REI while Alicia was Nordstrom's.

"What are you thinking about? Wondering what your ex is doing tonight?"

She blinked and realized her lascivious thought must be all over her face. She wondered if she'd said anything out loud.

"Shit, Penn! The chicken's burning!" Maya shouted.

Penn quickly returned to the grill, and soon afterward a plentiful spread covered the table. Although CC couldn't fully appreciate it, she was impressed by the assortment of serving bowls, plates and condiment trays.

Penn brought her a heaping plate of chicken kabobs, red potatoes, green beans, asparagus and fresh bread. Lynette sat in the redwood chair, and Viv returned to the chaise lounge next to her. It seemed everyone had assigned places, and she wondered whose she'd taken until she watched Penn, now carrying her own plate, head for the hammock on the opposite side of the patio. She sat down carefully, balancing her dinner while she gently rocked. Maya sat near her, and CC realized they formed a loose circle around the food and the mosaic table.

"So what's the surgery of the week?" Viv asked Maya.

"The surgery of the week was removing a spear from a man's ribcage after his best friend accidentally stabbed him."

"Are they sure it was an accident?" Viv asked, and everyone laughed.

CC studied Maya. There was something familiar about her—something distinct, but she couldn't place it. Maybe she'd met her before but that was unlikely unless she was from Bloomington.

Lynette grabbed another bottle of wine and gave everyone a refill. "I had an incredible day today. I finally had a chance to go through this box of albums I acquired at an auction, and I found a mint condition copy of Keith Moon's *Two Sides of the Moon*. Can you believe it?"

They smiled politely but it was obvious no one was as excited as her. She looked at them, dumbfounded. "C'mon, guys! It's Keith Moon!"

"I guess it's pretty rare, huh?" Penn offered.

"Oh, yeah," she said. "That was the only solo album he recorded, and he sang all the vocals and didn't play the drums except for a few songs. I'll be able to sell it for at least sixty bucks!"

Viv leaned over and said to CC, "Lynette owns a record store called Valley Vinyl. They specialize in old LPs."

She looked up at Lynette, surprised. "You mean like real records? Do people still play those?"

Lynette gasped at the question. "Some people do. Some of us aren't totally sold on iTunes as the music provider to the world. A few of us still believe in the preservation of history and loyalty to the local small business owners of this community!"

Everyone cheered, and when CC raised her glass in salute, half of the wine dribbled onto the grass. She was drunk, a fact she confirmed when she leaned forward to check her ice pack and the ground spun underneath her. Only when she returned to a reclining position did the world realign. *I'll just live out here in this chair. They can throw a blanket over me during the winter.*

She gathered that Lynette lived in the first cottage with all of the dogs, and she'd seen Maya run back to the cottage that barely looked as if someone lived there. CC imagined that Maya, as a nurse, kept erratic, long hours and was barely home. Since she knew Penn lived on the end, that left the cottage with the harp symbol on the limestone.

"Who lives there?" she blurted to Viv.

"That's Siobhan's place. She's a harpist with the Phoenix Symphony. Tonight they have a concert. But you'll have to hear her play sometime. She's incredibly gifted."

"You dedicated *Chloe Goes to the Symphony* to her."

Viv looked surprised. "I did."

"Do you always dedicate your books to someone in your life?"

"Usually," she said as she stood up.

"Who's Kiah?"

Viv froze and a pained expression crossed her face.

CC said quickly, "I'm sorry."

"She was a friend," Viv said simply before she walked away.

She felt horrible for opening her big mouth. Kiah was definitely someone very important to her and possibly part of the enclave's mystery. How did the five women come to live there? How did the enclave come to be? She doubted the cute little cottages and the park had always been a part of the land. Had Viv created this slice of heaven?

Lynette handed her some sweet potato pie, and she consumed the slice in ten seconds. It was heaven. She closed her eyes, the wine and Vicodin killing her pain, and found herself on the trolley car surrounded by people taking a ride. They were traveling down a major street passing old Buicks, Caddies and Plymouths. Across from her was a man in a suit—Jacob Rubenstein. He was reading the newspaper. She slid across the seat to talk to him when there was a sudden squeal of brakes.

"Sorry folks," a familiar voice called.

She glanced toward the driver, and Penn turned and tipped

her hat. She was dressed in a white uniform and when their eyes met, she winked.

Suddenly the trolley was empty, and Penn was patting her lap. "Come here, baby," she said, and CC obeyed.

She crawled into her lap and kissed her. Her cap fell off when CC's fingers explored her short curls. Penn unbuttoned her shirt and kissed the side of her breast. She threw her head back and groaned.

"Hey," a voice said, "you need to wake up."

She blinked. Penn's face was bathed in the moonlight, and they were alone.

"What time is it?" she asked.

"About eleven thirty."

"I need to go," she said, sitting up and sending a shooting pain through her leg. "Shit."

"I don't think you're going anywhere. You're half drunk and you couldn't operate a gas pedal with a stick. I could be disbarred if I let you leave in such a state." She looked around and threw up her hands. "I guess you're staying with me."

"With you?"

A look of interest crossed Penn's face, and she felt her cheeks grow hot.

"Put your arms around my neck," Penn said. She complied and Penn hefted her out of the chair with ease. "You're as light as a feather. It's those skinny legs of yours."

"What's wrong with my legs?"

"Nothing. In fact, Siobhan said you looked adorable, all curled up in the chair."

She was suddenly wide awake. "Siobhan saw me? While I was asleep?"

"Uh-huh."

"What else did she say?"

She looked uncomfortable. "Well, some typical bawdy Irish humor you probably wouldn't approve of seeing as you are from the Midwest."

"Why does everyone say that? We midwesterners have a great sense of humor."

"Uh-huh."

She pushed open the door with her foot, and CC was greeted by the faint odor of cinnamon. A long ceramic tile hung over the arch leading into the kitchen area. It said simply, *I choose*, just like the mosaics on the table.

"What do you choose?" she mumbled.

"Many things."

She set her down, and CC hobbled to the couch.

"Would you like some tea?" Penn offered.

She nodded, and Penn busied herself with the kettle and cups, perfectly at ease puttering around the little kitchen.

"What do you choose?" she asked again.

Penn glanced up from the teakettle. "Everything. I make my own life."

"Such as?"

She shrugged. "I don't do anything I don't want to do or be anywhere I don't want to be."

"And how can you afford that kind of lifestyle?" she asked cynically. "Lots of people, including me, would love to have that attitude."

"Then have it," Penn said, staring at her intently.

She laughed and caught Penn blushing. "It's not that simple. I have responsibilities."

"Everyone does," she said as the kettle whistled.

"Then how do you do it?"

She brought her a teacup and sat next to her. "You sound like you're mocking me."

"On the contrary," CC scoffed. "I want to know. How did you come to adopt this philosophy? Does it have anything to do with an ex?" When Penn nearly spewed her tea across the floor, CC said, "Bingo."

"Good guess, counselor. I thought she was innocent. And I'm usually pretty good at reading people. I screwed up twice," she concluded. "I helped a felon go free, and I lost everything in my life."

"Is that why you don't practice law in a firm?"

"That's part of it. After I got fired the second time, I gave up on the system."

"You were fired *twice*?"

"I was. And then I quit the last gig. The first time I refused to try a case when I realized our client had lied to us for over a year and he really *had* killed his little daughter. The senior partner was furious with me and threw me out on the sidewalk, literally."

"But you got another job, right?"

"Yeah, I was still worried about my loans and my career, so I called in a favor with a friend and got a job working in the DA's office in Sacramento. I thought it would be better for me being on the side of right."

"Then what happened?"

"I learned that right isn't always right. So many cases got pleaded out. I couldn't stomach it. I won't be a part of the law if I can't be right."

"But that's not what it's about," she pointed out. "It's about a system of checks and balances and hopefully justice prevails."

"Which law textbook are you quoting, Miss Carlson?" She shifted on the couch to face her. "The system doesn't matter to me, only justice. That's just how I am. If I can't be right, I won't participate." She pointed at the ceramic tile. "I choose." She paused and asked, "What do you choose, CC?"

They gazed at each other over the tops of the teacups, hiding their expressions behind the Earl Grey. She didn't know what to do. She was used to women making a move on *her*. That was certainly what Alicia had done. CC knew she was pretty and if she waited long enough, others took the risk before she had to.

But Penn just sat there. And then the tea was gone.

"It's time to get you to bed," she announced, taking her cup.

Penn carried her to the large king-sized mattress, and she craned her neck to examine the bedroom. It was filled with modern furniture and painted in earth tones, except for the opposite wall which was a rich rust color. Penn removed her shoes and used another pillow to elevate her ankle.

"I like your bedroom."

"Thanks," Penn said as she tucked her in.

Suddenly she felt amorous, the trolley dream triggering her senses. She was in a great bedroom, lying on a comfortable bed and staring into the eyes of a very attractive woman. She wrapped her arms around Penn's neck. Maybe it was the wine or the Vicodin, but she was willing to take the risk.

"I'm glad you invited me over even if you are trying to get me disbarred."

"I don't want you to be disbarred. I invited you over because… well, you seemed lonely."

For a moment Penn's eyes were a kaleidoscope revealing her complexity and goodness. CC pulled her into a kiss. It was like stepping toward a campfire, the heat instantly enveloping her. But just as she relaxed to enjoy Penn's yielding lips, Penn pulled away and untangled CC's arms from her neck. The campfire disappeared, and she suddenly felt vulnerable and foolish.

"That's probably not the best idea tonight," Penn said kindly. "You're hurt and on drugs. And I don't do hookups."

The judgment in her voice was unmistakable. Penn turned away without another word.

CHAPTER NINE

October, 1954

"Vivian Battle, you *will* wear a dress for your class picture tomorrow and that's final."

"I will not!"

"Yes, you will, or you won't have your sketchbook for a month."

She held up the dress in one hand and the sketchbook in the other. Art and my friendship with Kiah were all I had. I violently grabbed the dress but unfortunately it didn't tear in half. She watched as I changed into it then she pushed me into a chair and brushed my hair.

"This rat's nest is the worst I've ever seen it. Why can't you keep yours nice like Kiah? I thought you idolized her to no end."

"Not her hair," I snorted, and that got me a whack on the head with the brush.

"Don't sass me when I'm holding a weapon," she hissed. "You make it too easy."

She pulled and yanked until she was satisfied. I went to the mirror and scowled.

"Get that expression off your face or you'll never have any friends." She fluffed my hair and smoothed the skirt and said, "Appearance is important in a friendship and so is compromise. Look at me and the sewing circle. We don't always see eye-to-eye, but they're my friends."

"They're not your friends," I said.

She smacked me across the face, and we both froze in horror. She'd never hit me. I ran upstairs and collapsed on my window seat waiting for Kiah to come home from church. I longed to talk to Will, but he spent his time hanging out with a bunch of no-goods. He'd greased his hair back into a ducktail, and he reminded me of Billy Smith. And then one day I'd actually seen them together after school behind the mini-market. Both of them were smoking and taunting a black boy with the hot tip of their cigarettes. I couldn't believe it. Mama would've killed him if she knew, but they never talked either.

****

In the eight months that had passed, all of the trees had been destroyed except for the ones that would sit in the homeowners' yards, and little cement foundations laid in neat rows went on for a mile. I missed the orange trees terribly, but Kiah was living outside my front door so it seemed like a good trade.

But at school I couldn't find anyone to like me. So I spent my lunch hours hanging around the art room. Miss Noyce, the art teacher, thought I was incredibly talented. She let me make my own projects and even gave me some art supplies to take home, but only if I kept my grades up.

Tall with long brown hair that she wore in a bun, she was pretty, I thought. She stood perfectly straight, like she was pressed against a board, and when she talked about a piece of art or famous artists it was as if she knew them personally and had invited them over for dinner. She was the one who introduced me to Monet and Renoir and told me I could be as good as they were. I didn't believe her, but I appreciated her belief in my talent, which she praised every time I opened my sketchbook.

Kiah came up the drive with Mac and when she looked toward my window I motioned to her. She waited until he had gone inside before she climbed up the trellis. Even though she came into our house through the back door all the time, she still liked climbing.

I burst into tears when she hugged me and it took a few minutes to finally explain what had happened with Mama.

She rubbed my back and whispered, "You gotta understand what else you were saying to her."

I looked up through my tears. Half of the time she had to re-explain whatever she said because I was always three steps behind her.

"I didn't say anything else."

She shook her head. "We always do. Every time we speak there are the words that come out and the ones that don't. And you *didn't* say a bunch."

I looked at her dumbly.

"Think about it, Vivi. Daddy and I've been living over here in the cabin for two months and other than those nasty sewing ladies, I haven't seen one other car come up that driveway except Mr. Rubenstein's Cadillac and your daddy's truck once in a blue moon. Does your mama have any other friends I don't know about?" When I didn't answer she said, "Those ladies are all she has, and for you to say that they should quit coming around is like saying you think she should be alone."

I realized then Mama couldn't be alone.

****

I left for school on Monday wearing the horrible dress with the French braid Mama had insisted upon. By the time I got to my first period American history class, my forehead no longer felt like it was being stretched a mile away from my nose. I slid into my chair and nodded at Gloria Meyer, the only other girl who was as quiet as I was. With her dark hair and long nose, I knew she was Jewish, and I guessed that was why so many of the other kids didn't talk to her.

Mr. Corliss clapped his hands once and everyone immediately turned around and shut up. "We left off with the Pilgrims coming to America. What did we learn yesterday?"

"We learned that they came here to escape religious execution," one student said.

"*Persecution*," he corrected. "What else?"

"They taught the Indians all kinds of things, like hunting and fishing and sharing."

"They had a big feast with the Indians and that's why we have Thanksgiving because the Indians were so grateful."

I squirmed in my seat. The answers didn't make sense, but I wasn't going to say anything.

"Miss Battle, you seem to want to add to the discussion. What did *you* learn yesterday?"

I shrugged. Maybe he'd pick someone else. I hung my head and tried to be invisible.

He sighed heavily. "Miss Battle, I'm waiting. You are one of the most infrequent contributors to this class, and, for once, I'd like to know what you think. Or *do* you think, Miss Battle, about anything except the silly drawings that you make when you're supposed to be taking notes?"

My head shot up and I said, "It can't be right."

His eyes narrowed behind his horn-rimmed glasses. "What can't be right?"

"The story."

He shook his head and looked like he had indigestion. I could tell he was already sorry he'd called on me. "What are you talking about, Miss Battle?"

I glanced at the students, many of whom had turned in their seats to stare at me curiously. They either didn't understand what I was trying to say, or they couldn't believe I was challenging one of the meanest teachers in the school.

"I think it's ridiculous. How could the Pilgrims get to the New World and teach the Indians how to hunt and farm and fish?"

He closed his eyes like he was praying that I would disappear. "Please explain, Miss Battle."

"Well, wouldn't they be dead?"

"What?" he asked in total exasperation.

"The Indians were there first, right?"

"Yes."

"So if they didn't know how to hunt or fish or farm, how did they survive? They should've been dead. The Mayflower should've pulled up and found a bunch of dead Indians lying on the shore." I heard a cough next to me and his angry eyes immediately shot toward Gloria Meyer. She had her head down, but I thought I saw a smile from underneath the dark hair that fell in her face.

When he mumbled something under his breath and pulled out his packet of office slips, I knew I was in trouble. "Miss Battle, I don't appreciate your insubordinate attitude."

"I wasn't trying to be insubordinate, but I don't understand how they could be so stupid. Here in Arizona the Hohokam Indians built all kinds of canals and that was thousands of years before the Pilgrims came. I just don't get it—"

"That is because you are an impertinent girl stupider than any Indian." He thrust out the pass and waited until I trudged to the front to claim it.

"I'm not stupid," I muttered under my breath. "It's your story that's stupid."

"What did you say?"

His question hung over me like a raincloud waiting to burst. All I had to say was something simple like, "I didn't say anything, sir," but that wasn't me. I blurted, "The Pilgrim story is the dumbest thing I've ever heard next to that stupid story of Jonah being swallowed by the whale."

He pointed at the door and all his blood seemed to be in his drooping cheeks. "OUT!"

****

When Mama came to get me, her face was nearly as red as Mr. Corliss's had been. She disappeared into Principal Landy's office for a few minutes before she swooped out and grabbed my arm. She dragged me through the hallway, and if I'd had any friends, I imagined I would've lost some out of embarrassment.

We drove home in silence, but I knew from the way she twitched in her seat, played with the radio and took deep drags on her cigarette that she was ready to explode like Vesuvius. And when we screeched into the driveway she chased me into the house, smacking my butt as I walked through the door.

"Vivian Lucille Battle, you are the most ungrateful, disrespectful child I've ever known," she hissed as she followed me up the stairs.

"But it didn't make sense," I argued. "How could the Pilgrims—"

"I don't give a fuck!" She grabbed the wooden paddle off the bathroom door handle. "Bend over."

My jaw dropped. That was the foulest language I'd ever heard her use, and it was so beneath her as a lady. She shook the paddle at me and I took a step back.

"I'm too old for that. You ain't hitting me! I'm not a little kid."

"You're certainly acting like one. Now bend over."

"No! That's Pops' job."

And it was. She'd never paddled either me or Will but something changed in her when I spoke the truth.

"You lean your ass over right now! Right now!" she screeched.

And when I didn't do it, she swung the paddle and hit me in the hip bone. I cried out and started running as it slammed into my back and nearly knocked me over. I righted myself, staring at my door that seemed a mile away, wondering if she would bring the paddle down on my head.

I stumbled inside, gasping for air as I swung the door shut, certain she was right behind me. But as it closed, I glimpsed her leaning against the wall, the paddle dangling toward the floor. I fell on my bed and sobbed.

Later that night Kiah snuck up the trellis, and I cried again in her arms. I told her what happened, hoping she could explain it right like she always did.

"Your mama's not half as mad at you as she is at your pops," she said, stroking my hair.

"What does he have to do with it?"

"Everything," she said simply. "At least that's what my daddy thinks."

"I don't get it. And why doesn't your daddy come over anymore?" I asked, suddenly realizing that I hadn't seen Mac at our table in a long time.

"He's busy," she said, and I knew she was lying.

She stroked my cheek and kissed me. Soon the dark afternoon in the hallway was forgotten in the tenderness of her lips. When she pressed against me I felt like I was sitting in an orange tree and all the little branches were poking at me in a nice way. Neither of us knew what to do but it felt wonderful just to *know* we liked it.

We heard the creak of the screen door that Pops had never fixed, and I looked down as Mama appeared on the porch smoking her cigarette. She didn't look anything like she had earlier. She'd taken a bath, redone her hair and put on some makeup after our shouting match. It seemed like it had never happened. I didn't understand how she could forget everything so quickly. I'd heard of amnesia and maybe she suffered from it.

Kiah took me by the shoulders, suddenly very serious. "You can't tell no one about our kissing, Vivi. Not ever."

"Why not?"

"It's wrong, that's why. Double wrong, really."

"Why?"

"It's wrong for girls to kiss like we do, but even worse, I'm black and you're white and mixin' is illegal. Do you know what the Klan is doin' to couples who mix?"

I'd never even heard of the Ku Klux Klan until Mac and Kiah had explained it to me one night. Why grown men would run around wearing sheets seemed ridiculous and when I'd mentioned them to Mama, she'd called them a bunch of sons of bitches.

"But the Klan's not around here," I argued.

"You don't think so? I hear boys talkin' about the Klan all the time at my school. How they've run blacks out of the drive-ins or pushed us off the sidewalks. Don't you hear those kinds of stories?"

I nodded. I heard all kinds of foul-mouthed slurs as Mama

called them, not just about the Klan. Nigger, spic and kike were sneers regularly spewed by the white kids at the lockers between every class. It was like hatred took a break for fifty minutes at a time, just long enough for us to learn math, science, history and English before it started again. And lunchtime was the worst, which was why I was glad I spent mine with Miss Noyce.

A car rumbled up the driveway and both of us stepped to the window. Mr. Rubenstein emerged and joined Mama on the sun porch. She scurried away, leaving him to sit on the old divan with his hat in his hand. Two minutes later she came out with a piece of sweet potato pie and a cup of coffee.

"Why does he still come by?" I asked.

"He likes your mama. She's beautiful and funny, and she doesn't hate Jews."

"She doesn't hate anyone except maybe me," I added. A shiver ran down my back as I pictured her coming at me with the paddle.

"She doesn't hate you, Vivi. She loves you most of all."

She wrapped her arms around me and the shivering stopped. "How long are you suspended for?"

"Three days. Mr. Landy says I have to write a letter of apology to that son of a bitch Corliss. What have I got to apologize for, anyway? I just asked a question. Don't you think that's a good question?"

"It's a great question," she agreed. "I imagine those Indians were doing just fine without the white folks, just like my people were minding their own business over in Africa before the slave traders came."

She'd told me fascinating stories about the slave traders who came from America and imprisoned her people. I hadn't believed her and shown her and Mac my history book, which told us that the blacks *liked* coming to America. Mac had shaken his head sadly and shared some letters from his ancestors. Then I apologized profusely.

He'd grinned and said, "Miss Vivi, I believe that you will help change the world." Then he'd gone to his room and when he came back, he handed me his copy of the first Wonder Woman comic book.

"Mac, I can't accept this."

"Oh, yes you can." And then he'd kissed me on the cheek.

I'd sighed and hung my head. "I hate being white. It's so embarrassing."

And they'd both laughed for a long time.

Headlights appeared behind Mr. Rubenstein's Cadillac and my heart jumped at the thought that Pops might be home, but I quickly realized it was another car.

"Who's that?" Kiah asked.

We peered through the window as a figure emerged in the darkness. It was a woman and there was something familiar about her silhouette, but I didn't recognize her until the light of the sun porch shone on her face.

"That's Miss Noyce, my art teacher," I said. "I wonder why she's here."

I suddenly felt sick. She held my sketchbook in her hand, and I imagined she was returning it to me. She'd probably heard about my behavior in history class and now she was kicking me out of art too. Where would I eat lunch?

I started to cry and sniffle.

"Hey, it's okay," Kiah said, pulling me close.

She was right. When Mama came out to greet her they were all smiles, and I was surprised when Mama disappeared and returned with another piece of pie and coffee for Miss Noyce. It got later and later but nobody left. From my window I could see Mama's ruby red lips move each time she added to the conversation. She touched Mr. Rubenstein's arm periodically and the two of them seemed to be explaining something to Miss Noyce, who nodded politely. Once in a while Mama's laugh floated up to my window and soothed the pain of the afternoon.

"I gotta go," Kiah said as she crawled out the window.

"Say hi to Mac for me."

She gave me a quick kiss and snuck away.

I found a piece of paper from my schoolbag and began to draw a picture of the Pilgrims landing on Plymouth Rock, dead Indians lying on the shore while the white men hovered over them scratching their heads in bewilderment. The hinges creaked as Mama opened my door and I automatically thrust the drawing to the floor. I hadn't even heard our visitors leave.

She stood in the doorway holding my sketchbook under her arm. She looked like herself and I wasn't afraid, at least no more than I ever was. She carefully set it on the bed like it was breakable.

"Miss Noyce came by tonight. She wanted you to have this while you're out of school." Our eyes met briefly before she looked toward the window. "She showed me your drawings. She says you have talent, Vivi, a gift."

I thought of some of my sketches—the orchard, Kiah, one of Pops as I remembered him working in the groves, Will sitting on the front stoop thinking and the one of Mama with the expression I wanted her to have.

"She's right," she said.

I almost didn't hear it. She said it so softly that the words almost got sucked through the open window by the passing wind. I almost missed the only compliment she'd ever given me.

And it was another long while, long enough for the wind to announce its presence again before she said in a weak, flat voice, "Please, Vivi. You're so strong."

She headed to her bedroom, the tap of her pumps against the oak floor fading away when the door clicked shut.

Re: Definitely Friends First! – 27 (Central Phoenix)
Date: 2010-06-17 5:07AM MST

Dearest DFF,
The moon is a ghost now. I've fluttered beyond the horizon and past the oldest part of time. The golden yellow sun pierces my soul infuriarting and igniting me at the same time. Then I whisper.

Posted by: ????girl
Reply

Re: Definitely Friends First! – 27 (Central Phoenix)
Date: 2010-06-17 11:52AM MST

DFF,
This will be short—at work. Liked yor post. My stats: luv horses, working out, Zumba, long walks on the beach, and if yur a real redhead, I'll marry u on the spot. Gotta go. Boss alert.

Posted by: Cheekygal
Reply

Re: Definitely Friends First! – 27 (Central Phoenix)
Date: 2010-06-18 8:44PM MST

DFF,
Are you happy with the number of hits and the quality of the hits your posting has received? If not, please contact us as we can help you design and create a posting guaranteed to attract that special someone. She's out there waiting for the right words from you!

Posted by: Classyads
Reply

CHAPTER TEN

June, 2010

Ding!

CC woke to the smell of strong coffee. She gently rotated her ankle and was surprised that only a flicker of pain remained. She got up slowly and gingerly walked to the adjoining bathroom. It was tiny with only a pedestal sink, mirror and toilet, but Penn's choice of chrome fixtures and dark Italian tile impressed her. The woman had great taste.

Her need for a caffeine fix drove her to the kitchen. Penn had favored red shelves over kitchen cabinets, and a small island served as the dining table and prep area, which, considering the size of the cottage, was an excellent economical space choice. The steel appliances and bright countertops added to the kitchen's appeal.

She saw the note after she poured the coffee. It took three

attempts to read her horrible handwriting. *Hi. Had to do some work and errands. If you're reading this you must be up and your ankle is better. Otherwise, I guess I'll find you stuck in my bed when I get home. Not an unpleasant thought. Help yourself to whatever you want.*

It wasn't signed and gave no mention as to when she would return, not that CC could afford to hang around. She glanced at her watch. She was already late, and she'd need at least another hour to get home, shower and change before she went to work. But she kept rereading the part about Penn finding her in bed. She was flirting—in writing. For a lawyer, it was serious to commit words to a page that could be used in court. She shook her head, completely confused.

She sipped her coffee and reviewed her day, thinking of the meetings and the unappealing stack of files on her desk that never seemed to shrink. After draining the cup, she grabbed her handbag, portfolio and shoes from the bedroom. There was no way she'd attempt to wear the heels with a wobbly ankle, so she went barefoot out the door.

"Hello," a voice called.

Sitting cross-legged on top of the mosaic table was a woman with bright red hair. It flowed straight down her back and glimmered in the sun. She was rail-thin with milky skin, finely chiseled bone structure and perfect posture. The yoga pants, tank top and pose suggested she was meditating.

"Hi, I'm CC," she said, offering her hand.

The woman's handshake was delicate, as if she was protecting her fingers. "I know. I saw you last night when I got home. I'm Siobhan."

Her brogue was rich and thick and CC immediately wanted her to say something else. "Can you repeat that?"

She nodded with the patience of someone who was always asked the same question. "It's like the first syllable of Chevy, *Chev* and the word *on*. Siobhan."

"Siobhan," she repeated. "It's beautiful."

"Thanks. Are you feeling better?"

"Much. I'm sorry I wasn't awake when you got home."

She laughed and tucked her hair behind her ears. "That's

entirely forgivable. I heard Lynette and Viv fed you drugs and alcohol. You were helpless."

"I suppose I was. You were at work?"

"Yes, I'm a harpist with the Phoenix Symphony. We had a concert."

"Wow. You must be very good."

She grinned with humility. "I hope so. I don't make much money, but I enjoy what I do. Can you say the same?"

CC stumbled before she said, "I'm an attorney like Penn."

"No one's an attorney like Penn," she disagreed. "At least, I've never met anyone like Penn, have you?"

"I hardly know her."

"That makes two of us."

She uncrossed her legs and stretched her arms, freeing herself from first position. When she stood next to CC she towered over her. "After you went to sleep last night, Lynette and Maya pumped Penn and Viv for information, but they wouldn't say why you've shown up or what you want. What *do* you want?" She threw a glance at the portfolio. "Does it have anything to do with art? Are you a groupie just trying to spend some time with Viv?"

CC really didn't know what she wanted, and she couldn't understand why Viv and Penn hadn't ratted her out.

"It's complicated," she said lamely. "I'm involved in a legal matter with Viv."

She narrowed her gorgeous green eyes, disbelieving. "Penn is Viv's attorney. She'd never hire someone else."

"No, I'm not her attorney. Like I said, it's complicated." Siobhan studied her until she felt undressed. "I need to get going. I'm already late for work. It was nice meeting you."

"Take the day off," she said suddenly.

"What?"

"Play hooky. You've obviously been hurt so use that as an excuse. Spend the day with me."

"Uh, I can't. I have things I need to get done."

She reached for the sky and stretched, extending her frame to its full length and displaying the curves of her large breasts. CC caught a glimpse of her creamy white belly before she exhaled slowly and relaxed each muscle and vertebra.

"And what could be so important that it can't wait until tomorrow? Are you in the middle of a murder trial?"

"No—"

"Do you have an important death row appeal that's due before midnight?"

"Of course not. I—"

"Are they making you a partner?"

"No, I just—"

"You're just another lawyer having a typical day of paper pushing," she concluded. "At least that's what Penn always calls it. So just skip it."

"Skip it?" she asked incredulously. Siobhan made ditching work sound as harmless as throwing aluminum cans in the trash rather than the recycling dumpster.

"Yes."

She thought of the files, the handwriting sample and the report she still hadn't rewritten for Blanca—and her last student loan statement. She was about to hobble back to her car when Siobhan took her hand.

"Even though I'm taller than you, I've got some clothes you could wear. C'mon, we'll have some fun. You've read the mosaic above Penn's kitchen, right?" Siobhan extended her foot and pointed to the *I Choose* mosaic embedded in the concrete table. "Make a choice, the *right* choice."

****

Decked out in white capri pants, a stylish red cotton blouse and some black flats, for she and Siobhan were indeed the same shoe size, they took her portfolio and headed across the lawn for their first stop—coffee and scones with Viv.

She'd called and spoken with Blanca about her absence, stating that she'd taken a spill down some stairs and was spending the day with her foot in the air. She tried to sound injured and promised she'd be back tomorrow. Blanca had sighed deeply and dismissed her curtly.

They found Viv on the sun porch working on a picture of Chloe, taking advantage of the morning light. Beside her were a sterling silver tea set and a basket of scones covered by a linen napkin.

"Look who I brought with me," Siobhan announced, digging under the napkin.

Viv seemed genuinely pleased and patted the stool beside her. "Sit down and give me your opinion," she said.

She held up a two-page spread depicting Chloe packing for a trip. The various green hues of Chloe's skin, the rich brown tones of the old suitcase and the background choices for Chloe's cute bedroom would entice young readers to keep turning the pages. She said as much to Viv who thanked her for the feedback and picked up her portfolio.

"Now, let me see your little guy."

She protested, but Viv ignored her and found the page with Danny the Dachshund. "It's so basic," CC apologized. "I did it back in high school and forgot about it."

"I like it," Siobhan offered between scone bites. "He's cute."

"So what needs to change?" Viv asked like a teacher.

She wasn't expecting the question. She'd had a similar conversation with her art teacher over ten years ago. "Well, I need more of a blend to the browns and blacks of his coat, and his eyes aren't right."

"What do you mean?" she probed.

"They're not interesting. A character's eyes are critical to establishing a connection with a child reader. It's all in the eyes."

She smiled, pleased. "You have a wonderful beginning. Now, I want you to fix Danny and bring him back to me." She rose and assembled a box of supplies.

"What?"

"I think I've included everything you need. I certainly don't use the Sumi ink much so it won't be missed."

"But—"

"No buts," she said, handing her the box. "Now, if you want a scone you'd better eat one quick. Siobhan can finish an entire basket in less than ten minutes. How she keeps her twig figure I'll never know." She gave her a look and added, "Aren't the Irish a hearty people with girth?"

"We are," she said between bites. "I should weigh about ten pounds less but that will never happen if I keep eating your scones and pie."

CC took a scone and asked, "Viv, how did the enclave come to be?"

Her smile broke. "Well, when my father sold the groves, my mother insisted that we keep our home. Mr. Rubenstein liked her so much that he threw in some extra land, which originally housed workers' quarters. Back in the fifties there were three identical cabins that sat where the cottages are now."

"How did they transform into cottages?"

Viv stirred her tea and added some drops from a lemon wedge. CC sensed she'd hit on a difficult topic. When Viv looked up she said, "*Transform* isn't exactly the word I'd choose, dear."

"What happened?"

"They burned down."

****

The ER parking lot at Maricopa Medical Center was so crowded that people had created random parking spaces, obviously believing their medical emergency warranted the risk of a ticket or a tow. Siobhan's ancient Ford truck snaked through the lot four times until it finally came across a man wearing a huge cast and a boy piling into a Chevy Cavalier.

When the man tumbled into the passenger side and the boy, who couldn't have been more than eleven got behind the wheel, Siobhan said, "I hope today isn't his first driving lesson."

She put the truck in reverse to give him ample room to exit before claiming the prized spot. They wandered into the ER and the sounds and sights assaulted them immediately. Many of the waiting families held one or two screaming infants. People slept in chairs, contorted into uncomfortable positions, and a few men and women, who CC guessed were homeless judging by their lack of hygiene, shuffled past, each muttering nonstop to an invisible companion. A man in his thirties sat alone in a corner, his hand wrapped in a bloody bandage. The look on his face suggested he had a few painkillers in his system. A TV mounted to the ceiling blared an old seventies comedy, the laugh track a bitter oxymoron to the misery and exhaustion on the faces in the lobby. And CC noted none of the faces were white.

She stayed close to Siobhan, who seemed unfazed by the scene. She carried a pink gift bag in her hand that Maya needed at noontime. She'd been in charge of purchasing a gift for a baby shower and had left it on her kitchen table as she rushed out the door.

The desk clerk waved at her. "Hey, hey, girl. The cavalry has arrived. You saved her bacon."

Siobhan nodded at the large Hispanic woman. "It's good to know someone with a night job. Is she here? I'll feel better once it's no longer in my possession."

The woman nodded as she picked up the phone. "Yeah, go on back. She should be finishing rounds."

The double doors flew open and they headed into triage. Medical personnel raced in all directions, carrying charts and supplies or pushing gurneys. They spotted Maya surrounded by several young nurses who wrote furiously in their notebooks. She was discussing the diagnosis of a patient and as each one made an effort to impress her, she either pointedly disagreed or gave a quick nod before asking the next question. When she saw CC and Siobhan, she excused herself.

She kissed Siobhan on the cheek and took the bag. "I owe you."

"As usual."

Maya turned and gave CC an unexpected hug. "You're looking a hundred times better. How's the ankle?"

"Great, but I think I'll stay away from heels for a few days."

"Probably a good idea." She looked at her with wise eyes, and again she had the feeling that she'd seen her face before.

Maya kissed Siobhan again and returned to work. As they made their way out of the hospital, CC couldn't shake the nagging feeling that she knew her.

"Has she always worked here?"

"For a long time but I think that's about to change."

"Why?"

"Well, if you can believe it, she would prefer to work in a

clinic. These patients aren't needy enough. Many of them are getting help from the system, but not only is she very tired of the bureaucracy, she knows many families don't qualify. Those are the people she wants to help."

"That's very noble given the demand for nurses."

She nodded and maneuvered out of the parking lot. "Absolutely. She turned down an opportunity to do research at Johns Hopkins and a chance to be a surgical nurse at Sloan-Kettering. All for this. But I think the reason she wants to leave is personal."

"Why?"

"Her lover is the hospital's CFO. She's married, and Maya has finally realized she'll never leave her husband."

She groaned. "I hate those stories."

Suddenly Siobhan's cell phone barked. "Hi Lynette," she cooed. "How are you, love?"

All she could hear was a high-pitched squeak on the other end. CC checked her own phone and answered her e-mail, much of which was from Blanca who had questions about various cases. Clearly she would contact her endlessly as punishment for missing work.

"Are you serious? Lynette! Fine, we'll be there in a few minutes." She hung a quick right onto Central Avenue and explained. "That was Lynette. Charlie Parker ate something and now he's throwing up. She's alone at the store and needs help. So how are you at cashiering?"

"Who's Charlie Parker? I mean, I *know* who the real Charlie Parker is…"

"One of the mutts. Sorry, I didn't explain that very well. All of her canine friends are named after famous musicians. There's Charlie Parker, Muddy Waters, Janis Joplin, Chrissy Hynde, Ella Fitzgerald, Aretha—that's just Aretha—and in my honor, Turlough O'Carolyn."

"Who's that?"

"He was an influential Irish harpist who lived in the sixteen hundreds. I'm surprised you haven't heard of him," she said sarcastically.

"Sorry. I think the harp is beautiful, though. And what an

honor to have a dog named after you. What kind of dog is it?"

"Well, it's hard to tell. You may not have noticed last night since you were in a drug-induced stupor, but all of Lynette's dogs are rescues. She picks the homeliest dogs that are just a few hours away from the needle and adopts them."

"Then I'm surprised she only has seven."

"That's because we don't let her bring any more of them home. Lynette may love dogs, but Viv has a soft spot for feral cats. One afternoon we found the canines and the felines facing off in the front yard. It looked like the animal version of *West Side Story*. After we separated them, we told Lynette she had to find other people to take the dogs. She's a one-woman adoption center who's probably saved a few hundred animals. She's got a website, and she puts up flyers in her store. She does a lot."

Siobhan pulled into a driveway and parked behind a small strip mall. Two of the four shops were boarded up but the parking lot was half full, an indication that Central Music and Valley Vinyl were thriving. CC recognized the Smartcar from the enclave and assumed it was Lynette's.

A small patio faced the parking lot; huge plants and misters kept the June heat at bay and the entire side wall was plastered with flyers of lost cats and dogs. A hairy brown blob that looked like a cross between an Irish setter and a pug bounded through an open door, clearly excited to see Siobhan. The short, fur-covered mop wiggled and she laughed.

CC was grinning. "I hope Lynette puts her dogs on YouTube. People would crack up."

Siobhan leaned down and petted him. "She does. She is one of the most socially connected people you'll meet. This is Janis Joplin."

CC found the fur to be unexpectedly soft. "You're adorable."

"They're *all* adorable in their own way."

Punk music echoed throughout the store, which was incredibly bright and covered in aluminum siding that was hidden by dozens of concert posters for popular bands like the Ramones and the Pretenders, as well as groups CC had never heard of. Rows of album racks took up the floor space and a

Phono Bar lined the west wall. Customers could sit on stools, put on some headphones and listen to the albums. Several signs warned them to be careful with the LPs and to ask for assistance as needed. She shivered, realizing the Phoenix heat was a bitter enemy to the vinyl records.

"Her AC bill must be outrageous," she said to Siobhan.

"She's got some really good insulation and the aluminum helps."

They found her in a raised bandstand that served as the checkout and customer service area. A collage of old concert tickets from venues all across the country sat beneath the Plexiglas countertop. A few patrons waited for Lynette to scan their purchases with a hand-held computer that CC guessed was connected to the nearby MacBook with its giant monitor. The advanced technology struck her as odd since the store sold outdated LPs. She'd expected an old-fashioned register and a Cash Only sign.

Lynette's outfit was as eclectic as the shop. She wore a short leather skirt, a Rush concert T-shirt and Mickey Mouse ears. When the last customer took his receipt, she disappeared into a back room and returned with her purse, cradling a hairy black dog. She seemed distraught as she stroked his head. "Charlie's not doing so good. I promise I'll be right back. I just need to drop him off with Dr. Casey." She turned to Siobhan. "Can you mind the store since you know what to do?"

She sighed. "Of course." She turned to CC and murmured, "My advice is hang on to the grab bar above the door."

"I love you," Lynette said breathily.

Siobhan raised an eyebrow. "Do you?"

She blew her a kiss and looked at CC expectantly. "Can you come with me and hold him on your lap?"

She nodded and followed her out to the tiny Smartcar.

"Do all of your dogs fit in here?"

"Not all at once. Usually I only bring three or four with me to work so we're nice and cozy."

She had never ridden in a Smartcar and was surprised that she didn't feel claustrophobic, not even with Charlie Parker on her lap.

"How was your night with Penn?" Lynette asked as she whipped around a corner.

She immediately clenched the grab bar. "Uh, fine."

Lynette scowled. "Damn it. *Fine* means that she didn't make a move on you doesn't it?"

"I was under the influence of medication and alcohol."

"Hmph. Well, that might be a *good* excuse, but I still think it's an excuse." She glanced at CC who hoped her face wasn't crimson. "She likes you. I can tell."

"What's her story?" CC asked, hoping Lynette would shed more light on Penn's obvious gun-shy ways.

"Well, I know there was a really bad breakup. Her ex was a former client who she'd met while she worked in this big law firm in California. The woman was accused of embezzling money from her dot-com company. Penn was the only one who believed her and fought to take the case. So she gets her off, they move in together, and then she rips off Penn for everything she's got, dumps her for someone else and runs off to live in the Caymans on Penn's money *and* the money she really *had* stolen!"

"You're kidding?"

"Nope. Penn was crushed. She swore off women."

"So you've never seen her with a girlfriend?"

She shook her head. "Maybe you could change that."

She shifted slightly in the tiny seat. When she looked out the window and stared at the sidewalk next to her, she felt as though she were on a kiddie ride at a fair and the little car was tied to a track.

"New topic. You pick."

"I like your store. Do you get a lot of business?"

"You'd be surprised. A lot of people still like records. They're happy iPods came along, but they like the sound of the old records, too. It's that unwillingness to give up some of the best things from the past, like cover art. Album covers are so cool, and there just isn't the same level of attention paid to a CD cover. It's a quarter of the size and people don't even buy CDs anymore. They just want the hit songs. Back in the sixties and seventies album art was almost as important to sales as the artist himself. Tons of money went into deciding what graced the cover."

She gripped the grab bar tighter. Lynette was barely paying attention to the road and constantly jamming on her brakes just seconds before the Smartcar careened into someone's bumper.

"What do you think of the enclave?" Lynette asked.

"It seems like a wonderful place to live."

"It is. We're a family."

She whipped back and forth between two lanes, moving ahead of people until she had to stop at a red light.

"How long have you lived there?"

"Hmm. I guess Viv took me in about two years ago."

She chuckled. "You mean like you take in the dogs?"

"Yeah, that's about right. She chose all of us."

The little car whirred as it picked up speed again, and CC imagined twenty rubber bands turning frantically under the hood.

"How does one get chosen to be a tenant at the enclave?"

"Oh, we're not tenants. We don't pay any rent."

"You don't? You live there for free?"

"Uh-huh. Viv is the coolest. She doesn't need the money, so she's never charged us."

"That's incredibly generous of her, but why would she do that? Your rents could pay for her property taxes or upgrades on the house—"

"I know," she said. "We've tried to tell her that, but she won't take our cash. I guess it's been like that for a few decades. She just started taking in women who needed a place to live. Some stayed for a few months and some for several years. In fact Viv's partner was one of the first members of the enclave."

"Partner? What happened with her?"

Lynette's beaming smile broke. "She passed away five years ago from cancer. I never met her, but I heard she was amazing." She whipped between two lanes and said, "So, women come and go, and we just pay for the utilities and do a lot of the maintenance too. Penn's pretty handy, in case you're wondering," she added with a wink.

CC knew she was blushing. Every time someone mentioned Penn's name it affected her physically and chemically. She needed to stay focused. Lynette was sharing information that might be important to the case with Seth Rubenstein.

"How do you get chosen?"

"That was the weirdest part," she said with a little laugh. "She just showed up at the store one day with Penn and introduced herself. Then they asked if I wanted to live somewhere for free. At first I thought they were nuts or part of some sick sex cult, but then I went and saw the enclave and the cottage. I fell in love with the place. And when I met everyone else I realized I'd just won a really cool lottery."

"So did you ever find out why you were picked?"

She shook her head. "Nope. I asked once, and Penn told me not to look a gift horse in the mouth. Just be grateful. And I am."

"Viv said that there were originally cabins there instead of cottages, but they burned down. Do you know anything about that?"

"Seriously?" she asked, surprised. "I had no idea."

She managed to stop the car before it careened through the vet's front window. "Be right back," she said, grabbing Charlie Parker and bolting out of the car and toward the entrance.

She wasn't surprised that Lynette didn't know about the cabins. Siobhan had looked equally surprised and when CC had pressed Viv for more details, she refused to talk about it further, shooing them off the sun porch so she could get back to work.

She scrolled through her e-mail, feeling slightly guilty about missing work. Blanca had rescheduled three appointments for her and met a new client in her place. She wondered if she'd jeopardized her job by playing hooky and then zeroed in on the last paragraph of Blanca's e-mail.

Alicia had dropped by to deliver something to CC and gone to lunch with Blanca instead. Now Blanca wanted to know what she thought of Alicia as an attorney. She grew uneasy. Was Blanca considering hiring her?

She closed her e-mail without responding as Lynette jumped back in the car and zipped out of the parking lot.

"I'm sure he'll be fine," Lynette said worriedly.

"Absolutely," she agreed. "He seems to be a great dog."

She had no idea what to say. She'd never had a dog because

of her father's allergies. At least that had always been the story. She suspected her mother didn't want to clean up the mess or deal with the hair. And rodents were absolutely forbidden just on principle. For years she'd begged for a pet, and when her mother finally acquiesced and took her to the shelter to get a cat for her tenth birthday, he ran away to live at the neighbor's house.

Lynette peeled around a corner so fast that CC was certain two of the wheels left the street. She felt her whole body shift toward the door as she tightened her grip on the grab bar. Suddenly Lynette hit the brakes and pulled into a small parking lot in front of a mini-mall.

"Damn it!" she hissed.

"Why are we stopping?" she asked, but Lynette was already out of the car and headed to the entrance of a decrepit dollar store. CC got out and went with her. Attached to a pole was a panting and drooling German shepherd. CC could tell he was suffering from the June heat.

"People are absolute idiots. For every one good person there are at least eight imbeciles. I'll take dogs any day."

"What are you going to do?"

"Make a point."

She headed inside and asked for the manager. A pudgy, balding Hispanic man appeared. She tore into him, pointing to the dog outside and demanding he do something about it. When he answered her in Spanish, she easily switched languages and the man glowered. He held up his hands in defeat, and she went to the container aisle and retrieved a large plastic bowl which she filled up in the restroom.

They returned to the dog, who lapped up most of the water and wagged his tail gratefully. She flung open the passenger's door and withdrew two pamphlets written in English and Spanish. She handed one to CC and placed the other inside the dog's worn collar.

On one side were six black-and-white photos, all graphic depictions of dogs that had been victims of animal cruelty. The other side read, *You are not a friend to your pet! Be responsible! Animal cruelty carries severe fines and jail time. The WATCH is watching you!* She realized The WATCH stood for Women Against The Canine Haters.

They piled back into the car and, although she didn't think it could be possible, Lynette's driving worsened. She muttered under her breath about the stupidity of humankind while she yanked the little steering wheel left and right, veering in and out of traffic until they finally returned to the record store. All the while CC had closed her eyes and tried not to get sick.

Lynette marched in and threw her bag on the counter. Siobhan said blandly, "I take it you found another one?"

"Why in the summer?" she shouted, gaining the attention of the store's customers. "I'd love to take every single one of those assholes and put them in a fur coat, stand them on the asphalt at one in the afternoon *without any shoes* and leave them there for two hours. That should be their punishment!"

Everyone applauded, and as regulars, CC guessed they were familiar with her rants. Siobhan kissed her on the cheek and waved goodbye.

"She's really something," CC said as they got into the truck.

Siobhan threw a glance back at the store. "She is. And what did you think of her driving?"

They both laughed and headed west on Indian School Road. Siobhan regaled her with stories of growing up in Ireland and what it was like to come to America. CC watched her as much as she listened to her, hypnotized by the delicateness of her gestures and the curve of her perfect smile. And her brogue was enchanting.

"Are you bored?" she asked.

She shook her head. "No, not at all. I love listening to you. Can I ask you a question? How did you wind up living in the enclave?"

"It's interesting you ask. I was just thinking about that this morning. About a year ago I was playing at a civil ceremony for two women who knew Penn and Viv. They invited me to dinner and came to hear me play at the symphony. We got to know each other over the next few months, and then they just asked if I wanted to move. I'd been there for a barbecue and I loved it.

When I asked how much the rent was, Viv told me it was free. I was flabbergasted. I couldn't believe it."

"I've never heard of such a situation," she said. "How can Viv afford it?"

She shook her head. "I don't know. I've heard that she's lived there since she was a kid, and it's the only home she's ever known. Although it's unusual for a writer to be so successful, she's been very fortunate. The Chloe series is one of the most enduring and popular children's series of all time. And, *Chloe Goes to the Symphony* is dedicated to me."

"Wow, that's interesting," she murmured, pretending to be surprised.

They entered Maryvale, one of Phoenix's most depressed communities. The post-World War Two suburb hadn't fared as well as Viv's beautiful little area. Gang graffiti covered multiple buildings and shuttered businesses dotted every corner. It was struggling in the economy—and losing.

Siobhan turned into a residential neighborhood, and CC's heart dropped at the sight of the rundown homes. Cars sat on blocks in several driveways, nearly every fifth house seemed to be in foreclosure and landscaping was a joke. She imagined the city's blight inspectors couldn't keep up, if any of them bothered to call.

Amid the countless neglected homes, a beautiful, pristine stone church sat on a corner. She gazed at the tall bell tower and the vibrant stained-glass windows, imagining it was the neighborhood's hope and the gangsters left it alone.

They pulled into a parking space, and Siobhan turned to her, not bothering to shut off the motor. "Time to go to work," she announced.

"What?"

"Go through that side door and down the hallway to the third door on the right—no, left," she corrected.

She looked around in bewilderment. "Why are you leaving me here?"

"I'm not leaving you. I'm dropping you off. Penn's expecting you."

"You're not coming in?" she asked hopefully.

"No, I'm not coming in. And I need to be perfectly clear. You don't stand a chance with me."

Her jaw dropped. "Wow. That was harsh."

She swept her beautiful red hair to the left side. "No, I'm just being honest. I watched you all the way over here staring at me. Nuh-uh. Not going to happen."

She leaned toward her using all the charm she possessed. "Why not?"

Siobhan pointed at the door and she understood.

"I belong to Penn now? Is that what all of you have decided? What if I'm not interested in Penn?"

"But you are," she interrupted. "And even if you weren't, I'm not interested in *you*. There's someone else."

She studied her the way she studied a client. "Really?"

"Really. Now go."

CC sighed and headed into the church. She hadn't seen Penn's Nova, which meant it was either parked somewhere safe, had already been stolen, or they were taking the bus back across the valley, an idea she couldn't fathom.

An elderly African-American couple shuffled past a small sandwich board sign with the words *Lawyer/Abrogado* and an arrow pointing to an open door. She heard commotion and saw at least forty people waiting in the small room. Since there weren't enough chairs, many stood clutching papers and files and nearly everyone was Hispanic or Native American. At the sight of a white woman they stared suspiciously.

An older woman with steel-gray hair came through a connecting door, Penn following behind her, speaking in Spanish. When she finished, the woman pulled her into a hug and said, "*Gracias, gracias.*"

Penn finally broke free and smiled when she saw CC. Her chosen T-shirt of the day said in bright pink letters *Easily Distracted by Shiny Objects.*

"What are you doing here?" she asked.

She pointed toward the parking lot. "Siobhan said you asked me to come."

She rolled her eyes "Did she? Aren't you supposed to be slaving away on the thirtieth floor somewhere?"

"I am, but she convinced me to take a day off."

"I see." She paused to think and then asked, "This isn't some attempt to pump me for information that could hurt Viv, is it?"

"No," she protested. "I don't want to hurt her. I wish you'd understand that." She looked around. "Now, do you want some help or not?"

Penn studied her a moment longer before she said, "Come on back."

The room next door was much smaller and only contained two card tables and a few folding chairs. One table was empty, but the other was covered in files and notes. Judging from the list of scriptures on the chalkboard that covered the side wall she guessed the room was usually used for a Bible study class.

"Normally a church volunteer helps me with intake, but she got called to work. Since you're actually an attorney, we should get through everything twice as fast. Do you speak Spanish?" CC shook her head. "That's okay. They usually bring a kid to translate. What you need to do is determine the issue, and if it's something we can help with, then we do our best. Otherwise we might send them to another agency. We'll do the first one together before you solo."

She grabbed a clipboard and called for Ms. Mendoza. A plump woman who couldn't have been much older than CC walked in, a teenage boy behind her. She wore a skimpy tank top and cutoffs, the word *Destiny* tattooed over her left breast in bold black ink. Not surprisingly, she introduced herself as Destiny and pointed to her son Felipe.

They huddled around Penn's little card table, and Destiny withdrew some folded papers from her purse. "The school won't take him, and I don't think that's right."

Penn perused the copies of his school records. "When were you expelled, Felipe?"

"Over a year ago." He rubbed his eye, and CC spotted a small teardrop tattoo on his knuckle.

He was only twelve but had been expelled for attacking another boy with a pipe during lunch recess.

Penn looked at Destiny. "Has he been in school since the expulsion?"

She shook her head. "Nobody would take him. They said they didn't have to."

"They're right. That's the law. It was your responsibility, though, to find him a school."

Destiny threw up her hands and copped an attitude. "How in the hell am I gonna do that? I got two other kids to support, and I work two jobs. If he's gonna make trouble and give me a headache, then he can go to work with his uncle. And that's exactly what he did."

Penn raised her hand in understanding, and she backed off. "Sorry. I'm just so frustrated," she said, choking back tears.

"Okay, they have to take your son back now even though they may not want to. The expulsion period is over, and they have a legal obligation to do so."

Destiny clapped her hands. "That's what I thought. They lied to me. Big surprise."

Penn pulled out her cell phone and found the phone number. CC marveled that in two minutes she was talking with the principal about Felipe's re-enrollment. It didn't hurt that she'd mentioned she was an attorney who was thinking of calling the Department of Education. Mother and son left immediately afterward, and Penn warned the boy to stay out of trouble.

The whole exchange took less than ten minutes. At Hartford and Burns the idea was to maximize time and make money, but at Penn's church office she recognized the goal was exactly the opposite.

Penn handed her the clipboard. "Ready?"

She nodded and they called in the next two names. The young man who faced her didn't understand why his former boss told him he couldn't qualify for unemployment, but after a quick review of his file she realized he did qualify and told him what to do. Her next interview was with a young couple who'd been kicked out of their apartment even though they had a lease, followed by a destitute woman who needed medicine. The final clients were a little girl and the grandmother who wanted to adopt her, since her own daughter was a meth head and had disappeared.

By the time they crossed off the last name on the clipboard and the lobby was empty, the sun was setting. They filled two boxes with files and folders then walked across the inner courtyard to a covered carport with a gate.

"My only requirement was that my car was safe," Penn remarked.

They drove back to the east side, and CC paid particular attention as the poverty and blight gave way to wealth and entitlement.

"How did you get involved with this church?"

Penn shrugged. "Hmm, that's a good question. I'm not sure I remember. I was helping somebody, and then they mentioned that Pastor Renee needed a lawyer. So what did you think?"

"It's nothing like a real law firm," she mused, and although she meant it as a compliment, for she'd thoroughly enjoyed making a difference for two hours, Penn saw her reply as a criticism.

"I'm sorry my little card table and folding chairs don't live up to the Hartford and Burns standard, or is it the clientele?"

"That's not fair!"

Penn snorted. "Isn't it? Do you think any of these people would ever get past your lobby? Most of them aren't educated, don't speak the language and frankly, they're just plain tired. They work two or three jobs, have several kids and they don't have the energy to fight the system. Your firm would only take on the slam-dunk cases and probably screw the client over just because it's so easy to take advantage of poor people."

Her voice echoed in the car, and she abruptly stopped talking and put both hands on the wheel. CC stared blankly out the window, stunned by the attack. She'd spent the afternoon helping her and Penn hadn't bothered to say thank you, and now she was being treated with contempt.

As they sat at a red light, Penn blurted, "So my third question is, do you like being a lawyer?"

"No," was her flat and immediate reply.

Whether it was the terseness of her response or the simplicity of the answer, Penn said nothing else for the rest of the drive. She'd barely stopped the car, and CC was out the door with her purse and portfolio and heading for the street.

"CC, wait!"

She ignored her and kept walking.

"Aren't you going to check and see if Siobhan's home?" she taunted.

"Why are you being so horrible?" she cried. "You rejected me last night after I kissed you. Then I help you all afternoon but you never say thank you, and now you're suggesting I want to screw your friend."

Her eyes widened. "I didn't say that! You're the one trying to kick Viv out of her house!"

"I don't want that to happen! I'm doing everything I can, but no one will tell me anything. I can't help if I don't know the whole story."

She shook her head. "The whole story is too hard for Viv. She can't tell it."

"Then you tell it to me."

She hesitated, thinking about the possibilities. "I don't know everything either, otherwise I'd know what to do. And you're the attorney for the other side. I can't imagine how many ethics we've violated today."

The evening silence drifted between them until she finally asked, "Why are you here?"

CC shrugged. "I don't know."

Penn sighed heavily and reached into the car for the file boxes. "I appreciated your help. And whatever you want to do with Siobhan is your business. And about the kiss last night… that was a mistake," she said, her gaze far away.

"For the record, I don't want to kiss Siobhan."

"What about your ex?"

She didn't have an answer, and she knew Penn would see through a denial. "The jury's still out," she said flatly. "But I like you a lot, Penn, and you were right. I am lonely."

Penn's biceps bulged under the weight of the pain and suffering of complete strangers in the file boxes she held, but her face was wracked with fear.

She was completely defenseless when CC pressed their lips together in a soft kiss.

"I choose, right?"

CHAPTER ELEVEN

December, 1954

I could never get used to Christmas without snow. I loved all of the Iowa winter nights when I'd sit next to the Christmas tree and watch the snow fall, especially during a full moon when all of the flakes looked like tumbling lights. I thought Santa Claus loved us best because it had to be the greatest place in the world to deliver presents. I could just see him grinning as he flew into Cedar Rapids, grateful to be back each year.

While we always had a tree in Phoenix and kept many of the traditions we'd had in Iowa, it wasn't the same. Something had always seemed to be missing, like the one gift I wanted and never got. But this year I was really looking forward to the holiday.

After our big fight, Mama and I had a new understanding, forever unspoken but present nonetheless. We'd gotten used to Pops' absence, and when I discovered most of his clothes missing from his half of the closet, she admitted that he'd moved out.

Will had become a ghost. Once in a while he stole into the kitchen to eat and then disappeared into the night. I knew he still slept in his bed occasionally because I'd hear him climbing the trellis after midnight, but he was gone again before breakfast. I'd seen a letter from the school marked *Urgent!* and when I asked Mama about it, she said that he'd dropped out and there was nothing she could do about it.

"It's his life, Vivi. If he wants to spend it hanging with lowlifes then I've got no use for him at all."

For some reason he blamed her for Pops and Shirley West, and he told her once that he had no respect for her at all. She'd told him to get out and never come back. He must have taken that to heart.

I know she longed for the old Will, but she didn't seem to miss Pops at all. I'd never seen her happier. There were people all over the property now as the houses appeared—plumbers, contractors, electricians, bricklayers—and all of them loved her sweet potato pie thanks to Mac.

Whatever problem they'd had between them was over, and Mac and Kiah spent lots of time at our kitchen table eating and laughing with us. One evening Will came through the door unexpectedly just as we were sitting down to dinner. He stopped suddenly at the sight of Mac planted in Pops' usual spot. He got a sick look on his face and bolted out before she could explain. Several days passed before I heard him climb the trellis again.

People came and went all the time, including Mr. Rubenstein, who was usually accompanied by Miss Noyce. The four of them—Mama, Mr. Rubenstein, Miss Noyce and Mac spent many evenings laughing and talking on the sun porch. Mama wasn't alone anymore, and it showed on her face.

Sometimes Mr. Munoz joined them. He was the young Latino man who lived next to Mac and Kiah in the second cabin. Mr. Rubenstein had hired him to do all the electrical work. He was quiet and polite, and Mama said he was a true gentleman. The third cabin was occupied by Mr. Benson, a master mason who supervised the many bricklayers building the houses. I didn't much care for him. He was about a hundred and fifty years old and always scowled. He did his job and kept to himself which was fine by me.

Kiah and I were closer than ever, and I fretted over what to give her for Christmas. She'd liked my drawing so much that I decided to do one of Mac for her. He willingly sat for an entire hour while I did my best to capture his likeness.

When he saw it he said, "You've done real good, Vivi. You're an artist."

He kissed the top of my head just like I'd seen him do a hundred times with Kiah. It was as if I was his daughter too.

We'd made our Christmas plans that included all of our new friends—Mac, Kiah, Miss Noyce and even Mr. Rubenstein, who would join us for Christmas dinner. When I'd asked him if that was against his religion, he'd laughed and said there was no law against having dinner with friends.

Then on December twenty-third Pops walked through the door.

It was after dinner, and we were doing the dishes when he waltzed in carrying his suitcase. Mama looked up and her jaw dropped.

"Chet, what are you doing here?"

"Can't a man come in to his own house at Christmastime?" he asked pleasantly.

He'd been living with another woman while everyone whispered behind her back. I waited for her to hurl the cup she was drying at his head. It's certainly what she would do to me.

But she didn't. She didn't seem happy or sad. She didn't seem like she was really there.

"Do you want some coffee?"

"Yes," he said.

He went upstairs while she raced around the kitchen reassembling the coffeepot we'd just cleaned. When I heard his feet tromping across the ceiling and I was sure he couldn't hear us, I said, "Mama—"

"Don't," she said sharply, pointing at me. "Don't."

She returned to the coffee, but I couldn't let it go. "How can he just come back? Aren't you furious?"

When she finally looked at me it was with pity. "You're too young to understand, Vivi."

And it was just like the last six months had never happened. Will clomped down the stairs the next morning having appeared out of nowhere, and we all sat around the table for breakfast.

"When's Christmas service?" Pops asked.

"Usual time. Ten thirty."

"Is my dress shirt pressed?"

"Of course."

"Christmas dinner at five o'clock?"

Her fork stopped midway to her mouth, but she quickly recovered. "Yes."

I started to ask about Mac and Kiah and Mr. Rubenstein and Miss Noyce but she offered me the slightest shake of her head, and I chewed on my waffle instead. Even though Mr. Rubenstein had bought his land and saved him from a life of tending the orange groves, Pops wouldn't dare break bread with a Jew and a black man. I guessed she would be making phone calls, apologizing to everyone for ruining their Christmas.

Tears pooled in my eyes as I thought about Kiah and Mac having Christmas all alone. I must have looked sad because he noticed.

"What's wrong, Vivian?"

"Nothing."

"Wouldn't have anything to do with that little black girl you're so chummy with, would it?"

I swirled my waffle in the syrup. I could feel her eyes on me. I thought about everything I loved about Christmas and when I looked up, I smiled.

"What do you want for Christmas, Pops?"

His face softened. He loved getting gifts from me and Will. "I hadn't thought about it. I'm sure whatever you come up with will be fine."

He winked at me and returned to his paper. When I glanced at Mama, her face hidden behind her coffee cup, she winked too.

****

Pops hung around the house on Christmas Eve fixing the things he'd neglected with Will as his assistant. I realized I'd never get a chance to see Kiah. I moped about my room, drawing and listening to a jazz album Mac had given me. I loved jazz and bopped to the beat while I colored my latest drawing of a tree frog.

Over the wail of Charlie Parker's horn I didn't hear the ladder clunk against the side of the house.

"What in the hell are you doing listening to that nigger music?"

I fell out of my chair and landed next to the bed. Pops' face sat in the window, his upper body edging through. He wore an awful sneer as he reached over to my record player and slapped the needle. A high-pitched scratch warbled through the speaker, and I felt sick. How could I ever tell Mac?

I quickly retrieved the record and put it back in the sleeve carefully.

"Give it to me," he said.

I held it to my chest. "It's not mine."

He motioned for it, and I knew better than to argue. He charged down the ladder and pounded on Mac's door. When Mac appeared, he thrust the album at him and poked him in the chest. He was at least a head taller, but Mac had a good fifty pounds on him. He kept poking and pointing while Mac stood there silently. Finally Pops made a little sweeping motion with his hand, as if he was excusing him, and Mac went back in the cabin and closed the door. He stood on their porch for a long while, his head hung and his hands on his hips. I saw motion from the corner of my eye and Mama leaving the sun porch and returning to the kitchen.

I stayed in my room the rest of the day. I kept looking at Kiah's cabin longingly, hoping she missed me as much as I missed her. We'd had so many wonderful plans for Christmas and now they were ruined. At dinner no one said anything, and by nightfall Mama was out on the sun porch, smoking her cigarette and drinking vodka. I gazed at her through my window wondering if she was as disappointed as I was. I knew Kiah wouldn't dare visit with Pops around, so all I could do was stare toward the point where the sky touched all of the little roofs that were popping up beyond the row of trees that separated our property from the subdivision. It was hard to believe that over a year had gone by since Mr. Rubenstein had appeared.

I heard a creak and saw Kiah's front door open. Mac stepped out holding his pipe and tobacco. He leaned against the porch post and his face glowed as he struck the match and started to puff. Then he was a black man in the dark night. I could tell from the way he stood that he was facing Mama, watching her. She was illuminated by the soft bulb of the floor lamp that we kept on the porch, and she seemed to be staring at him too. I glanced back and forth but neither held up a friendly hand or called across the yard. They had a conversation without words, and I suddenly realized it was private and I was an intruder.

****

It may have been my imagination but when the four of us walked into Faith Lutheran Church, everyone turned and whispered. It had been months since Pops and Will had joined us and while Mama always had an excuse for their absence—Pops was working extra hours or Will was sick—people just nodded in kindness. She squeezed my arm as if she knew how painful this was, but Pops didn't blink an eye. Will looked mighty uncomfortable and kept tugging at his tie, and I noticed when Pops motioned him into a pew next to another family, the father quickly changed places with his teenage daughter. Will Battle was now a boy with a bad reputation. Everyone knew that.

While the pastor talked about why Christmas was the greatest day of the year, I decided I couldn't disagree more. Mama had run out on Christmas Eve to get Pops presents from all of us—a hammer, a set of wrenches and a new tie, which I knew he hated and he knew *she* hated it too. He'd gotten me a sketchbook, Will a Zippo lighter so he'd look cool when he smoked and Mama a bottle of his favorite perfume. We'd gone through the motions, each thanking one another politely. The whole charade lasted about fifteen minutes before we gave up and went to our own corners of the house.

When the service finally ended we followed the procession outside. Groups of men clustered together, and Pops sidled up next to his drinking buddy Hughie Larch. Mama flashed a Hollywood smile and joined the sewing circle ladies. She commented on Agnes's Christmas dress, which gained her invitation into the group. She was smooth. There was no doubt about it.

I sat on a retaining wall that bordered the back of the church property, admiring the way she could make the best of any situation. They talked like they were the best of friends, but on the wall, where I couldn't hear the constant flatteries and little comments, I saw the truth. Whenever she spoke, they all gritted their teeth, especially Mary Rose, Billy's mama. They gave her the respectful attention deserved of a speaker and then their heads turned away quickly once she'd finished a paragraph.

I was plotting a way to see Kiah that night after Pops had finished a few scotches, when hands gripped my shoulders and pulled me backward into a shallow ditch. I looked up at Billy Smith—and Will. When I tried to stand up, Billy pushed me down. My shoulder hit a concrete pipe jutting out from the ditch, and I yelped in pain.

"Will tells me you're a nigger lover," he said.

I wouldn't answer so he dropped dirt clods on me. I knew if I tried to get up, he'd just shove me down again, so I laid there and took it. I could see Will's face, but he wouldn't look at me. He was watching Billy, his hands jammed in his pockets. When Billy ran out of clods, he grabbed a long stick and pressed it against my chest.

"No boy is ever gonna want you, Vivi. You're too ugly to look at."

"Is that what your boyfriend tells you?" I asked with a grin.

"You bitch," he snarled and smacked my face with the stick.

I felt blood running down my cheek behind my ear.

"No, Billy," Will said firmly.

He pulled the stick away and tossed it back in the ditch. Infuriated, Billy gave him a hard shove, but he didn't pick up the stick again. I guessed there would always be a part of him that was afraid of Will. Instead he hacked a loogie in my face before he stepped away.

"C'mon, Will," he said, heading out of the ditch. "Let's go steal some plum wine in honor of the holiday."

Will didn't move. Billy stopped walking when he realized Will wasn't following. "Let's go, Battle! Quit bein' a pussy!" he shouted before heading for the street.

Will helped me up and handed me his handkerchief.

"Why?" I asked.

It was a question I'd been dying to ask him for months. Where had my brother gone? Why wasn't he ever there anymore? Why didn't he love me and Mama? Why had he dropped out of school and become friends with a boy he'd hated?

The look on his face was the old Will, the one who cared. "Everybody's talkin', Vivi. You and Mama, you gotta keep 'em out of the house. Stay away from 'em."

"Who's talking?" I demanded to know.

"Everybody," he said again before he ran to catch up to Billy.

I wiped my face and held the handkerchief over my bloody cheek. The front of my dress was covered in dirt, and I couldn't imagine how bad the back looked. My head was throbbing and there was blood on my scalp from hitting the drain pipe.

When I climbed over the retaining wall, Mama was still standing there talking to the ladies, but her smile dropped at the sight of me.

"Vivian, what happened?"

I looked into her eyes, hoping she could read my mind like I'd come to read hers. "I fell," I said.

My answer sent a titter of chuckles and disapproval through the group, but she saw that I was holding Will's handkerchief in my hand.

"Vivian Lucille Battle, I cannot believe you! How can you be so careless on Christmas Day?" She took my arm far less forcefully than she'd ever done. "Excuse us, ladies. My daughter needs to learn some manners."

They all waved goodbye recognizing that she had her hands full with such a delinquent as me. When we got out of earshot she whispered, "What happened? Where's Will?"

"He's gone. Billy Smith pushed me down, and Will left with him."

She stopped walking and stared at me. "Will didn't—?"

I shook my head and she sighed. I didn't have the heart to tell her that he'd just stood there and let Billy abuse me. She checked me over and determined my injuries could all be handled with some iodine and bandages. We got into the car and waited for Pops while he jawed with his friends.

He acted like he had all the time in the world. I imagined he hadn't seen some of them in a long while, and when he glanced toward the car I guessed he was bragging about having a wife and a mistress.

"Is he home for good?"

"I don't know," she said. I heard her voice catch, and I knew she wanted him gone as much as I did.

"Will says we need to stay away from them. He says everybody's talking."

She didn't ask me to explain and she didn't ask any questions. She pulled out her compact and checked her face. She looked perfect as usual, but it didn't stop her from powdering her nose.

He said his goodbyes and shook each man's hand as if he wouldn't see them again for a while. I guessed he didn't go to church with Shirley West.

As he started toward us she said, "I don't much care what everybody else gossips about and neither should you, Vivi. It's just talk. It can't do any harm. And as for Will, well, I don't think he'll ever get over what your father did."

What Pops did? If Will was mad at him, why was he taking it out on us? It didn't make sense. All the way home I thought about Will's message. I knew he still cared even if he was a loser, and I worried he knew something we didn't. Pops drove home without a word to either of us, not even commenting on the state of my dress when we got out of the car.

We spent all afternoon preparing the dinner while he sat in the living room reading or listening to the radio. At one point he went to the icebox and grabbed some beers, and I stiffened in his presence. When I looked at Mama, she'd stopped peeling potatoes until the door shut and he shuffled away. Even though he was in another room it was as if he was next to us, nearly on top of us.

I imagined Kiah and Mac wouldn't have much of a celebration at all. I could tell Mama was equally depressed as we dressed the turkey, mashed the potatoes and cleaned the green beans. I doubted Will would return to partake in the feast, not wanting to step in front of Pops if he was drunk.

"Maybe we could take some of the leftovers to Mac and Kiah," I suggested quietly.

She nodded, and I guessed she'd already thought of that.

Dinner was served at precisely five o'clock without Will. Pops didn't ask where he was, and it occurred to me that his appearance on Christmas Eve was a command performance. While we were clueless as to his lawlessness and new friends, Pops was probably informed. Maybe Will was living with him and Shirley West.

I passed the bowls between them so neither had to speak directly to the other. Once our plates were full we ate in silence with only the clank of silverware to keep us company. I'd grown accustomed to the laughter and conversation with Mac and Kiah and the loneliness around the table made me miss them even more.

Mama finished her third vodka and stood to refill her glass.

"You've had enough," Pops said sternly.

It was the first time he'd ever commented on her drinking and it surprised her as much as it surprised me. His face was dark and unforgiving and she glared at him. It was a test of wills.

She reached for the bottle.

"Lois, put it away." He might as well have added *or else* at the end of the sentence.

They stared until she finally put the bottle in the cupboard. He returned to his dinner, but she stayed at the counter fingering her empty glass, unwilling to join us again.

The phone rang and I jumped to get it, grateful for something to do and hoping it was Miss Noyce. She always talked to me as if I had something important to tell her.

"Hello? Battle residence."

"Well, hello there, sweetie. Is your daddy home?"

I frowned. I didn't recognize the voice and no one called me sweetie. "Who is this, please?"

She cackled, and I was pretty sure she'd been drinking. "Oh, honey, this is a *friend*."

I must've looked entirely perplexed because Mama yanked the phone from me. "This is Lois Battle. May I help you?" she asked in her usual pleasant tone.

The woman's voice carried, and I could hear her through the earpiece. She prattled on for over a minute, and Mama stood very still for a long time. She coiled the phone cord tightly through her fingers and dropped the receiver against her shoulder as if she didn't care. I'd seen her do it a few times with salespeople, but she'd always looked amused then.

"Who's on the phone?" Pops asked.

She held out the receiver, and we all heard the woman's jibber-jabber. "It's Shirley."

He dropped his fork in a second and yanked the phone from her hand. He stepped into the living room pulling the phone cord as far as it would extend. I stayed near the doorway determined to learn about his new life.

"What the hell are you doin' calling here?" he asked harshly.

I couldn't hear Shirley's part, but he gasped and groaned a few times as she talked. He was pacing, raking his hand through his hair, clearly annoyed.

"I can't talk right now," he said. "I'll be home soon."

I'll be home soon. He'd told his girlfriend that her house was his home. I supposed I'd known this for a long time, ever since the sewing circle announced it to Mama, but hearing him say it was just like being shoved to the ground by Billy Smith.

I looked over at her. She'd wasted no time in retrieving the vodka bottle. If he was going to talk to his girlfriend, she was going to have a drink. He said something else, offered a few grunts and hung up. He sat back down with no intention of explaining himself or apologizing.

"Sit down, Vivian," he ordered.

I stood next to him. "No."

He offered a passing glance like I was a fly. "Sit down, young lady. Right now."

"No."

He reached for me, but I stepped away and all he grabbed was air. I chuckled, and he flew out of his chair and held me in a vise-like grip.

"You little ungrateful bitch! You will sit down right now, or I'll tan your fanny until you bleed!"

Something flew by us, and it wasn't until the vodka bottle shattered above the stove that we noticed Mama. The sound was deafening as shards of glass rained against the O'Keefe and Merritt stove. She bolted from the counter to the sink and held up the pitcher of hot turkey grease.

"Get...out...of...my...house."

She gulped air between each word, and her eyes were wild. He had let go of me when the bottle shattered, and now he faced her with a crooked smile. She was just a woman. His woman. Kiah had explained to me how it all worked.

"You mean *my* house, don't you darling?" he said, pointing at himself.

He advanced toward her, but she motioned with the pitcher and a little of the steaming grease sloshed to the floor between them.

"Oh, ho!" he cried, like a radio character. "My girl's got some vinegar in her, doesn't she? If I'd known you were a tomcat, I might've stayed home more often."

She laughed sharply and her red lips curled into a sick grin. "That's hysterical! You think that's supposed to hurt me? The fact that you left me for that slut, Shirley West?" She threw her head back and more of the grease splattered onto the floor. "Do you have *any* idea how many guys I fucked while we were married?"

All of his playfulness vanished. He loomed over her like he was ready to strike. "Don't you talk like that, Lois. Don't say those things."

"Say what? How else was I supposed to keep this house going? Money is a *commodity*, Chet. Sex is a *commodity*. For some men, they're interchangeable. And there are a lot of men in this town who think I'm a commodity."

He looked stricken, as if she'd already thrown the grease at him.

"I know you hate my big fancy words," she said in a superior tone, "so there's two you can go look up, commodity and interchangeable."

I don't think she expected him to charge, but he barreled into her and the grease flew everywhere. He screamed, backing up immediately and ripping off his dress shirt in one motion. He grabbed a towel and ran to the laundry room.

"Turn on the faucet," she moaned, and I threw on the cold water while she bathed her hand. It had gotten the worst of it, but I noticed her chest was covered as well.

"Mama, you need to change your blouse," I said.

She shook her head, and I saw the tears. "It hurts, but nothing like this. Get some butter."

I brought a block of butter from the icebox, and she squeezed it like it was clay in Miss Noyce's class. I heard her gasp in relief.

Footsteps charged up the steps and Mac ran to her.

"Oh, no," he murmured, taking her hand.

"He's still here," she whispered. "In the laundry room. You need to leave."

He shook his head. "Uh-huh. I'm not leaving you with him. There's no telling what he'll do."

"Mac, please," she pleaded. "You've got to go."

"Well, I ain't."

He appeared in the kitchen doorway without his shirt. His muscles rippled every time he took a breath. He looked *strong*. I didn't remember him that way. He was always lanky, but I imagined lifting huge planters and digging tree holes was great exercise. His chest was beet red, and I could see the blisters already forming over the angry skin. It had to hurt like crazy. He held a towel in his hand which at the sight of Mac, he wrapped around his knuckles.

"Chet, don't," she pleaded. "Just let it be."

He ambled closer wearing a disgusted expression. "Man can't

leave it alone, Lois. Will says he's eating at your table and from the looks of it, he aims to take my place."

I noticed Mac had his hand over Mama's, and they looked as if they were together. Pops smacked his wrapped fist against his palm, and I saw him wince. Mac faced him as if he was accepting his fate.

"You fucking my wife?" Pops asked.

Mac said nothing while Mama pleaded for him to leave but it was like no one could hear her.

Pops took the first swing. He brought his arm over in a roundhouse, his favorite punch, but Mac immediately held up his giant hand and stopped his fist. It was like watching a cartoon. The expression on Pops' face was pure amazement and surprise, his hand suspended in midair, clenched between Mac's fingers spread like a claw. When he tried to pull back, Mac held it in place.

He pulled Pops closer until it looked like they were dancing. Mac set his free hand over Pops' beet-red chest.

"You need to leave," he said quietly. When Pops stared at him with sheer hatred, he touched the skin with his flat palm and Pops whimpered. "You need to leave *now*." He pressed harder and tears streamed out of Pops' eyes. He nodded furiously and Mac stepped back.

He rushed out of the room and up the stairs. Thuds and crashes echoed through the ceiling, and I imagined he was destroying Mama's things in the process. Eventually it all went quiet, and he trudged down the stairs with his suitcase.

"You'll regret this, Lois," he said as he passed her on the way out the door.

We heard his truck start followed by a terrible screeching sound. We ran outside to find the mailbox toppled over and a huge tire tread through Mama's flower bed. Kiah and Mr. Munoz ran out from the cabins, having missed all the excitement.

"What happened?" she asked me, looking at the mailbox.

"Pops," I said. "What do you think he'll do, Mama?" I asked her.

She bent down and shook her head at her destroyed red roses. "Nothing, honey. I think the roses got the worst of it. It's over now."

I looked up at Kiah and Mac. Both wore worried expressions. They knew more about hatred than anyone I knew. And if they were worried, I supposed Mama should be too.

Re: Definitely Friends First! - 27 (Central
Phoenix)
Date: 2010-06-20, 12:15AM MST

Slut! Whore!

Posted by: BrooklynBornBaby
Reply

Re: Definitely Friends First! - 27 (Central
Phoenix)
Date: 2010-06-20, 9:39AM MST

We were <u>already</u> friends. Then lovers. Now
I want more again. Be with me. Second
chances are so wonderful.

Posted by: LawyerAlicia
Reply

PhoenixConnect.Com (Women Seeking Women)
Re: Definitely Friends First! - 27 (Central
Phoenix)
Date: 2010-06-23, 6:00AM MST

This is a message from PhoenixConnect.Com
regarding your posting Definitely Friends
First! Your posting is scheduled to expire
in two days. Please reply if you would like
to remain active.

Reply

CHAPTER TWELVE

June, 2010

As CC stood pinned against a wall in the foundations department of Nordstrom's, she concluded that Alicia knew which stores had the best dressing rooms. It was spacious with two mirrors, a chair and several hanging fixtures. She imagined the women in adjoining cubicles were busy admiring the lift a bustier provided or grumbling over their muffin tops. She doubted any of them was holding back an orgasm like she was now.

Alicia was on her knees with CC's left leg flung over her shoulder while she dug for treasure. When CC glanced in the mirror across the room at the woman wearing the leopard-skin bra and panties, she hardly recognized herself. She looked good. She looked sexy. She pushed the image of Penn's cherubic face out of her mind and allowed herself a small groan when she couldn't hold back any longer.

"Don't they have cameras?" she asked Alicia as she dressed.

She smiled knowingly. "No, honey. Only rich kleptomaniacs steal and there aren't that many of them. So they don't want to know what most people are doing in here." She wrapped her arms around CC and sighed. "Didn't that feel good?"

"Uh, yeah it did."

"Well, you can thank Nadia. This is another one of her favorite rendezvous."

Her face fell. "*Nadia* took you here, too? Are we just replaying the great moments of your life with her?"

"Get over it, CC," Alicia said. She kissed her softly. "I have." She stepped back and caressed the panties with her index finger. "All you need now is some fabulous fuck-me pumps to go with this little ensemble."

CC frowned. "I can barely afford this. There's no way I can add shoes."

She kissed her sweetly on the shoulder. "That'll be my *second* present to you. Daddy sent me a message from the trust."

A message from the trust was code for money. The trust was her safety net, and she'd convinced her father to disburse it on a monthly basis since she'd finished law school with straight A's.

"Meet me downstairs," she whispered, closing the door behind her.

CC collapsed into the overstuffed chair, sexually satisfied and emotionally despondent. She'd replayed the kiss a thousand times—and Penn's immediate exodus after their lips had parted. CC had enjoyed that delicious moment like the first bite of a great dessert. She'd opened her eyes just in time to see the panic on Penn's face before she fled, practically running away with the boxes in her arms.

She'd felt dejected all week, especially when Penn never bothered to call again. She rationalized that it probably wasn't worth it. She'd dated women like her before, who couldn't overcome a bad breakup and were a relationship mess. She really didn't want to deal with that yet. And there was the issue of Alicia...

She couldn't decide what to do. They had met during their first year of law school, and she'd been impressed by her worldliness and her ability to command any situation. She was from a wealthy family in Chicago, who'd agreed to let her move away—but not too far. A dozen co-eds had lusted after her, so when she picked CC for a girlfriend, she'd felt honored, as if she'd been claimed like a prize.

Maybe Alicia was worth a second chance, as her reply had suggested, so she became the *first* person CC had actually responded to since taking out the personal ad. Definitely ironic.

She tried to forget that she was most likely replaying a previous Saturday tryst between Nadia and Alicia, and headed to the shoe department. She was in the midst of trying on the tallest stilettos she'd ever worn when her phone rang—Penn. Alicia was studying summer sandals at a display table near the front so she answered the call.

"Hey."

"Um, hi, CC," she stammered.

"Hi, I'm so glad you called," she said sweetly.

"Uh, well, uh, I was wondering if you had any plans tonight. Viv and I, and maybe Lynette were going to the symphony."

"Tell her it's at the park downtown and Siobhan has a solo," Viv called from the background.

"Did you get all that?" she asked, sounding perturbed.

"Uh, yeah. That sounds great. I'd love—"

"Which one will make my feet look sexier?" Alicia held two sandals up in front of her face.

She stepped away and tumbled over the stack of shoes, dropping her phone into one of the open boxes. She searched frantically amid the tissue paper and expensive heels, all of which seemed horribly slutty now.

Alicia picked up the ones CC hated the most, a pair of bright red Gucci ankle-straps with gold buckles. "I think these definitely say fuck me. And that's exactly what I intend to do, baby."

She searched faster, certain that Penn could hear all of the flirtatious comments. She finally found the phone between two of the boxes. Her heart sank when she realized Penn had hung up.

Alicia insisted on paying for the Gucci shoes and demanded an opportunity to see her wear them—immediately.

She was still in a funk over the phone call, but Alicia's soft kiss was too enticing. And her midwestern manners compelled her to thank Alicia for the gifts.

"Are you staying here?" CC asked as they drove along Central Avenue.

"For now," she said simply.

"What about Nadia?"

Alicia caressed her cheek and slid her hand down her breast. "I'm undecided."

She'd driven by these old condos a few times and was rather certain Mr. Hartford of Hartford and Burns lived in the same building, one that boasted a doorman and laundry service. They pulled into the underground parking garage and took the residents' elevator to the tenth floor, which housed only two apartments because of each one's massive square footage. The living area faced Central Avenue, and a spacious patio provided the best view for the downtown parades that occurred throughout the year. The modern kitchen contained all of the trappings found in trendy magazines, and CC especially liked the stylish pendant lights that hung over the stove and the island. It was a place she could only dream about.

"How do you know this person?"

Alicia flashed a mysterious smile and busied herself at the bar cart. "One of my clients owns this place. It's where he keeps his mistress, but she's in France right now." She handed her a highball glass of whisky. "I know it's the middle of the afternoon, but what the hell? Cheers."

She downed it quickly and felt the buzz immediately. Alicia refilled their glasses and gave her a tour of the guest quarters. By the time they returned to the kitchen, she was almost drunk, and she was glad. Penn kept intruding on her thoughts. She imagined their single kissing session was all there would ever be.

"You know," Alicia said, "I've been thinking a lot about us, remembering all those late nights when we'd study and then wind up making love."

She laughed. "You would do anything to escape torts."

Alicia pulled her into an embrace. "It wasn't just about torts. Your body is a total turn-on. It always has been."

"What about Nadia?"

"I've learned a lot about relationships from her—and sex. She's taught me to be free with my body. She was an experiment. I had to know if our love was just a school thing or if it was real."

"And what do you think?" she asked, unsure if she wanted to know the answer.

"I'm still thinking, but I'm leaning heavily in your favor. What about you? Now you have this incredible career with a major law firm. Why would you want me back?"

"My career's not so great," she said, sidestepping the relationship question.

She looked at her incredulously. "Are you kidding? You work for one of the most powerful firms in the city with terrific opportunities for advancement. I'd kill to have your job."

"I hope you're exaggerating."

"Only a little," Alicia said, unbuttoning CC's shirt. "I'm really enjoying our new sex life."

"I can't believe some of the things I'm doing with you," she said. "You're different."

"We can thank Nadia."

She groaned when Alicia's fingertips massaged her nipples. She couldn't believe how ready she was again and how quickly she responded to her touch.

"You haven't seen the best part of the house."

They went down a short hallway into a large bedroom with an adjoining bath. She stepped to the large picture window across from the king-sized bed and gazed at South Mountain. It made her jealous when she thought of the tiny one-bedroom she lived in now.

Alicia held up the Nordstrom's bag. "There's a pair of scissors in the bathroom so you can cut off the tags. Why don't you go change for me? Let me see the whole outfit together."

Alicia stretched out on the bed and fiddled with the lighting and some mood music via remote control while CC disappeared into a bathroom that was the size of her kitchen. She changed and leaned over the vanity. She'd become everything Penn hated.

But Penn had waited nearly a week to call her back.

When she returned, Alicia howled in delight. "Wow!

My imagination couldn't do that justice. Now give me a little attitude."

She laughed and felt her face redden. "I'm not a model. I can barely walk in these things."

"What you need is a little courage," she said emphatically, holding up a bottle of tequila and a full shot glass. CC gulped the tequila and Alicia refilled it. "You're not drinking?"

"I will," she said. "Who were you talking to on the phone before? Was that one of your new paramours, or was it the butch dyke from the charity event?"

CC's face reddened and Alicia chuckled. "I thought so." She kissed her ear. "Forget her. She's not what you need. This is about new beginnings."

After two more shooters she was feeling no pain. When Alicia turned on some Janet Jackson and commanded her to strut, she imagined she was on a runway during Paris fashion week. She pranced across the room swaying her hips with extra gusto every time Alicia whooped and clapped.

"Let me see some dancing!" she shouted.

She waved her off, but Alicia prodded until she was shaking her booty and whipping her hair to the sides. She was free. When the song ended, she downed another shooter.

"You are too good," Alicia called from the bed. And a flash of light blinded her. "God, your gorgeous!"

Alicia held a camera. Before she could protest, the flash popped again.

"Don't," she said. "Please."

"Oh, baby, yeah," she said playfully. "You are too hot *not* to. Now give me a little pose."

She grew uncomfortable each time she glanced at the camera and Alicia's face behind the view finder. "No. Let's go to bed now."

"Not yet," she said. "Lean back against the dresser and spread your legs. I want the full effect."

She shook her head and Alicia dropped the camera to her chest. "CC, please. It's just a few pictures. You have no idea how beautiful you look right now. This is just between us, for old time's sake, or maybe for *new* time's sake."

Her voice matched the softness of her expression, and CC felt a burst of hope. She laughed seductively. "How do you want me?"

★★★★

Eventually they went to bed, but only after Alicia had posed her twenty different ways—against the wall, on the bed and straddling a chair. Some of the photos were merely seductive while others bordered on soft-porn and could never be put on her Facebook page. She'd noticed Alicia's libido increased with each click of the shutter, and it wasn't long before she was naked. Then CC didn't feel nearly as uncomfortable, but Alicia never turned the camera on herself or took a picture of them together.

Despite the fabulous view and the soft bed, she'd found the sex unfulfilling. Perhaps it was all the posing or her drunken state, but she guessed it was really Alicia's lack of interest in doing it in a bed. They had finished without much fanfare, and she'd dressed while Alicia called a cab.

Dropping the Nordstrom's bag into a corner of her closet, she felt like she'd completed a walk of shame. She showered and faced the depressing thought of a night alone when she could've been listening to music with people she liked. She pictured Viv, Penn and Lynette relaxing under the cool June sky enjoying Siobhan's lilting harp. Maybe Penn would've kissed her. Unlikely. She'd come to realize that her self-confidence as an attorney was balanced by a coyness in her personal life. It was like there were two of her.

Ding!

She sighed and decided to delete the personal ad. She had enough drama in her life, and she'd be happy to never hear from BrooklynBornBaby again.

Ding!

She took slight comfort in her portfolio and worked on Danny the Dachshund for the rest of the evening. She found a classical station on her satellite radio and pictured herself at the park while she drew.

Ding!

Ding!
Ding!
Around midnight she stood and stretched, pleased with her progress. The evening hadn't been a total waste. Her e-mail had chimed incessantly, but she'd never been curious enough to abandon her drawing to see who'd commented on her Facebook page or which vacation destination Travelocity was hyping. Or to see which women were responding to her ad.

When she checked the inbox she was surprised to find nearly three dozen replies to her personal ad and an e-mail from Alicia.

I've taken the liberty of spicing up your personal ad. (Honey, you really should choose different passwords.) Hope you get some great hits. Maybe we could do a threesome? And because I KNOW the first thing you'll do is delete my little gift, I've changed your password for you. Wasn't that nice of me? New beginnings, babe! LOL.

Her face drained of color as she navigated to the ad. Alicia had added four of the pictures she'd taken that afternoon but was kind enough to crop out CC's face. One showed only her buttocks, another displayed her cleavage and in the other two she stood in the doorway, her leg extended over her head, her face turned away.

She thought she'd be sick. She checked the activity log and watched another five replies fall into the queue. She counted thirty-eight replies since she'd returned home.

She had to scroll through the photos a second time just to make sure they were real. She held her head in her hands, the throbbing hangover blocking her memory. She couldn't remember much except constantly leaning, twisting, turning, and at various times taking off the bra or pulling down the panties just far enough to tease.

And the smiling. She'd smiled through the whole thing. Alicia had insisted on it. She had no recollection of anything else thanks to the high quality tequila Alicia had provided.

But there had to be a hundred photos, and this was only a sampling. How many other pictures existed and what would Alicia do with the rest of them?

She stared at the e-mail message again. Alicia had ended it with *LOL.* Laugh out loud. But CC wasn't laughing at all.

CHAPTER THIRTEEN

February, 1955

The world outside my bedroom window was completely foreign. Shingled rooftops surrounded us and stretched to the base of Squaw Peak. And with all the houses came more people and their cars. What once had been simple dirt paths between the rows of trees were now streets with names like Georgia, Oregon and Michigan.

"Why don't they name them after indigenous plants?" Kiah asked. "Like Cactus Road or Saguaro Avenue?"

After she explained to me what indigenous meant I agreed.

The traffic increased greatly as Mr. Rubenstein sold all of the houses in the first subdivision quickly, and Mama said people were on a waiting list for the ones near us. It seemed he couldn't build them fast enough before people moved in. There wasn't a Saturday that went by without moving trucks pulling up into the brand-new carports. Barbecues, neighborhood meetings and children's birthday parties were common sights. Our neighborhood had a new designation—suburb.

I'd asked Mama if she ever wanted to live in one of the little ranch houses and she'd said, "No, honey, this is our home."

She also shied away from the neighborhood festivities, politely refusing offers by baking a sweet potato pie to forgive her absence. While she appreciated the invitations, I think she felt like a table with two legs. We weren't a regular family anymore, and she didn't want to discuss where Pops and Will had gone.

Still, everyone loved her pies. Word quickly spread about her talent, and she soon had a side business that helped keep us afloat. I'd never understood what had happened to all the money from the orange grove, but I'd guessed Pops had kept it all for himself and maybe Shirley West.

I'd heard Mama talking to Mac one night in the kitchen about finances. It seemed that when Pops first left, guilt forced him to provide for us a little, but after the scene at Christmas there was no help at all.

"Thank goodness people want to buy my pies or they'd probably turn the lights off," she'd said one night at dinner. Mac had squeezed her hand and offered his reassurances. That always seemed to make her feel better.

I worried that Pops would come back and kick us out since it was *his* house, but as each week passed my worry lessened. Maybe spending the money on Shirley West helped keep him away.

Mac and Kiah were over all the time and ate dinner with us often. Sometimes Mr. Munoz did too, but Mr. Benson never joined us. I'd once heard him grumble that he wouldn't sit at a table with niggers, kikes and spics, but he never said it above a whisper. He didn't make a scene about it the way other people did. Kiah called it quiet prejudice where people just grudgingly tolerated others. It wasn't good but it wasn't destructive either.

Sometimes Mr. Rubenstein and Miss Noyce came by, and when we were all sitting around the table it felt like a real family where everybody laughed and told jokes. We loved listening to Mr. Munoz's stories about his uncle Juan, who lived in Mexico and had a little dog named Rojo that always got in trouble.

It was at one of these dinners that Mr. Rubenstein tapped his glass with his fork to get everyone's attention before he announced that Miss Noyce had agreed to marry him. We all clapped, and then he asked Mama if they could get married in our house. She agreed immediately, and we set about preparing for the wedding, which they'd decided would be on Valentine's Day—just two weeks away.

For the next fourteen days, Kiah and I rushed home after school to help Mama clean the windows and floors and polish the silver. She was determined that the entire house would shine, even the parts that nobody would see.

"Do you think you'll ever get married?" I asked Kiah while we scrubbed the floors, our last task before the wedding the next day.

She shrugged. "I don't know. I haven't met a boy yet that I liked enough. I'm not sure I ever will."

"Well, I'm not. All boys care about is cars and drinking. And they all smell bad." Kiah laughed, and it made me smile. "I'd marry you," I said.

She stopped scrubbing and stared at me. At first I thought she was angry. She had a queer look on her face but then she smiled back. "I'd marry you too, Vivi."

"I wish we could," I said.

"Me too."

"Maybe someday."

"Yup," she agreed.

Mama stormed in, hands on her hips. "Are you two jabbering or working?"

"Working," we said simultaneously and resumed our scrubbing.

"Good. We've got a ton of food to cook before tomorrow afternoon, and I can't have you girls dilly-dallying with your chores. Understood?"

We both nodded and she flew away, leaving us to giggle quietly. "Why do you think Mr. Rubenstein and Miss Noyce wanted to get married here? I thought people had to get married in a church."

"They can't," she explained. "He's Jewish, but she isn't, so they can't get married at his church and nobody else would ever let a Jew in. So they're stuck."

"So who's gonna marry them?"

She shook her head. "I don't know. I guess somebody who doesn't care."

Somebody turned out to be a judge that Mr. Rubenstein knew. There were only about twelve guests, including all of us and his brother and little sister, one of Miss Noyce's teacher friends and only two people from her family. She'd come over one night and cried for an hour with Mama because most of her family hated her for marrying a Jew, and they had made a pact to skip the wedding. Mama patted her hand and told her that we were her family now and the rest of them would probably come around once they saw what a wonderful man Mr. Rubenstein was.

It was a fine party, and Kiah and I ate like crazy. Mr. Rubenstein, being as rich as he was, had hired Mama to do all the cooking except the wedding cake. For that he'd gone to a Jewish bakery. She'd studied up on finger food and something called canapés, which were really good. And, of course, there were eight sweet potato pies. When it came time for the champagne toast, Mac snuck Kiah and me each a little glass while Mama pretended to be upset.

The best part was the dancing. I got to dance with Kiah to all of Mac's jazz records, and it was really nice watching Mr. and Mrs. Rubenstein make googly eyes as he twirled her around the living room. Even Mrs. Rubenstein's people had a good time. At first the two of them, an aunt from Topeka and her daughter from Wichita, wouldn't talk to anyone, but as the afternoon wore on, they had fun. Mr. Munoz asked the aunt to dance, and she shook her head so hard I thought it might fall off, but he was a charmer, and after two more glasses of champagne, she asked *him* to dance and then wouldn't let him sit down.

I finally plopped into a corner chair and just watched. Kiah was dancing with Mr. Rubenstein, and Mac was dancing with Mama. I'd never seen her dance with Pops. I didn't know she knew how, but each time Mac spun her around she went in the right direction and flew back to him. I found myself bopping in my seat it was so entertaining.

Then the song changed to a slow one, and Mr. Rubenstein traded Kiah for his new wife. She came and sat by me, and we watched the four adults. Mr. Rubenstein gazed into his wife's eyes and whispered in her ear. Mac held Mama closely as they circled around, and she pressed her forehead into his chin. I glanced back and forth, comparing the couples. I didn't see a difference.

"Oh, no," Mama murmured over the music.

They'd all stopped dancing and were gazing out the window.

Kiah and I jumped up and followed Mac out the front door despite Mama's protests. Billy Smith strutted down the walk with a brick in his hand. Out on the street I saw a dark blue truck, and I couldn't be certain, but I thought I saw Will sitting in the passenger's seat. When Mac sauntered down the steps, Billy stopped.

"We don't want any trouble today, son," Mac said.

Billy looked at him with disgust. "I ain't no nigger's son. And I saw you dancing with her." He spat the words and held out the brick like he was preparing to throw it at Mac.

"That's none of your business," Mac replied.

"It's everybody's business. This is a house full of nigger lovers, kike lovers, spics and homos."

Mac took a step toward him, and he moved back.

"Chicken!" one of the boys called.

"Don't be a pussy, Billy!"

He glanced at them and charged Mac with the brick held over his head.

"Mac!" Mama screamed. She started to run down the steps, but Mr. Rubenstein grabbed her.

Mac ducked when Billy swung the brick and punched him in the stomach. We all heard him groan and saw him double up in pain. He dropped the brick in favor of holding his sides while Mac stood over him, urging him to take some deep breaths before he stood up.

"Nigger!" Billy screamed.

He ran back to the truck still hunched over. His four friends pushed him into the back and drove away, but not before they flipped the bird and said a lot of swear words. I noticed the boy I thought was Will had slunk down in his seat.

"I'm sorry, Jacob," Mac said when he returned to us holding the brick.

"Nothing to be sorry about," he declared. "We'd be a lot sorrier if that brick had gone through the window. I owe you a debt of gratitude, Mac. Thanks for saving the day." They shook hands, and then Mr. Rubenstein looked around the startled guests and grinned. "Now, who wants some wedding cake?"

We headed back inside, but it didn't take long before a police car showed up. I imagined that Billy Smith had run home and told his mother what had happened—a black man had assaulted him. The officer asked to talk to Mac but Mr. Rubenstein insisted on being present, bringing along the brick for evidence.

We watched from the sun porch as the police officer and Mac listened to Mr. Rubenstein. I could tell he was explaining what happened, and he kept pointing to the brick. The police officer read from his notes, and Mr. Rubenstein listened for a while and then started shaking his head and pointing to the brick again. While he talked, the cop gazed at Mac who stood quietly with his hands in his pockets. He didn't hang his head and he didn't look mad. He just looked respectful. Then the officer scratched his ear as if he was trying to decide what to do. He motioned for Mac to go back inside, and Mac joined Mama on the sun porch, taking her hand.

I turned back to Mr. Rubenstein and the police officer. They stood close, and I didn't think he was talking about the brick. He pointed toward the north, and the officer nodded slowly. He scratched his head, and then shook his hand before he drove away.

"Is everything all right, Jacob?" Mrs. Rubenstein asked as he stepped back into the house.

He smiled and kissed his new bride. "Everything's fine."

Mama touched his sleeve. "What happened? What did you say to him?"

"Well, first I pointed out that the brick is from Smith Brickyards and actually has the Smith stamp on it. There's no question who it belongs to. Then I pointed out that there were twelve eyewitnesses who knew the truth, and they'd be happy to testify in court to support Mac. And then I asked him if he was taking advantage of the special discount for law enforcement officers on the subdivision going up on Michigan Avenue. When he said he hadn't been able to get on the list, I told him he was on the list now *if* this all went away."

"You bribed him?" I asked.

Mama gasped. "Vivian!"

He squatted down and faced me. "Miss Vivi, I want you to think about what I'm going to say. It's okay to do a little wrong if it's for a big right. Remember that."

****

I sat perched in my bedroom window late that night. We'd had so much noise and commotion that I wasn't ready for the quiet. My brain was still hungry for action. Other than the whole part with Billy Smith, it had been the best day of my life. We'd had our picture taken on the front stoop with Mac and Kiah, and Mr. Rubenstein promised to get us a copy of it.

Eventually everyone left, and Mac said Kiah could sleep over. I glanced at my best friend snuggled under the blankets. The moonlight was just at the point where it cut right through the window and straight to the place where she lay. It shone on her face in just the right way, like she was a movie star.

Apparently Mama couldn't sleep either because she sat on the sun porch. She'd changed into her capri pants and a simple print shirt for the cleanup, but her hair was still up in the chignon and she'd left her fancy makeup on too. She was staring into the night, and I wondered what she was thinking about. Maybe it was her own wedding to Pops, or maybe she was reviewing the day. It had been a wonderful party.

A squeak broke the silence and Mac walked out on his porch carrying his pipe. I'd seen this at least a dozen times in the past few months, Mama on her porch and Mac on his. It was like they carried on a conversation without words. Once I'd stayed at the window, determined not to leave until one of them did, but then I fell asleep and woke up the next morning, my cheek pressed against the cold window and a terrible crick in my neck.

I was about to get up and go back to my bed and enjoy Kiah's warmth next to me when the oddest thing occurred. Mama stamped out her cigarette and came down the steps into the yard. She stood in front of her rose bushes, her hands behind her back. It was dark, and I couldn't tell if she was looking at him or the ground. He leaned against the post but even from a distance I could tell he was aware of her.

Then with a spring in her step she crossed the yard and climbed up the two little steps. She walked like she was delivering a sweet potato pie, which she'd done for over a year. Why she'd hesitated so long to cross the yard I didn't understand until she faced him, for she didn't have a sweet potato pie. It occurred to me that she had no reason at all to stand on a man's porch, particularly in the middle of the night.

They were as close as they'd been when they were dancing, and I thought they might start again when she reached up and touched his cheek. He stood perfectly still, leaning against that post, one hand holding his pipe while the other remained at his side. Her hand slid down his face and followed the line of his open-collared shirt. He was still wearing his Sunday best, but he'd taken off his tie and there was enough moonlight to see her hand over his heart.

Kiah stirred but a raging fire on my bed wouldn't have moved me from that window. A little worm of shame wrapped around my heart, telling me this was private and I wasn't supposed to know. I wasn't supposed to look. But I couldn't take my eyes away, not until he took her hand and led her inside the dark cabin.

CHAPTER FOURTEEN

June, 2010

CC spent the weekend tethered to her computer and her phone, desperately searching for a way to delete the posting and remove the horrible photos. She'd started with the basic idea of cracking the password, until she realized Alicia had probably chosen something nonsensical rather than a favorite movie they had shared or a restaurant they loved. She didn't *want* CC to delete the ad. She wasn't being funny. She wasn't playing a game. She was cruel.

CC yanked the locket from her neck and put it where it belonged—the trash can—before she attempted to navigate the PhoenixConnect website and determine how to delete the ad with the company's help.

But fear returned as the elevator ascended to the H and B offices on Monday morning. There had been no direct way to contact the website except through an e-mail exchange. As she left for work it was still up, and she had no idea if she could have it removed. And what if Alicia showed it to Blanca? If straight-laced law firms were anything it was fearful of bad press.

When she sat down at her computer she saw an e-mail from the tax department.

Shit.

Lydia Liles, a secretary to somebody important, informed her that she'd caught CC's mistake and had personally made sure the handwriting request was routed through the right channels. In fact, she'd pleaded for an expedited review, and because she was so persuasive, she'd been assured that CC Carlson would have those results in two days.

She slumped back in her chair. She'd have to send her a gushing thank-you e-mail, praising her for her keen initiative and promising that she would mention the catch to her boss. Perhaps a promotion would be on the way.

She tapped her foot madly. Once the handwriting analysis was confirmed it was only a matter of time before it went to a judge. As far as she could tell, there was nothing Penn could argue. It was obvious that Viv was holding back. Maybe there was something she knew that could save her house, but she'd have to share her story. Since CC didn't have any appointments until the afternoon, she grabbed her purse and headed for the enclave, telling the receptionist that if anyone asked, she'd gone to the law library at Arizona State.

The Nova and Beemer were in the carport, and Penn was sitting in one of the chaise lounges surrounded by files. When she saw CC, she stood up and crossed her arms over the powder-blue T-shirt that read in white bubble letters, *The Cops Never Think it's as Funny as You Do.*

"Get out," Penn said.

She shook her head. "We need to talk. I know you're mad—"

"Get out—now," Penn repeated. "You have no business being here."

"I just want to help. The handwriting analysis is coming back—"

"And I'll deal with it. Go."

"Penn, please, I want to talk to you," she pleaded.

"Nope."

In a second she was slung over her shoulder like a bag of flour.

"Put me down!" she screamed.

"There's nothing to talk about. You are clearly one of the most unscrupulous people I've ever met."

"Unscrupulous?" she repeated, wiggling every which way to break free. "I'm trying to help! I care about Viv! And I care about you, too. Let's talk about this."

"Not on your life," Penn replied. "If I—"

She let out a cry and suddenly they were careening to the pavement. CC found herself on top of Penn. She glanced back and saw that they had fallen into the same pothole.

"Son of a bitch," Penn said. "How in the hell does that keep happening?"

"Are you all right?"

She stared at the sky. "I don't know. Can you get up, please?"

She decided to take advantage of the situation. "No, not until you hear me out. I am *not* unscrupulous. Confused, probably. Possibly unemployed."

Penn blurted, "CC, we're lying in the middle of a *road*. If Lynette barrels around the corner like she always does, we're dead!" Then she comprehended what CC had said. "Wait. You're unemployed?"

She shrugged. "Hard to say but it's all the more reason for you to listen," she said calmly.

Penn tried to lean forward, but CC pressed her shoulders into the pavement.

"Damn it. Let me up!"

Her cobalt blue eyes stormed with anger, and CC almost released her, somewhat fearful of her expression. But as their bodies collided she saw that hint of interest from the first day, a flicker that occurred every time they were close.

"I'll be quick and then you can get up, and I'll leave if you want me to. First, Seth Rubenstein will be happy to see Viv sleeping in the street. Second, the handwriting analysis will be back in two days, so we don't have much time to fix this, if there's even a way. Finally, if you care at all, I have absolutely no interest in my ex. She's a horrible person who's done something really unscrupulous. You can't call me unscrupulous compared to her."

She took a breath and thought she might cry. Penn touched her neck obviously looking for the locket. When she didn't find it, she asked, "What happened?"

"She showed her true colors," she said simply. "You really want to talk about that now? We need to save the enclave."

Penn looked distraught. "I've told you. She's not going to help us. She probably can't even remember anything."

"She's got to try, and you've got to make her, or you all get to find another place to live."

They got up and headed for the farmhouse, Penn limping slightly.

"You really broke up with your girlfriend?" she asked suspiciously.

"Definitely," she said confidently. "It's over." An idea came to her. "And I may need your help with a computer problem, but let's talk to Viv first."

"Okay," Penn said slowly.

They found Viv on the sun porch, adding details to her stagecoach. "You girls out having a little fun?" she asked without looking up. When they didn't reply she set down her brush and slowly turned around.

CC had never seen Penn look so serious. She stared at Viv and said, "It's time. We need to talk—about everything."

"I've told you—"

"No," Penn interjected. "You've told me what you wanted to tell me. Now I need to know the rest. You could lose your house. *We* could lose this place, too. It's not just about you. Where will Lynette go with all those dogs?"

Viv's telltale strength, that was as bright as the watercolors she used for Chloe, washed away from her face, and, for the first time, CC saw the muted tones and faded edges of the old woman she really was.

"You've resorted to guilt," she accused Penn.

Penn stared at her steadfastly. "I'll do whatever I need to do to help you, Viv."

"It won't matter," she said softly.

"You don't know that," Penn replied.

She set down her brush and stood up slowly. "Let's go inside."

****

At Viv's request Penn retrieved a tray of iced tea and three servings of sweet potato pie while she perused a tall bookcase in the hallway that was filled with Chloe books. Her finger trailed across the spines as she studied the titles.

"You'll find, my dear, that art imitates life," she said as she pulled five titles from the shelf and handed them to her—*Chloe Makes a Friend, Chloe Bakes a Pie, Chloe's Mom, Chloe and the Bully* and *Chloe Says Goodbye*.

They passed the hutch by the dining room, and Viv picked up the two black-and-white photos that CC had noticed on her first visit. Penn joined them and served the pie.

"This is the best pie I've ever tasted," Viv said, spearing the tip. "My mama couldn't do much, but she could make a pie."

Penn set her plate down, her impatience evident. "Viv, we don't have a lot of time—"

"I'm tellin' what I know, missy. Hush up," Viv scolded. She picked up *Chloe Makes a Friend* and opened it to the dedication, *For Kiah*. "Kiah was my best friend in the whole world. She came here when they built the subdivision but, like in the story, she was different. She was black." She held up *Chloe and the Bully*, and the dedication read, *For Mac*. "Her father was Mac, who was the love of my mama's life, but it wasn't easy for any of us," she said gesturing to the book. Her voice crumpled for a second, and she took a sip of tea.

She handed CC the other two books, *Chloe Makes a Pie* and *Chloe's Mom*. CC read the respective dedications—*For Jacob* and *For Mama*.

"I understand why you would dedicate a book to your mother, but how does Jacob Rubenstein fit into your family?"

"He was an amazing man. This city is indebted to him."

"How so?" CC asked.

"He helped everyone, him and his wife Della. She was my art teacher for a time, and Mama introduced them. A lot of businesses in this town wouldn't have made it without a little charity or understanding from them."

"So, I guess he was very powerful," she summarized.

"Not really powerful," Viv disagreed. "Power implies abuse. Jacob was careful and often the victim of anti-Semitic hatred. But he had money, unlike the Mexicans and the Blacks. Money creates power, which can command respect, but he chose to earn it." She stopped suddenly and waved a hand. "Sorry, I get on my soapbox sometimes. The point is he did things for people. He was a true collaborator and not afraid to right a wrong even if it meant breaking the law sometimes."

CC leaned forward, fascinated. "Can you give me an example?"

Viv smiled as she wandered into the past. "A young Chinese couple opened a market right on the edge of the area that was Phoenix's unofficial Chinatown. But they didn't realize they were on the wrong side of the street. In fact, they'd opened their shop on a block with white-only businesses who didn't take too kindly to all the Chinese people traipsing down the sidewalk speaking their funny language. Nor did the whites appreciate the odd smells coming from the store. So the businessmen decided to push the Chinese couple out."

"How could they do that?"

"At first it was subtle. They tried some intimidation tactics, like having a group of teenage boys hassle the customers so they'd stop shopping there, and then they managed to get the zoning changed so that no one could park in front of the stores, which didn't bother the whites because they had a parking lot they shared nearby. It didn't take long before the market was in trouble. But one of their customers was Della. She had a great appreciation of Asian art and culture, so she'd befriended a lot of people in the Chinese community. When the couple told her what was happening, she told Jacob."

"What did he do?"

"Plenty," she said. "You see, the white businessmen didn't own the parking lot. Jacob did."

She pieced together the scenario quickly. "So if they lost the parking lot, they'd have as much trouble keeping customers as the Chinese couple."

"Exactly," she said. "Since they'd had the zoning changed at the front of the store, they needed that lot."

"So he threatened to take it away," she concluded.

Viv shook her head. "No. That's what most people would've done but not Jacob. Instead, he showed up one day around noon and invited the businessmen out to the parking lot for lunch with the Chinese couple."

Penn laughed. "What?"

"He'd paid them to prepare a wonderful Asian lunch and invited everyone to dine in the parking lot. I'm sure that it was uncomfortable at first, but the businessmen thought the food was delicious, and eventually they were all laughing and trying to communicate with the Chinese couple."

"Were they serving sake?" CC asked.

"Of course," Viv said, laughing. "But it worked. The businessmen realized this was Jacob's polite way of asking them to share the parking lot and they did."

"That was brilliant," Penn commented.

"That was Jacob," Viv said. "He was wonderful to me and Mama." She handed CC one of the framed photographs. "And Mac and Kiah," she said as an afterthought. CC realized it was one of the photos she'd seen at the diner—the wedding photo of the Rubensteins, Viv, her mother, Mac and Kiah standing in front of the farmhouse.

"I imagine you and Kiah were close," CC concluded.

Viv offered a sad smile. "I loved her. Mac was the foreman who built the subdivision, and Kiah was his daughter. Mama loved him, and I loved Kiah."

She said it plainly as a truth. And while it was a lovely sentiment, CC realized that such relationships wouldn't have been tolerated in the fifties.

"Where's Kiah now?" she asked.

Viv looked solemn. "She's gone." Her hands started to shake.

"I can't speak of this anymore, and it doesn't have anything to do with this." She poked a finger in Penn's direction. "Stay out of the attic!" she commanded before she excused herself.

"What's in the attic?" CC asked Penn.

"It's stuffed with every memory Viv has. I had to go up there after Christmas one year. You wouldn't believe what she's got."

"Then we've got to convince her," CC said adamantly. She picked up the wedding photo and held it out. "For them."

Penn offered a sad smile and took CC's hand. "I believe you want to help. But you're jeopardizing your career. Let me figure this out. Go back to work and salvage your job while I convince Viv to let me search."

She gazed at Penn's hand covering her own, imagining that it took a tremendous amount of effort for her to create such a connection and not pull away immediately. She decided that she'd make a move—a simple gesture—and if Penn recoiled, she'd leave.

She flexed her hand and entwined Penn's fingers between her own. "Do you think you could help me with a little computer problem?"

CHAPTER FIFTEEN

August, 1955

Mama always said extreme temperatures meant extreme tempers, and the blistering heat of August was the most dreaded time of year. Once the mercury reached one hundred and ten, sensibility went out the window. Will and I had never needed a thermometer. Once it became too hot to go barefoot, we'd ask Mama for an egg and fry it on the tin shed's roof. I'd stare into the sky at the searing tentacles reaching down to earth feeling my skin burn as each second passed.

When Mama saw me she would say, "Vivian Battle, if you keep looking at the sun, you'll go blind. Then where will you be? What man wants to marry a blind moron?"

The summer of fifty-five saw record-breaking temperatures, and the swamp cooler was no help unless I stood directly underneath one of the vents. The house was even more wretchedly hot since Mama baked from morning to night.

Mac broke up several fights between the construction workers at lunchtime, all of whom boiled after eleven a.m. when the sun peaked in the sky.

He came by for lunch every day to eat with us. Kiah was at summer school getting ready to be a senior. She'd taken so many extra classes they were going to let her graduate at the end of next year at seventeen. Losing her depressed me fiercely and we'd decided not to talk about it. But sometimes she'd get so excited thinking about Tuskegee that she couldn't help it. At those times I just smiled and let her talk.

Orangedale Estates was nearly finished. When I gazed out my window at the gray shingled rooftops, the little streets between the rows of houses and the clusters of remaining orange trees that decorated the front and backyards, I couldn't remember the grove, and I was sorry to lose the memory.

I knew Mama didn't want the construction to end. Every time Mac or I mentioned how fast they were finishing, she'd look away. I knew why. When the subdivision was done, Mr. Rubenstein wanted him to move to his next project in a neighborhood called Arcadia.

Mama and Mac were officially a couple. That night I saw Mama go into their cabin was the beginning of something special, and it didn't take Kiah very long to figure out what was happening. She was the smart one, and they couldn't hide their affection very well. Mama was always smiling and laughing whenever he was around, and sometimes he got so bold he'd just pull her into his arms and kiss her. Then she would scold him for his carelessness, and he'd look properly remorseful until they both started giggling. Often they just disappeared to her bedroom, the only place they could really be alone.

I guessed Mr. and Mrs. Rubenstein knew, and Mr. Munoz, since they visited frequently. After dinner they'd sit out on the patio furniture Mr. Rubenstein had purchased for Mama's birthday, and drink and talk deep into the evening.

I'd never seen her happier. She was a full-fledged business owner thanks to Mr. Rubenstein. He'd helped her get a license, and she ran her pie business out of our kitchen. Mac had made her a wonderful sign that read *Farmhouse Pies* that sat on the edge of the road. Tourists and neighbors turned up our driveway to buy sweet potato pies throughout the day. People seemed to put aside their concerns and prejudices when it came to food. The same women who frowned at Mama when she entered a store would doll up a smile to match their dress as they knocked on the back door asking for a pie.

I was Mama's primary helper, doing some of the prep work and delivering the pies on Will's old bicycle. I didn't think he'd care since he spent all of his time riding around with his loser friends in that old beat-up truck we'd seen the day of the Rubenstein's wedding. One time his gang saw me making a delivery, and they pulled up alongside the bicycle. I tried to ignore them until someone hit me with a rock and I toppled over, the pie splattering on the road. When I told Mama she just shook her head and made another one. She didn't ask about Will. She never did.

His words from Christmas Day had stuck with me, and I felt like we got little reminders from time to time that our circle of friends, including blacks, Jews and at least one homo—me—could be in danger.

I'd realized I was the homo Billy Smith was talking about after Mrs. Rubenstein explained it to me one day while we were sketching together. Even though she'd quit teaching after she married Mr. Rubenstein, she'd agreed to give me private lessons.

"Is it bad to be a homo?" I'd asked.

She shook her head. "No, it's just another way God made us different."

It had been such a great answer that I'd immediately announced, "I love Kiah."

She'd smiled and said, "I know, honey."

But as wonderful as our friends were, things were changing. Someone came along one night and wrote *Nigger Lover* in black paint across Mama's pie sign. And then she was asked to resign from the sewing circle, which didn't seem to bother her at all. She was so happy with Mac and the Rubensteins that she didn't need any pretend friends. But I worried that it was all part of something bigger.

Every time I rode Will's bike through the new neighborhoods, I felt the city getting hotter and more oppressive. If I stopped at Lacy's drugstore to pick up some medicine, or if I went to the market with Mama, people seemed to avoid us, even the people we knew. The cashiers stared at us with unfriendly expressions, and sometimes I thought they might tell us to put all of our groceries back. It didn't seem to bother Mama, who always offered her mega-watt movie star smile. She could melt anyone's prejudice.

"What's that word when you think something bad is coming?" I asked Kiah.

"Ominous?" she said.

"Yeah, that's how I feel."

We were lying on the grass behind our house. I was sketching, and she was doing her homework as usual. Mama was taking a break from the pie making and had given me the afternoon off to be with Kiah. Sometimes we didn't talk for hours but we always held hands and sometimes we kissed.

A car approached and we looked over to see Mr. Rubenstein and Mac hurry up the back steps. We followed them inside just as Mr. Rubenstein finished calling for an ambulance.

"I just don't know what to do," he said after he hung up. "This is the third time the machinery has been vandalized, but this is the first time anyone's been hurt."

"Will John be all right?" Mama asked.

"They think so. He's got a broken clavicle."

"How did it happen?"

"He was driving the bulldozer and the brakes gave out. He couldn't stop and ran into a ditch. Threw him right off," Mac explained.

Mama asked, "What happened to the brakes?"

Mr. Rubenstein shrugged. "I don't know. The inspector came out a month ago to check on all the equipment. If there was something wrong, he'd have caught it."

"It was intentional," Mac said sadly.

"Oh, that can't be true," she exclaimed. "Why would anyone want to hurt someone like John? He's a lovely person."

Mac took her hand. "Sweets, whoever did this didn't care. They didn't know who would be driving that bulldozer but that wasn't the point. They wanted to hurt Jacob."

She looked at Mr. Rubenstein with a pained expression. "Oh, Jacob."

He threw up his hands and said, "I'm tired of this whole mess."

He tipped his hat to Mama and left. When he saw Kiah and me listening on the sun porch, he nodded and tipped his hat again. We gazed through the window at our parents. Mac held her in his arms and kissed the top of her head. When he glanced over his shoulder he saw us and offered a sad smile before leading her upstairs to be alone.

"What's going on, Kiah? Do you think this has anything to do with the funny feeling I had?"

I gazed up at my wise friend. She'd grown another few inches and towered over me now. I waited for an answer, but then she turned and walked into their cabin without saying a word. "Kiah?" I called, but she ignored me.

I slumped onto the back porch steps and rested my chin on my fists. I didn't know what to do. She didn't want to talk, and if I went upstairs to my room I'd be close to Mac and Mama, and I didn't want to interrupt their privacy. So I just sat on the steps staring into the yard—my entire world.

I didn't have any other friends except Kiah and Gloria Meyer, who also liked art. After my suspension during freshman year, we'd started tossing notes back and forth when Mr. Corliss wasn't looking, and we ate lunch together in the art room with Mrs. Whittier, the teacher who replaced Mrs. Rubenstein. But I didn't see Gloria outside of school. I didn't see anyone.

On Friday nights I didn't cruise down Central Avenue like the other teenagers, stopping at Bob's Big Boy for a hamburger. I didn't go to the movies on Saturday nights, and I didn't date boys. I wondered if there was something wrong with me. I hated going out in public because all I felt was Kiah's absence. She'd have to sit in the Negro section at the hamburger place or the balcony at the Palms, and we'd never—ever—be able to kiss in public.

As I stared across the lawn at her cabin I felt the miles grow between us, like the distance between Birmingham and Phoenix. Tuskeegee was only a year away. When she left me here, what would I do?

I pondered that question for another hour until dusk crept across the yard, and Mac joined me on the sun porch. He sat down next to me and gave me a hug.

"Where's Kiah?"

I nodded toward the cabin and he sighed. "It's gonna be okay, Vivi. Kiah's just worried about me and your mama."

"She doesn't think it's right," I said.

"Well, she doesn't know everything, least of all about what it means to be in love."

"Yes, she does," I replied, almost shouting.

He blinked at me and started to ask why, but he stopped himself and looked away, thinking. "Well, it'll be all right," he concluded before he got up and went into the cabin.

I couldn't focus for the rest of the evening. Kiah had refused to join us for dinner, and I felt lost. So I just roamed around the house, from my bedroom to the kitchen and then to the living room.

"Vivian, go find something productive to do," Mama said in an aggravated tone. She was making her shopping list in the kitchen while Mac read the paper on the sun porch. I'd come in and out at least five times bored out of my skull. When I reached for the icebox handle she said, "If you open that icebox one more time, I'm going to shove you inside and leave you right next to the bottle of milk."

I groaned and went out the front door that creaked from lack of use. I strolled down the brick path, listening to the hum of the cicadas and enjoying the cool night air. Millions of stars breached the darkness casting a glow over the streets. I leaned against the wooden gate and stared at the little houses across from us. Oddly, none of our neighbors were out tonight. Usually people sat on their porches and chatted or gossiped when it was so hot, but it was completely quiet. A string of glowing porch lights was the only sign of life until I heard a low rumble.

Headlights appeared at the corner of the next block—a truck.

I had a fleeting thought of Will and his buddies until an older man stepped out, whistling and carrying his lunchbox up the driveway of the end house. I exhaled. I'd been holding my breath and hadn't even realized it. My pulse was racing, and when I held up my hand it was shaking.

"You're beyond ridiculous, Vivian Battle," I whispered.

But my nerves and the stuffy house kept me up for much of the night. I'd stuck my head under the bathtub faucet and climbed into bed with dripping wet hair. Maybe a breeze would sneak through my bedroom window and give me relief, but it didn't work.

I threw the covers aside and decided to sleep on the sun porch just like Pops had done all those nights. After an hour of staring into the black night toward Kiah's cabin, my eyelids finally closed.

A steady, soft scraping interrupted my light sleep, and I sat up on the divan. The moon was only a sliver and the sun porch nothing but a series of shadows. Two figures stole up our driveway. One was carrying a sack and the other was dragging a large piece of wood. They stopped in the yard between our house and the cabins and busied themselves with the wood. I went to one of the windows and stared into the darkness. My mind registered the planted cross just as they lit it on fire.

I screamed.

They ran, but not before they threw three burning fireballs toward each of the cabins. I watched in horror as the night turned yellow, crimson and orange. A flurry of noise came from the house and Mac tore past me to the cabin.

Kiah.

I started after him, but Mama grabbed me from behind and held me. I writhed until I broke free, but she blocked the door. I had to get to Kiah. I had to help. I ran back inside and out the front door, determined to circle back down the driveway. I burst through the small cluster of trees that lined the property and stopped suddenly. Standing behind some bushes watching the fire was Pops. I took a step and a twig snapped. His gaze shot toward the trees. I stood very still hoping he hadn't seen me.

Neither of us moved as precious seconds vanished. I could

hear Mac and Mr. Munoz shouting for the hose and my worry for Kiah nearly propelled my feet forward, but I'd have to step in front of Pops. If he grabbed me, I'd never reach her. Maybe we both thought we were invisible, or maybe we both knew we weren't.

The fire truck's wail grew closer until it pulled up the drive. A moving blur of red, it passed between us, and when I blinked he was gone. I stood there a second longer, wondering if I'd imagined the whole thing, before I shot around the side of the house. I felt the fire first, the heat announcing its presence, but what I saw sent the air out of my lungs. The flames were so ravenous they fed off each other, and the three cabins were indistinguishable.

Firemen hurried around the yard, running lines, trampling through my mother's roses and shouting orders to each other. Thick smoke swirled around me, and I nearly gagged. I scanned the yard for Kiah but only found Mr. Benson, leaning against an orange tree in his pajama bottoms and a T-shirt. Another fire truck rolled into the yard, and it wasn't until the motor died that I heard my mother screaming.

I knew it was her, somewhere near the flames. I followed the sound of her voice, wincing at its agony, knowing the cause. *Mac. Kiah.* She was locked between Mr. Munoz's strong arms. Her legs dangled in the air as she writhed to break free, just as I had done only minutes before. I fell to the ground, not caring that the fire's heat was burning my face. I couldn't get any closer, but I wouldn't move back. A group of neighbors huddled together in a corner of the yard, their backs to the fire. What was so interesting?

More sirens. Ambulances. Mama's cry.

A man with a satchel pushed his way through the crowd. When it parted for a split second against the angry light of the flames, I saw the familiar pattern of roses—Kiah's nightgown.

I ran into the crowd, pushing to the front until I finally reached her. She was unconscious, and the man was tending to her wounds. Her left leg and arm were badly burned, and he was applying a salve. The crowd was telling a tale I didn't understand.

The ambulance forced us back and gently lifted her onto a stretcher. I rushed to her side, walking with her as they took her to the ambulance.

"Kiah," I cried, not knowing if she could hear me. "I'm here."

I said a prayer as they snaked out of the driveway, tears streaming down my face. Only then did I realize that Mama wasn't screaming anymore. She wasn't with Mr. Munoz or near the fire trucks. I tripped over the hoses and slipped in the muddy grass searching for her.

The sun porch glowed behind me. She sat on the divan watching the fire, as if it were a television show. She didn't look at me when I flung open the screen door. An unlit cigarette shook in her hand, as if it were alive, and a guttural sound escaped her lips.

I stared toward the fire. Kiah. Mr. Munoz. Mr. Benson. But where was Mac? A hand touched my shoulder, and I stared up into Mr. Rubenstein's kind, watery eyes. He went past me and knelt before her. When he touched her shoulder, she burst into tears and threw her arms around him.

Amid the thick smoke I still could smell Mrs. Rubenstein's perfume, so I wasn't surprised when she slid next to me and pulled me into an embrace.

"Where's Mac?" I whispered.

"He's gone, sweetie. He managed to get Kiah out through the back window, but then the fire was too much."

She squeezed me tighter before the first sob pushed through my throat.

****

I spent most of that night lying on the fancy sofa in the living room, Mrs. Rubenstein at my side. The firefighters and policemen came in and out of the house for a few hours, interviewing Mama and Mr. Rubenstein, trying to understand what happened. Pieces of their conversation floated into my brain—names, times and details. At one point they started to discuss Mac's family and my eyes opened wide, but then the conversation dissolved, and I knew Mr. Rubenstein had led them to the sun porch.

Mama remained at the kitchen table, the bottle of vodka next to her. She didn't cry and her strength was tremendously comforting. All of the unfamiliar people eventually left and only the whispered exchanges between Mama and the Rubensteins remained. At one point she started to whimper, and Mrs. Rubenstein pulled her against her chest. I got up and went to the doorway.

"Mama? When can I go see Kiah?"

At the sound of my voice all three adults stopped talking, and Mama rubbed her eyes with a tissue. "Honey, I don't know," she said, searching for her strong voice. "She's in the black part of the hospital. We'll just have to wait and see. Mac's family…"

Her voice trailed off and she stared at the table, fighting back the tears. I retreated to the living room and stared out the front window. The yard looked no different than it had the night before. Yet I knew that if I followed the brick path around the house, the picture would show the end of our quiet life with Mac and Kiah.

My feet were moving before I could stop them—until I reached the end of the driveway. The cabins were a tangle of smoking, charred remains, rising up from the foundations. Black and gray debris had suffocated the lush grass that connected our house with the cabins, leaving only a muddy bog and the burned cross.

Mac and Kiah had explained its origins from the Middle Ages and what it meant now. I kicked it and a clump of charred wood disintegrated. So I kicked it again and again, pulverizing the remains under the force of my sneaker. I didn't realize I was screaming until I had to catch my breath. When I glanced toward the sun porch, I saw Mama and the Rubensteins watching me.

I gave one final kick and said, "Mr. Rubenstein, there's something I need to tell you."

CHAPTER SIXTEEN

June, 2010

"Um, well, this personal ad is...personal."

Penn stared at the screen, and CC knew she wasn't focused on the words.

"Can you delete it or figure out the password, or something?"

"Maybe. This website has a low level of security, so I'm hoping my cracking program can hack it." She clicked through several screens expertly, and the computer started to whir. "So, I think this entitles me to three more questions."

"I don't think so," CC argued. Penn pushed away from the keyboard, and CC collapsed onto the sofa. "Okay, what do you want to know?"

Penn returned to her work. "How did your ex get you to pose for these pictures?"

"With a lot of tequila. Next question."

"If she's so mean and manipulative, why were you ever with her, and why would you ever want to subject yourself to her twice?"

She groaned loudly. "We don't have time for that answer. I'm sure it's all rooted in my childhood. One more question."

"There," Penn said, hitting a few keys. "Done."

She sat up. "You got it? That was quick. What was it?"

"Just a series of five meaningless letters and symbols."

She sighed. "Thanks."

"I still get one more question. Why would a smart, gorgeous woman ever take out a personal ad?"

There wasn't a trace of sarcasm in her voice and the cobalt blue eyes showed sincerity—and opportunity. The question lingered in the silent cottage, a world away from the ringing phones, clicking keyboards and endless negotiations that defined CC's responsibilities. She abandoned her suit jacket on the couch and went to Penn, whose hands were folded in her lap. When CC unbuttoned her shirt and revealed the leopard skin bra from the photos, Penn's eyes fluttered and CC worried she might run away. They needed to forge a connection that would conquer her fear of the past.

She took Penn's shaking hand and placed it on her breast, stroking her fingers until they came to life.

"I…I haven't…It's been two years." She looked embarrassed, as if she couldn't believe what she was saying.

CC closed her eyes and enjoyed Penn's caress. "That's too long," she murmured. "It's time to end the drought." She unbuttoned her suit pants so Penn could peek at the matching panties. "Touch me."

CC felt her piercing gaze, knew she was deciding whether to take another chance. The chair squeaked, and she sensed her nearness before warm lips kissed her belly.

****

She woke up alone. The luxurious sheets kissed her skin, but Penn was gone. The clock on the nightstand read four p.m., and she realized she'd taken a nap. She never napped. Her brain was always cluttered with work. But after a few hours with Penn she'd contracted professional amnesia, and she couldn't think of a single thing to worry about except where Penn was.

Her cell phone vibrated and she looked around the room, realizing Penn had draped her clothes over a chair along with the Droid. It was Blanca. While she didn't want to speak to her boss naked, she loathed the idea of listening to the terse message that would obviously be left if she didn't.

"This is CC," she said.

"Where are you?"

"Um, I'm standing outside of a garage, actually. My car died on my way back from the law library right in the middle of an intersection. Fortunately, a few guys helped me move it off the street, but then I had to wait for the tow truck."

"I've left four messages," was her curt reply.

She sighed. "I was just about to call you. I accidentally left my phone on the passenger's seat of the car, so I was separated from it all the way back from Tempe. They're working on it now." When Blanca didn't answer she said, "Are you still there?"

"I am. And quite frankly, CC, you're living up to the abysmal employment statistics associated with your age group. When will you be returning to the office?"

She glanced up. Penn stood in the doorway. "I'm sure it won't be too long," she said hopefully, knowing that Blanca would send a secretary to pick her up if necessary. "Probably within the hour."

"I'm setting my alarm," Blanca said before she hung up.

"You're not a very good liar," Penn observed. "Don't ever go to court naked."

"I'll write that down," she said. She turned off her phone and started to dress. "Do you have anything I can wear in case we find ourselves in the attic?"

She wanted to climb back into bed, but Penn's body language suggested she was incredibly uncomfortable. Penn barely looked at her as she picked through a drawer and found her a Gumby T-shirt and a pair of cargo shorts.

"I'm not sure these will fit you. We're not exactly the same body type."

She handed the clothes to her and disappeared into the kitchen while CC dressed. The shorts were two sizes too large, but they managed to stay around her hips.

"Are you okay?" she asked, sliding onto a stool.

Penn poured them each a cup of tea. "I got scared after you fell asleep. I'm thinking we made a mistake. I mean it was great," she quickly added, "but I just don't know if it was the right thing to do. I don't know if I was ready."

She glanced at CC, waiting for her reaction. CC took a sip of tea and said, "I think it was a great experiment."

"An experiment?"

"Well, you wouldn't buy a bicycle without taking it for a test ride, would you?"

Penn chuckled. "Are you comparing yourself to a Huffy?"

She leaned across the counter. "Kiss me." Penn obliged, and she said, "We can take it slow. I'm fine with that. We've determined that we have excellent chemistry, but if you want me to leave, I will. What do you choose?" she asked.

"Maybe we could get to know each other better," Penn said.

"I agree. I think it's time for me to ask *you* some questions."

"Okay, what do you want to know?"

"What kind of a name is Penn?"

She sighed. "My last name is Pennington…and my first name is Posey."

She bit her lip to ward off a burst of laughter. "Like the flower? Your name is Posey Pennington?"

"Yes, *Cleopatra*, it is."

"Good point. How did you come to live here? Siobhan and Lynette said they were handpicked, and they don't pay rent. Is that true?"

She nodded slowly. "Viv chose us, me included."

"Why? How? I guess I just don't understand that level of generosity. I mean, Viv's heart is clearly enormous, but she's got to survive."

"And she does. She's very wealthy. Chloe the Chameleon has made sure of that. But money isn't a big factor in her life. It never has been. After her mother died she didn't want to run a B and B, and she also didn't want to deal with landlord laws, which in a rental situation would have been the case. She just wanted friends, and Kiah."

"What happened to her?"

Penn stopped to think. "I don't know," she finally said. "When Viv speaks of her she confuses the present and the past, and I'm not sure what happened after their childhood. I know that Viv had a lover for about fifteen years. That might've been Kiah. I *do* know that woman died of breast cancer."

"Has there been anyone else?"

"No," she said without any sadness. "Viv is content to surround herself with good friends and her passion. I'm sure, though, that if Ms. Right strolled up the driveway she'd resume her skinny-dipping ways."

CC's eyes widened. "Skinny-dipping?"

Penn shook her head. "You don't want to know."

"So there's been a long list of members at the enclave."

"A few dozen."

"How did she find you?"

"I guess we saved each other," she said. "I kept her from going to jail, and she gave me a place to live."

"What happened?"

"It was about four years ago. I'd quit my job, had my heart broken and my bank account emptied by an unscrupulous girlfriend—and that's another story I won't tell now," she added quickly. "You're way past three questions with this one."

"So noted," she said. "Continue."

"I was destitute and standing in Walgreens debating whether to spend the extra twenty cents for a toothbrush with an angled head, when I heard the alarm sound at the front of the store. I peered down the main aisle and saw Viv arguing with a young guy I guessed was the store manager.

"She's yelling that she's being assaulted, and the guy accuses her of shoplifting a bag of medication. Apparently she'd told the pharmacy clerk that she had some more shopping to do, and the girl allowed her to keep the bag while she hunted for her other things. But she didn't see what she was looking for so she decided to leave—"

"But she hadn't paid for the medication."

"She forgot. So I help Viv try to explain to the guy, who wasn't the manager but the *assistant* manager, and who obviously wished he was the manager. He wouldn't let it go. That's when I took the bag from Viv and hurled it across the store."

She choked on her tea. "You did what?"

"I chucked it as far as I could. They were completely dumbfounded. I told him that since it was clearly somewhere in his store, he had no case and no reason to detain my client. I identified myself as her attorney and asked him how much money he had in the bank because when Walgreen's found out how he treated a customer, he was going to lose his job and never be manager of anything. That's when he went and found the bag, let her pay for it and told her to have a nice day as she left."

"That took a lot of guts," CC said.

Penn waved it off. "Not really. I had nothing to lose. I wasn't employed, and I didn't answer to anyone. So she offered me some money, which I refused, and then I thought we'd part ways. She saw my car packed with my stuff and asked me if I wanted some lunch. I never left."

"She's so generous," CC mused.

"Yeah, it's her way. Her life is the enclave."

CC squeezed her hand. "Then we've got to do everything we can to help her keep it, even if it's difficult to discuss the past."

"That's not so easy since there are so many bad memories, particularly the fire."

"Viv mentioned it once. What happened?"

"The KKK burned down the cabins around the farmhouse and left a huge burning cross."

"What year was that?"

Penn shrugged. "I'm not sure. In the fifties. Why?"

"I'm wondering if the note is related."

"How?"

"Seth Rubenstein told me that his father got out of the housing industry in fifty-six, and the note he found from Chet Battle is dated August of fifty-five. If the cabins burned down then…"

"It's awfully coincidental. There could be a connection." She curled a finger through CC's hair. "Are you sure you want to help? I mean this could hurt your career if we find something to save the enclave."

Like a kaleidoscope spinning, she saw the colors and responsibilities of her life—the monstrous student loan she owed, her parents' pride every time they announced their daughter was a *lawyer*, and the thousands of hours she'd spent studying for the bar. All she had to do was hop in the Honda and hurry back to H and B.

And then she thought of Chloe. And her sketchbook.

"I can do this," she said finally. "I choose."

****

Penn called Maya, Lynette and Siobhan and explained the situation. Once they'd gathered in the common area, they marched through the hedge and confronted Viv, just as she was carrying out a sweet potato pie for their weekly barbecue.

"Where are you going?" she asked suspiciously. She looked at Penn. "You need to start the grill."

"Viv, let us help," Siobhan said.

"Please," Lynette pleaded. "No apartment would let me keep all the dogs."

"There might be an answer, a way," Maya added. "Finding out the truth might help."

Viv's gaze landed on Maya, and she stared at her intently as if she'd said something wrong. "That's not always the case," she said cryptically. Eventually she sighed and turned to Penn. "I'm not going up there. You're on your own."

****

The upstairs hallways were antiquated and dreary. CC noticed that the wainscoting needed some paint, and the yellowing wallpaper was peeling away. While Viv had modernized the downstairs, it was obvious she'd neglected the second floor.

Penn grabbed a cord attached to a pull-down ladder, and they all climbed up into the musty air. CC realized that whoever had built the farmhouse valued storage space, and while visitors needed to hunker down to avoid smacking their foreheads against the low-angled ceilings, there was plenty of room to preserve a lifetime of memories. And that was exactly what Viv had done.

"My God," Lynette said. "I've seen thrift stores with less stuff."

"This will take forever," Siobhan said, marveling at the endless stacks of boxes, trunks and crates amid the various miscellaneous items such as a canoe, sporting equipment, an ancient bicycle and a sewing mannequin.

Penn put her hands on her hips. "Okay, we know we're looking for papers or documents—"

"And photos, too," CC said. "We might be able to piece some of this together if we see some photos."

She scanned the room. "Any ideas?"

Maya strolled across the few bare patches of floor, studying the contents of the room. She peered into the dusty corners and checked some of the labels. "I think it's actually in order."

Lynette laughed. "Are you crazy?"

"Think about it. My parents had an attic like this in Oakland. When my mom hauled something up there she tossed it in the most convenient place. Once in a while they moved some stuff against a wall—"

"But they just put more stuff in front of it," CC said. "My parents do the same thing in Bloomington with their basement."

"Exactly."

Maya scanned the stacks of boxes and hodgepodge of items before she finally pointed to the area underneath the stained glass window, the place closest to the entrance. "I'm guessing the fifties are over there."

They each took a corner with Penn in the middle. Dust particles swirled around them and every fifteen minutes someone went into a hacking fit after swallowing an entire cloud. A few bottles of wine and plates of crackers and cheese sat amid them, their compromise for forfeiting barbecue night in favor of what Lynette was affectionately calling a snipe hunt.

They quickly realized that Lois Battle lived at the far side of anal and had categorized and compartmentalized her and Viv's life systematically. A stack of long boxes labeled *Vivi's Schoolwork* contained three other boxes nested inside, each one dated with a year. Christmas cards, bills and receipts were equally well sorted. All of them were captivated when Maya stumbled upon a box of IOU's from the forties.

"People were an entirely different breed back then," she said.

After an hour, Siobhan complained, "It would really help to know specifically what we were looking for."

"Anything that mentions Chet Battle, Jacob Rubenstein, nineteen fifty-five or the enclave," Penn said.

CC took a sip of wine and pulled another trunk in front of her. So far she'd discovered that Lois was astoundingly beautiful, smart—according to her report cards—and an incredible pie maker. She imagined that she'd eventually come across invoices, recipes and possibly thank-you notes since Lois kept *everything*, and Viv had inherited her penchant for pack-ratting.

Lynette groaned as she shut another folder. "Why are people so complicated and mean? I can't imagine anyone throwing Viv out on the street. What a greedy bastard this guy must be."

"I agree," Maya said.

"Is this something?" Siobhan asked, showing a letter to Penn.

CC crouched next to them and read over her shoulder. It was a letter from someone named Gracie to Lois, dated November of nineteen fifty-five. She skimmed the contents which included the usual references to the weather and the changing seasons in Birmingham, where Gracie apparently lived, but it also mentioned Kiah and her ongoing recovery.

"What was she recovering from?" Siobhan asked.

"I don't know," Penn said. "Read any other letter you find from this person."

CC returned to the small box of family photos she'd found, sandwiched in a larger box labeled *Mom's Things*. The photos were almost exclusively of the four Battles, and judging from the scenery, she guessed they were all taken in the Midwest. They were a good-looking family, and Chet Battle was as handsome as his wife was beautiful. Perhaps his roving eye had been the cause of their divorce.

She shared her thoughts with the group and Lynette snorted. "I'm not surprised. So typical of a man to cheat on a woman, typical of anyone I guess. No one's faithful," she said off-handedly.

"Damn it, Lynette!" Siobhan shouted. "Does anyone rate in your life that doesn't have a tail? Are all human beings worthless?"

"Of course not," she sputtered, clearly taken aback. "But interpersonal relationships are so..."

"What? Complicated? Messy?" She stood up and a stack of photos cascaded to the floor. "And exhilarating, fulfilling and *sensual*. There is nothing like spending a weekend holed up in a cabin with your lover and a roaring fire."

Lynette blinked. "Who would take care of the dogs?"

She threw up her hands. "I'm done. Good luck, ladies," she said before she stormed down the ladder.

"Siobhan?" Lynette called after her. She looked at the others. "What's up with her?"

Maya shook her head in amazement. "I'm surprised it took this long," she said to Penn. She leaned toward Lynette and said, "Honey, you are the dumbest smart person I know. You can spot a stray dog three blocks away, but you can't see what's right in front of you."

She adjusted the beret she was sporting. "What are you talking about?"

"She's in love with you, stupid," Penn said slowly.

"She is?"

Maya set aside the stack of letters she was holding. "Honey, think about it. Who stayed with Janis Joplin when she was so sick? Who always comes to your rescue every time you run out of gas because you just can't remember that E means *empty?* Who offered to go to dinner with your parents and you when you told them you were gay? C'mon, honey, it shouldn't surprise you. You love music, and she's a musician. You fit together."

Her gaze dropped to her lap.

"Are you okay?" Penn finally asked.

She shook her head and picked up a box. "I can't discuss this now," she said. "Let's just worry about Viv."

They returned to their work, and CC poked through a trunk full of knickknacks. Buried deep at the bottom she found a shoebox without a label. Inside was a row of letters pressed together so tightly that she had to part them in half to pull one out, still in its original white envelope. She saw there was no return address, and the postmark was from Phoenix in nineteen sixty-one. It was addressed to Lois Battle and the script was awkward, as if it was written by a man.

August 12, 1961

My dear Lois,

We returned from our summer vacation last week. Disneyland is indeed a magical place. Seth most enjoyed the Submarine Voyage, and Moira liked King Arthur's Carousel, but by the fourth time she felt sick. Della liked driving the little Autopia cars, which is a car of the future, but I preferred the Astro Jets.

Vivi and Maude would love it, and if you ever want to take them…

Business is booming, and we're talking about opening another restaurant. I had the idea because of your pie. A customer wanted to know how he could get one and not drive ten miles. What do you think?

I miss you terribly. It's been three weeks since we stopped by, and my eyes long to gaze into yours. I hope Maudie isn't giving you too much trouble. Five-year-olds are a handful. I certainly know this. I can't believe Vivi will turn twenty in just a few months. She's such an amazing young woman, Lois, and certainly the godsend you described in your last letter. Della and I will visit next week. I promise.

All my love,

Jacob

All my love. Jacob had signed his letter by proclaiming his love, but was it romantic or platonic? She wrestled with the box until she could free the very first letter. The envelope was dated nineteen fifty-six, and when she pulled out the white sheets of paper, a black-and-white photo fell to the floor—of a very pregnant Lois standing on the farmhouse's porch with a teenage Vivian.

The conversations and experiences of the last several days started to form a picture, like a child's connect-the-dot game. She looked over at Penn, who was shuffling through a stack of memorabilia.

"Who was Maude?" she asked.

"No idea," Penn mumbled. "But your theory that Lois Battle had a system is falling apart."

"How so?"

"I'm in this box marked nineteen fifty-nine, and I'm finding pictures that were obviously drawn by a small child. Viv was seventeen."

She stared at the photo in her hand. "Has anyone heard Viv talk about Maude?"

"The only Maude I know was my birth mother," Maya said.

CHAPTER SEVENTEEN

November, 1955

When I told Mr. Rubenstein that I'd seen Pops hiding in the bushes while the cabins burned, he calmly nodded his head. I'm not sure if he ever told Mama, but no one ever spoke of it again. He thanked me, and said I shouldn't repeat it to anyone and I didn't. It was probably one of the few secrets I kept.

And three months later when I saw Pops walk out of the drugstore with Shirley West, I decided it hadn't been important. Even though I didn't want him back in our lives, he was my father, and if he wasn't in jail it meant he didn't have anything to do with the fire or Mac's death. I got some comfort from that.

Mac was gone, and Kiah was stuck in the hospital, badly burned. Mr. Rubenstein arranged for me to visit once. I snuck up the back steps to the colored wing but at the sight of my best friend—the love of my life—wrapped in bandages and looking like a mummy, I burst into tears and ran out of the room. I decided I would just wait for her at home.

Orangedale Estates was a thriving community. I didn't need to sit on my window seat for confirmation. It was all around me. And I loathed staring out my window anymore. The yard below was an awful memory of that night. The debris from the cabins had been hauled away and the ground in front of them, once beautiful, lush grass, was again dirt, circling the cement foundations of the destroyed cabins.

"What are they going to do with those?" I asked Mama one night while we sat on the sun porch.

"Jacob says he's going to build some cottages there."

I looked at her funny. It didn't make sense. "Why?"

She glanced up from her sewing. "So we can make money. He says that travelers like the idea of staying in a place that reminds them of home. It's called a bed-and-breakfast. They can stay in the cottages, and I can cook for them."

"Where are they from?"

"All over," she replied.

I returned to my sketching, trying not to stare at her swollen belly. Two weeks after the fire she'd told me her secret—she was pregnant with Mac's child. He'd been so happy to learn he was going to be a father again, regardless of the problems it created. Mr. Rubenstein had found someone to deliver the baby, and an attorney who'd handle her divorce from Pops. It had all been planned—everything except Mac's death.

"And I've got some more good news. Jacob and Della are starting a restaurant, and they're going to feature my sweet potato pie." She offered a slight smile, the most she could muster after everything that had happened.

"That's great. Your pie's the best. I can't wait for me and Kiah to try it at the restaurant. I wonder if it will taste different."

She set down her sewing. "Honey, Kiah's going away to live in Birmingham with her Aunt Gracie."

"What?"

"That's where her people are. She doesn't have any family left."

"She's got us!"

She bit her lip and looked at me sympathetically. "Honey, she'll always have us, but we're not her family."

"That's not true," I cried. "You make your family. It's not always about blood," I said, repeating some wise words that Della Rubenstein had said to me.

She pulled me into her arms, and I cried for a long time. It wasn't fair. I knew Kiah was going to move away eventually, but I'd been robbed of the precious time I had before she went to Tuskeegee.

"When does she leave?"

"Next week. But she'd like to see you before she goes."

****

The girl who ascended the steps was covered in scars and used a cane to support her right side, which had been terribly burned by the flames licking the window frame as she tried to escape. When she saw me she smiled her big smile, and I took her strong left hand. Mama had warned me not to embrace her. It was still far too painful.

We sat on the sun porch drinking Mac's lemonade and eating Mama's sweet potato pie.

"I've missed this so much," she said. "I miss everything," she added softly.

She looked up to see if I understood, and I nodded.

"How are your grades?" she asked.

I shrugged, embarrassed. All I wanted to do was draw. "They're okay. They'll never be as good as yours."

"I don't have any," she snorted. "I've lost a lot of time. I may have to wait a year for Tuskeegee."

"I doubt it. You're too smart to keep out of college."

She smiled again, and we both kept eating. It was awkward between us, and I threw a glance at the destroyed backyard and the cause of our changed relationship.

"What do you think about the baby?" she asked suddenly.

"I like it, I guess." I said.

"It'll be our connection, Vivi. The little boy or girl will keep us together even though we're far apart," she said, a note of excitement in her voice. It sounded as if she was trying to convince herself at the same time. "It'll be a way to keep Daddy..." Her voice trailed off as she forced a sob down.

"Yeah," I agreed. I couldn't bear to see her cry or hear her talk about Mac.

Mr. Rubenstein and Mama joined us, and I knew it was time for her to go. He was going to drive her all the way to New Mexico and leave her with a family friend until her aunt could pick her up.

She stood and took my hand. "Why can't you stay?" I asked.

She shook her head. "It just can't be that way, Vivi, at least not now. But someday I'll come back to visit."

Mama kissed her gently on the cheek, and we all walked out to the car, sensitive to her slow gait as she dragged her right leg across the dirt. Once she'd settled into her seat I stuck my hand through the open window and offered her a gift—an orange.

"Where did you get this?" she asked in amazement. "It's only November."

"I found it on the tree closest to the road. I doubt it's ripe yet, but it looks ready."

We both studied the freak of nature. While most of the other orange blossoms were still green, I'd found one all by itself on a branch. Maybe extra water reached its roots or maybe the sun kissed it frequently, but for whatever reason it was more mature than the others, and it reminded me of her.

The motor rumbled to life and I stepped away, feeling the comfort of Mama's strong hands on my shoulders. We all waved, and while I knew Kiah was a person who kept her word, something told me this was goodbye.

The car slipped out of the driveway, and I ran after it. I could hear Mama calling me, but I ignored her. As it picked up speed I ran faster. Even after it turned onto Missouri Avenue, I kept running past the endless rows of orange trees I remembered, wanting them back more desperately than ever. And hating Mac for killing the first one.

CHAPTER EIGHTEEN

June, 2010

CC realized she'd accidentally unearthed a family secret, and judging by the blank expression on Maya's face, she guessed Maya had no clue that she was related to Viv. But the resemblance between Maya and Kiah's portrait was now obvious to her, perhaps because she was an artist.

She set the information aside and focused on the problem: how to keep Seth Rubenstein from claiming the enclave. She pulled more letters from the box, realizing that the key was the relationship between Lois and Jacob.

"CC," Penn said. "Who's Maude?"

CC waved her off. "It's not important right now. Probably just a friend of Lois's," she said glancing at Maya. "I need to sort through this box, but I need better light."

CC took the shoebox and went downstairs. Viv wasn't

around, and she imagined she might be on the sun porch working. She settled onto the couch across from the oil painting of Kiah. As she read Jacob's letters to Lois, she periodically looked up at Kiah's strong expression and wise eyes. She felt like she was reliving some of the moments Jacob recalled, such as the time when he'd first visited and offered to buy Chet Battle's orchards. She glanced at the antique dining table, imagining the two of them haggling over the price under the glow of the ornate chandelier.

Her phone rang and she glanced at the display. Alicia. She was about to divert to voice mail, but suddenly felt the urge for confrontation and picked up the call.

"Hey. I've got two suite-level tickets to the Diamondbacks game tonight. Interested?"

"Oh, I can't. I've got to work."

Alicia snorted. "Really? What if I told you that I'm calling you from *your* office?"

She immediately became wary. "What are you doing there?"

"I came by to see if you wanted to go, and Blanca told me you were at a garage?"

She realized Blanca might be standing right next to her, listening to every word she said. "You of all people know how my car is. I barely made it off the freeway before it died. They're still working on it, but it's taking longer than I thought."

"So which garage are you at?"

"Uh, I'm not sure. It's either Tony's or Al's or Tony's *and* Al's, something like that. It was a place that the tow truck driver recommended. They take Triple-A."

"Well, that's convenient," Alicia said, and CC knew she saw through the lie. They'd lived together too long. There was a long pause and she wondered if she'd hung up. "Are you still there?"

"Seriously, CC, are you with your new friends?"

"Actually, yes, I'm at the enclave. I'm spending some time with Viv. She's helping me with my drawings."

"During a work day? Are you crazy? You're sure it's not that cute little butch dyke who was glued to your side at the charity event?"

"Alicia…"

"Seriously, CC, are you and the butch together now? Because having any contact with them during this case is unethical." Her voice rose. "I know you'll probably hate me for this, but I'm demanding that you meet me at the game. It will save your career and get you some hot sex in a luxury suite."

She wasn't paying attention. She was sifting through some old black-and-white photos she'd found in one of the letters—pictures from the grand opening of Della's, the flagship restaurant on Grand Avenue. Toward the bottom of the stack she found one of Jacob Rubenstein between his wife and Lois Battle. Lois was signing something but it wasn't a piece of paper. She peered at the picture bringing it as close to her eyes as possible.

"CC!" Alicia snapped. "Listen to me. Come home now. You can't get involved with these people."

She held the picture at arm's length and studied it differently, forgetting the center and focusing on the background, just as an artist might. They were standing in Della's, and she even remembered the exact location—the wall by the hallway. And on that wall…

She grinned. She had it.

"CC!" Alicia spat.

"I can't."

"Of course you can, but it sounds like you won't. It's the butch, isn't it? Don't lie to me anymore. Get home right now, or I'm sending those pictures to your boss! I broke up with Nadia. I'm all yours."

Alicia suddenly had her full attention. When she was certain she could speak with a steady voice she said, "That's great, Alicia. You threaten to ruin my career, and, in the next sentence, tell me you've finally split with the woman you left me for. Wow. That's quite an offer. It makes me wonder how many times I fell for similar offers when we were together. This time I think I'll wise up and decline."

"I'm serious about those pictures. Blanca offered me a job, and I'm thinking it might be *your* job."

"And you can have it."

She hung up and dropped her phone because her hands were

shaking so badly. Penn appeared as she was crawling under the coffee table to retrieve it.

"Are you okay?" she asked.

She shook her head. "I'm pretty sure I'm unemployed and possibly an Internet sensation as well."

"Really? Um, well…it'll be okay."

"So have you two figured out how I'm going to keep this place?" Viv asked from the doorway. Her granite-like expression was intimidating, and CC knew she needed to tread lightly.

She picked up the stack of photos. "I think I've found something, but I need to ask you some difficult questions. Did your mother and Jacob have an affair? I only ask," she said, motioning to the shoebox, "because there's at least a hundred letters in here."

She joined them on the couch and stared at the box. She plucked one from the middle and read the envelope. "Where did you find these?"

"They were inside another box, almost as if your mother was hiding them," Penn said. "Have you read any?"

Viv scowled. "Of course not, and I don't have any intention of reading them now. That was her personal business."

"But what if it helps us keep the enclave?" CC pressed.

Viv shook her head. "It won't. All you need to know is that Mama and Jacob Rubenstein were tremendously close. They always were. How close, I don't know, but he would've done anything for her. And maybe he did. But Mama loved Della too." She replaced the lid to the shoebox, minus the letter CC still held in her hand. "Maybe they had an affair while Della was alive or maybe not. And they may have waited until Della was gone. She died about two years before Mama's mind started to go. But it's not important."

CC and Penn looked at her skeptically and she sighed. "What is it with your generation? You're just fascinated with everyone else's dirt. Nothing can be left as a mystery. Who *cares* where Amelia Earhart crashed? And what if Lee Harvey Oswald had help? As if it matters? *Now*? All you need to know is what I said. Jacob loved my mother, and without his help we wouldn't have made it."

"Who was Maude?"

Viv leaned back into the corner of the sofa and licked her lips. "Maude was my half-sister. After my father left, my mother fell in love with Mac, Kiah's father. For a while it was wonderful, but then the cabins burned down one night and killed him. She'd just realized she was pregnant." Her voice faded away, and CC saw tears in her eyes. "I'm almost positive it was my father who set the fire," she added distantly. "That's what I told Jacob Rubenstein."

"What?" CC asked, startled.

"I saw two men, and then I saw my father hiding in the bushes watching the cabins burn. Afterward, I was pretty sure it was Pops who'd done it. So I told Jacob."

She thought of the note that had started the legal proceeding. "What month was that?"

Viv looked away. "It was August of fifty-five. It was so hot. And even after they put out the fire it felt like our house was ten degrees warmer than usual. That was the worst summer of my life."

"What are you thinking?" Penn asked CC.

"The note that gave the enclave to Jacob Rubenstein is dated August of fifty-five as well."

Penn looked at her seriously. "That can't be a coincidence."

"No, it can't," she agreed. "Viv, did Jacob call the police? Was your father ever arrested or even questioned?"

She shook her head. "I know he wasn't arrested. Mama just wanted it to go away. She missed Mac so much, and then all she cared about was making a life for me and Maude by selling her pies and running the B and B Jacob had built."

"So that's how the enclave came to be," CC concluded. "What happened to Kiah?"

Viv gazed at the oil portrait. "Kiah's death was the most tragic of all. She was beaten to death by a racist police officer during a freedom march in the South. Her death was a blow to all of us, Maude especially. Maude was such a beautiful child."

"Where is she now?" Penn asked.

"She's gone too." Viv stared out the window, refusing to look at her. "Life wasn't easy for her. It wasn't easy for anyone who grew up mixed in the sixties. She didn't belong anywhere. Mama and I did the best we could but the older she got, the wilder she became."

"What happened?"

"She ran away when she was thirteen, after Kiah died. We'd kept in touch all those years, and Kiah said that after she graduated from law school, she'd take Maude in. None of her people would. They were as prejudiced against mixed folks as much as anybody. But then she was killed, and Maude ran away. It was all so sad."

"Where did she go?" Penn asked.

"She headed for California. Mama was heartbroken. Maude was the second child she'd lost. First, my brother Will was killed in a knife fight in sixty-four, and then Maude, who was her only link to Mac, leaves her. Mama went from being the happiest person I knew to the saddest. Thank goodness for the Rubensteins. They were the only people who helped her."

"What happened to Maude?"

She glanced toward the attic. "Somewhere up there is a little box of her things," she added. "But in seventy-two, Jacob showed up on our doorstep. He'd received a call from the San Francisco police. Her body had been found in Golden Gate Park. She died from exposure, but I'm sure it was drugs."

Looking distressed, she paused and ran a hand over her face. "Apparently Maude had kept an envelope of pictures in her knapsack, and one of them was of Della's Restaurant. Mama had written Phoenix and the date on the back, and they looked up Jacob. She had to go claim the body. It was awful. She was never the same after that."

"And Maude had Maya before she died?" CC asked gently.

Her gaze shot up at CC. "Damn. How did you know?"

"Maya told us her mother was Maude."

She shook a finger at her. "You should be a detective." She stood and went to Kiah's portrait, setting her hand on the frame reverently. "Maude also had a picture of a newborn in her bag. I think Maya was probably born in somebody's house, and then Maude gave her up for adoption. I guess a lot of women did during that crazy time. Mama found a slip of paper with an address in her bag, so before she left San Francisco, she visited the people who'd adopted her. She decided not to make trouble, and they all kept in touch. And when Maya's adoptive parents' health started to fail, they moved out here." She offered a slight smile. "I doubt that was an accident."

"But she doesn't know you're her aunt?"

She turned and faced them. "Do you understand now why I didn't want to get into all this? It's not important. She knows she's adopted. That's enough. She loves me and we're family, not just in the blood sense. What would be gained from telling her? Her biological past is full of pain." Her gaze shifted from Penn to CC. "This is what I'm trying to tell you girls. The past is the past. It's not always good to know everything." She gazed at the portrait again. "You make your family, and I've made mine."

CC stood. "Viv, you said Jacob would do anything for your mother, right?"

"Absolutely."

"Would he commit a felony?"

****

CC, Penn and Viv rode in Penn's Nova as CC explained her theory. "I think Jacob confronted your father about the fire, Viv. He threatened to turn him into the police for arson and murder unless he signed over the enclave."

"Why would he do that?"

"Because he wanted something good to come from Mac's death," Penn concluded. "In all likelihood nothing would've happened if he'd gone to the police. There was no real proof. Chet would've denied it, and you didn't actually see him set the fire."

"And unfortunately in those times the death of a black man wasn't a big deal," CC said. "But he could help your mother if he got the land away from Chet."

Viv's head seemed to swim with the information. "Why didn't he have Pops sign over the place to Mama?"

"Because property law was vague and ambiguous back then. Most states didn't allow women to own property on their own,"

CC answered. "Jacob threatened Chet to sign over the land, and then he held it for Lois."

"But he should've signed it back in the seventies when the laws changed," Penn growled as she turned on to Grand Avenue.

"Mama was already in trouble by then, Penn. Her brain wasn't working right. And I imagine Jacob had his own box of letters. They probably just forgot about it."

Penn glanced at CC. "Are you thinking duress, counselor? Are you hoping to prove that the contract between the two men isn't binding?"

She shook her head. "Nope. That could be an angle, but there's no proof. I've got another hunch," she said with a grin.

"Where are we going?" Viv finally asked.

"Here," she said, pointing to the big sign.

Viv shrugged, puzzled. "Della's? Why are we here?"

"Good question," Penn agreed as they slid through the front door of the restaurant.

She asked for a table against the far wall, noticing Seth Rubenstein wasn't around, but his Lexus was parked outside. After the waitress took their pie and lemonade orders, she motioned for Penn to help her remove the *Farmhouse Pies* sign that hung above them.

"What in tarnation are you doin'?" Viv asked.

They lowered it onto the table and stared at the message on the backside, written in the long, angular script that CC had seen on the letters in the shoebox.

Della's Restaurant Est. March, 1957
Jacob Rubenstein, Della Rubenstein and Lois Battle
Founding Partners

"Well, I'll be damned," Penn said, kissing her cheek.

Viv leaned over the sign as the waitress appeared carrying a coffeepot. "Excuse me, but you're not allowed to do that."

Viv looked up with a victorious smile. "I most certainly am, young lady. I own this joint." She pointed at the message and explained who she was.

"Cool," the waitress said. "I love the sweet potato pie. It's the most ordered item on the menu."

Seth Rubenstein hustled out of the kitchen. "What's going on? Why are you here?"

CC pointed at Jacob Rubenstein's message and he shrugged. "So?"

"It means we're partners," Viv said. She stuck out her hand. "Put her there!"

He stared at her extended hand.

"You knew, didn't you?" Penn accused him.

He shuffled his feet, but said nothing.

Viv gasped. "You son of a bitch. If your parents were alive they'd tan your fanny but good! You're not half the man Jacob was."

His face turned completely red and clashed with his bright pink Hawaiian shirt. "I'm calling my lawyer, my *new* lawyer," he said to CC as he walked away. "You're fired."

A few minutes later, on the drive home Viv asked, "Will I get to keep the enclave? I really don't want to own a restaurant, even part of one."

"I think so," Penn said. "His new attorney will advise him to drop the suit. The Della franchise is worth a ton more than the property. He's not going to want to cut that *pie* in pieces."

They laughed so loud CC almost didn't hear her phone. She groaned when she saw Blanca's name and put the phone on speaker.

"Yes, Blanca."

"Your things need to be removed from our office by noon tomorrow."

"I understand," she said, glancing at Penn and Viv who were listening intently. From the echo on the line, Blanca's phone was also on speaker.

"And you should know that I intend to file a formal complaint against you with the state bar association for ethics violations."

"I understand," she repeated, imagining a giant toilet with wads of cash that represented her education circling in the bowl.

"And I'll need our new attorney to speak with Ms. Battle's attorney. Who might that be?"

"She's right here," she said, holding the phone out.

"This is Penn."

"Uh, hello, this is Alicia Dennis. I'll be taking over the Rubenstein matter. Hi, CC, I assume you're listening as well."

Penn shook her head. "That was quick. You people at Hartford and Burns give new meaning to turnover."

"Let's stick to business," Blanca directed. "What does your client want?"

Penn glanced at Viv. "You sure you don't want part of a restaurant?" Viv waved her off and leaned closer to the phone. "Ms. Battle will be perfectly happy with a deed to the property. She'll gladly forfeit her portion of Della's."

"I'm certain that will be acceptable," Blanca said. "I'll have Alicia draw up the paperwork."

"It'll be done by Friday," Alicia said quickly.

"Oh, and Alicia you may want to write a few things down. Are you ready?"

"Yes."

"First, when we come down to sign those papers, I expect you to return CC's Melissa Ferrick CD, got that?"

"Uh, okay—"

"And I'm not sure what you've got on her, but if anything appears on the Internet that defames her in any way, I'm coming after you personally and Heartless and Burned, too. And I won't care if the whole world sees. Do you understand that, Blanca?"

"I do," she said tersely.

"I think that's it," Penn said.

"Oh, no, wait one second!" Viv cried. "Vivian Battle, here."

"Yes, Ms. Battle," Blanca said flatly.

"As the president of the Alzheimer's Association, and a personal friend of Bill Hartford's, I'm requesting that you forget about filing that complaint with the bar." She let the message sink in before she said, "It won't turn out well for you, dear."

Her voice was as sweet as if she was reading a Chloe book, but the venom lurked under the surface. It took several beats but Blanca finally said, "I understand. Consider it forgotten. Are we through?"

Penn piped up. "Just one more point, Alicia. I really need to thank you."

"Why?"

"For being a moron. You gave up a total babe who's fabulous in bed. Thanks a lot. My rediscovered sex drive is very grateful."

She disconnected, and Viv slapped her back. CC stared out the window too stunned to speak. Penn kept her eyes on the road and her hands at ten and two on the steering wheel. When they stopped at a red light, she turned to CC and appeared to be three times larger than she was.

"Sometimes I absolutely love the law!"

They parked the car, and CC's head fell against the dashboard. "What have I done?"

Penn stroked her back. "You're miserable. You *hate* being a lawyer."

"But it's all I know how to do! And my student loans…"

"You have us."

She sat up and touched her cheek. "Penn—"

"Listen to me, CC."

"Yes, listen to *us*, CC," Viv said.

Viv held up her portfolio and displayed her most recent drawing, a picture of Danny the Dachshund leaping through the grass, playing with a butterfly. "This is excellent. This is what real talent looks like. You want a job? I'm giving you a job."

"What?" CC asked.

"I can't stop old age from interfering with my life. God knows I try every day. But the arthritis is getting to me, and it's harder to hold my brush. I need someone to help me with Chloe. I may not be able to control what happens to me, but Chloe can be timeless. She never has to die."

She couldn't believe what she was hearing. "You want me to be your apprentice?"

She shook her head. "You're far too talented for that word, but yes, I want you to learn from me, and in exchange I'll introduce you to my publisher." She tapped the picture and smiled wryly. "He's going to love this little guy and all the money he'll make. Kids love wiener dogs!" Her expression shifted, and she said seriously, "So when can you start? When can you move in?"

She blinked. "You want me to live here?"

"Of course! This is my home, and I'm loaded. It's that simple. And I want people around me I admire, love and trust. This is my family. I decided on Maya, Penn, Lynette and Siobhan, and now I'd like to add you."

"Uh, Viv, where will CC live?" Penn asked warily.

"With you," she replied, and Penn sputtered an unintelligible response that made her laugh. "I'm kidding, Penn. She can either stay with me, and Lord knows I've got the room, or she can move into Siobhan's place, which I imagine will be empty soon."

Penn snorted. "I don't know about that."

"I do," Viv said, pointing toward the cottages.

They got out of the Nova as Siobhan stormed toward her truck with Lynette and the dogs following after her.

"Siobhan, wait! I need to talk to you."

When she opened the tailgate, Lynette gave a shrill whistle and motioned. The five dogs jumped into the bed.

Siobhan pointed. "Get out!" The dogs ignored her and focused their stares on Lynette who was shaking a finger at them.

"I'm going to be late," she cried. "Lynette?"

"I really need to talk to you."

"I can't right now. I have a concert. You need to get these mutts down!" she shouted in her thick brogue.

Lynette wrapped her arms around her and kissed her passionately. As Lynette walked away, she whistled again, and the dogs tumbled out of the bed, nearly knocking a dazed Siobhan to the ground.

Lynette threw up her hands and said, "I think I'm trainable."

CHAPTER NINETEEN

September, 2010

From my childhood bedroom on the second floor I watched their exchange. They'd been playing this cat and mouse game for over a month but neither could become a cat. Both were just timid mice, afraid of love, too scared to try again. CC sat at the drawing board inside the sun porch perfecting her version of Chloe. She was naturally gifted, and I knew when I could no longer hold my brush, the young readers would be just as pleased with her Chloe. Only a few would catch the subtle differences in our styles.

Penn stood on her porch on the other side of the hedge, her arms folded, leaning against a post. She gazed at CC without being able to see her, picturing her through the thick foliage I'd planted decades ago. My breath caught, and for a moment fifty-five years evaporated and Mac and Mama appeared, he outside the cabin, and she on the sun porch. It disappeared when I heard the annoying ring from CC's cell phone. She answered, and I knew without looking across the hedge that it was Penn, wooing her to abandon her work and take a break.

Her face broke into a smile, and she quickly set her brush down and bounded outside. By the time she reached the hedge, though, her pace had slowed, she'd straightened her back and adopted a cool, somewhat indifferent expression.

They met at the hammock as they always did each afternoon—the halfway point between Penn's cottage and the farmhouse. It was what each could give right now. After their embrace and a little kiss, they cuddled on the hammock locked in each other's arms for an hour of sharing the past, healing the hurts and building the bridge. I stepped away from the window, unwilling to intrude further. They'd figure it out soon enough. The smart ones always did.

About The Author

Ann Roberts lives with her partner of seventeen years in Phoenix, Arizona. Recent empty nesters, their Rhodesian Ridgebacks, Duke and Sadie, keep them busy as do frequent phone calls to their son, the college student who needs money. A life-long educator, Ann is currently collaborating with Medal of Freedom winner, Gerda Weissman Klein, on a play about diversity and bullying. Please visit her website at annroberts. net.

Publications from
Bella Books, Inc.
Women. Books. Even Better Together.
P.O. Box 10543
Tallahassee, FL 32302
Phone: 800-729-4992
www.bellabooks.com

CALM BEFORE THE STORM by Peggy J. Herring. Colonel Marcel Robicheaux doesn't tell and so far no one official has asked, but the amorous pursuit by Jordan McGowen has her worried for both her career and her honor.
978-0-9677753-1-9

THE WILD ONE by Lyn Denison. Rachel Weston is busy keeping home and head together after the death of her husband. Her kids need her and what she doesn't need is the confusion that Quinn Farrelly creates in her body and heart.
978-0-9677753-4-0

LESSONS IN MURDER by Claire McNab. There's a corpse in the school with a neat hole in the head and a Black & Decker drill alongside. Which teacher should Inspector Carol Ashton suspect? Unfortunately, the alluring Sybil Quade is at the top of the list. First in this highly lauded series.
978-1-931513-65-4

WHEN AN ECHO RETURNS by Linda Kay Silva. The bayou where Echo Branson found her sanity has been swept clean by a hurricane—or at least they thought. Then an evil washed up by the storm comes looking for them all, one-by-one. Second in series.
978-1-59493-225-0

DEADLY INTERSECTIONS by Ann Roberts. Everyone is lying, including her own father and her girlfriend. Leaving matters to the professionals is supposed to be easier! Third in series with *PAID IN FULL* and *WHITE OFFERINGS.*
978-1-59493-224-3

SUBSTITUTE FOR LOVE by Karin Kallmaker. No substitutes, ever again! But then Holly's heart, body and soul are captured by Reyna... Reyna with no last name and a secret life that hides a terrible bargain, one written in family blood.
978-1-931513-62-3

MAKING UP FOR LOST TIME by Karin Kallmaker. Take one Next Home Network Star and add one Little White Lie to equal mayhem in little Mendocino and a recipe for sizzling romance. This lighthearted, steamy story is a feast for the senses in a kitchen that is way too hot.
978-1-931513-61-6

2ND FIDDLE by Kate Calloway. Cassidy James's first case left her with a broken heart. At least this new case is fighting the good fight, and she can throw all her passion and energy into it.
978-1-59493-200-7

HUNTING THE WITCH by Ellen Hart. The woman she loves — used to love — offers her help, and Jane Lawless finds it hard to say no. She needs TLC for recent injuries and who better than a doctor? But Julia's jittery demeanor awakens Jane's curiosity. And Jane has never been able to resist a mystery. #9 in series and Lammy-winner.
978-1-59493-206-9

FAÇADES by Alex Marcoux. Everything Anastasia ever wanted — she has it. Sidney is the woman who helped her get it. But keeping it will require a price — the unnamed passion that simmers between them.
978-1-59493-239-7